MERCILESS

Valeria Heights

CONTENTS

Dedication V

Epigraph VI

1. Chapter One 1

2. Chapter Two 10

3. Chapter Three 20

4. Chapter Four 24

5. Chapter Five 38

6. Chapter Six 43

7. Chapter Seven 57

8. Chapter Eight 71

9. Chapter Nine 80

10. Chapter Ten 90

11. Chapter Eleven 99

12. Chapter Twelve 110

13. Chapter Thirteen   123

14. Chapter Fourteen   136

15. Chapter Fifteen   145

16. Chapter Sixteen   166

17. Chapter Seventeen   170

18. Chapter Eighteen   182

19. Chapter Nineteen   197

20. Chapter Twenty   206

21. Chapter Twenty-One   220

22. Chapter Twenty-Two   225

23. Chapter Twenty-Three   239

24. Chapter Twenty-Four   254

25. Chapter Twenty-Five   263

26. Chapter Twenty-Six   275

27. Chapter Twenty-Seven   286

28. Chapter Twenty-Eight   295

29. Epilogue   302

Bonus Chapter Lucas   311

Bonus: Reckless Chapter One   312

Acknowledgements   322

To my husband,

who always believes in me.

I could never dedicate this to anyone else but you.

Nemesis

/noun/

A person who specifically brings about the downfall of another.

CHAPTER ONE

Clementine

I was thirty seconds away from parking in front of my house. As usual, I grabbed my bag from the passenger seat and placed it in my lap. I wanted to get inside as fast as possible.

It wasn't cold or raining. We were living in Southern California, so I wasn't hiding from bad weather. It was already dark but not particularly late, not that anyone was keeping tabs on me, and we lived in one of the richest and most pretentious neighborhoods in the state, so I wasn't afraid of being mugged.

I was scared of a pair of ocean blue eyes that belonged to my neighbor. It was ridiculous and childish of me to think that Lucas Cole would try to ambush me here. Or anywhere else for that matter. My avoiding him was more of a habit than a necessity, but I wasn't ready to test that theory.

I popped out of the car with the speed of a cartoon character, and, another ten seconds and approximately one thousand heart attacks later, I was inside the house. Lucas Cole had been successfully avoided once again.

I was trying to take deep, calming breaths by the front door when a smell I thought was in my past for good hit my nostrils.

Not the fucking candles again.

I went to the living room and found the boxes filled with these bioweapons my mother made two years ago in another of her post-divorce hobbies. An empty bottle of wine was standing next to the speaker. Ed Sheeran's voice was deafening every sound around the house. I laughed at the irony; my mother was always so concerned with her image, and yet she was harassing the neighbors with loud music like a fifteen-year-old.

I had no desire whatsoever to see her and, presuming she was in the kitchen, I went upstairs to my room.

And there she was, standing by my desk looking through my drawings with a judgmental look on her face. Her glass of wine had made a spot on one of them and I wanted to scream. There were at least twenty candles burning in different corners of the room. The stench was beyond repulsive. The smells had gotten so mixed together that the aroma could make you vomit faster than two fingers in the throat after drinking half a bottle of tequila. I presumed. I wasn't into drinking, unlike my mother.

But first things first. I had to close my curtains, as I had done every night for years, like a ritual. Not that I thought Lucas would look at me. He never did. I was dead to him, and yet every time he passed me by in the hallway in school with a new girl clinging to his neck as if I wasn't there, the hurt and humiliation echoed in every bone of my body.

I saw the lights in his room were on, but he wasn't there, or at least I couldn't see him. When we were little, our curtains were always open. He used to come up with funny faces just to make me laugh. I needed those laughs back then.

After I made sure I was protected by the thick black curtains, I turned to face my mother. I wanted to kick her out of my room, but I preferred to piss her off first.

"Are you trying to get high?" I asked as I walked around blowing out candles. "'Cause it's only been a minute since I got home, and I already have a headache, and you look like you are about to pass out."

Not that it would be a surprise. Every night for some time now she had passed out on her favorite expensive white sofa she had bullied my father into buying just months before he left her.

A chuckle. That's all I got from her. I was about to sleep in that stench, and she just chuckled at me.

"Is wine not enough for you anymore?"

A burning memory of me spending my early childhood wishing she would stop criticizing me, that she would stop yelling at me for everything she hated about me, flashed before my eyes for a moment. These days, I was going out of my way to make her scream again.

Pretty pathetic, huh?

"Watch it, Clementine!" she hissed, still looking at my drawings.

Clementine...

Everybody knew I hated my name. Not only because it was completely inadequate and so rare I had never met anyone named Clementine, but because she was the one who gave it to me. My siblings had normal names. But then again, Tyler and Madison were the wanted children, as my mother reminded all of us when we were still a pretending-to-be-functional family before the divorce.

"Don't get me wrong," I started again, crossing my arms over my chest. "I'm glad you got bored with the gourmet cooking, because you were definitely not good at it. This, however, suits you perfectly, but it's still a cliché, you know? A drunk middle-aged divorcée burning handmade candles. You're not working. You're just sucking cash from your ex-husband's pocket." I paused for a moment and cocked my head sideways. "Does Dad know how much money you spend on booze?"

She laughed.

"If you think your father cares about what we're doing, you're stupider than I thought," she slurred.

I couldn't say she was wrong about Dad. His approach to everything even before the divorce was to put some cash on the problem and run in the opposite direction. That's how I got my car. I was constantly bitching about my mother, so for my sixteenth birthday, he decided to buy me a fifty-thousand-dollar ride I had never wanted. It was completely inappropriate for a high school student. It took me three months to summon the courage to take it for a spin.

"I heard about your little hobby," she said, and her gaze fell on the drawing under her glass. "Oops. That one's ruined." She picked up the wine, then the piece of paper; I snatched it from her hand. She was right; it was ruined. I squeezed it in my fist.

She was a nasty person. Not that I didn't poke her every time I got the chance, but telling Dad about her alcohol abuse was an empty threat and she knew it. I wouldn't tell him. It would benefit her. She would get help. Sympathy. Eventually she would get better.

I wanted her to get worse.

I wanted her to suffer. To feel lonely, deserted, rejected, and weak. Like she made me feel every single day of my life.

Sylvia tried to walk towards me, but those stilettos she always wore weren't the best option if you want to get hammered. She lost balance, leaned over my bed, spilled her drink on my blanket, and laughed like a maniac.

"It's barely ten, Sylvia," I growled and rubbed my forehead. Sometimes I wanted to do violent things to my mother.

She ignored the fact that I called her by her name. When I started doing that a few years ago, she threw tantrums like a toddler. It pissed her off so much, she lost control over herself, and the perfect facade she maintained her whole life cracked each time. These days it didn't even make her roll her eyes at me. I had to up my game.

"How long have you been doing these?" she asked, pointing at my desk.

"Let's not pretend you care."

"I don't. But I don't want to be embarrassed either. Do you have any idea how it looks to people when they talk about stuff like that and they find out I don't know what you're doing?"

"It probably looks exactly like it is," I murmured.

"Are you suggesting something?" She was half-sitting, half-lying on my bed.

"Only that you stopped being a mother the moment your son left this house, even though you had a fourteen-year-old to look after?"

"Cry me a river," Sylvia dragged. "Your constant whining is so annoying. I can't even look at you."

"Soon you won't have to," I smiled. The school year started the next day.

"Yes, finally. I'll get rid of you after graduation. Like I always wanted to."

"Well, not exactly like you wanted to," I reminded her.

She didn't deny it. I always knew I was an unexpected child. Not a surprise, but bad news. She joked about my dad convincing her to keep me ever since I was a little girl.

"Obviously," she finally said. "I could have had a few good years, but no. You had to happen."

"Get out of my room," I said through clenched teeth.

"With pleasure."

I could probably go wash my hair in the time she spent taking her shoes off and getting out, but I waited silently. When she was finally out the door, I cracked a window behind the curtains just to get some fresh air. Then I collected all the candles and dumped them in her room.

I kneeled next to my bed and pulled out the shoe box. I wanted to make sure she hadn't found it. I started counting. Everything was as I left it. I could still pull it off. Not now, because the amount I had wasn't enough. But I could do it by graduation.

And it was going to crush my mother. I wanted to say that it would break her heart, but a long time ago I found out she didn't have one.

The next morning, I woke up in total darkness. The left side of my face was numb since I had probably spent the last few hours sleeping on my book instead of my pillow.

It was the first day of my senior year. Even though it was the beginning of the year, it felt like a kind of ending. I sat up in my bed, facing my thick curtains, thinking about Lucas.

Soon we won't be living across from each other.

The thought ripped something inside my chest, and, in a moment of weakness, I went to the window. I drew the curtains open. The sun blinded me for a second. Lucas's curtains were wide open. He wasn't scared that I might watch him. He loved being watched; it was a part of his personality.

The whole thing was ridiculous. Me, playing hide and seek with a guy that I hadn't spoken to for four years. Sprinting from my car to my front door like a criminal every time I got home. But I just couldn't bring myself to stop. It felt like everything would fall apart if I did.

I quit stalking the moment I saw movement in Lucas's room. I went to the hallway to go to the bathroom, and the smell of the fucking candles reminded me of the sight I was about to see on my way out to school this morning. I was breathing through my mouth only, but I could still somehow sense the stink on my tongue.

By the time I got out of the shower and back in my room, I had three texts and one missed phone call.

Hannah: You should get your ass to school like NOW. You won't believe who's here.

Tyler: Hey, sis. Call Dad back. He's acting like a dumped chick again.

Dad: Clem, are you mad at me?

I rolled my eyes mostly at my father and I typed back replies.

Me: Do I care?

Me: You should know. You've dumped a significant number of chicks yourself.

Me: No, Dad. I'll call you back.

I got dressed as my phone vibrated with messages from Hannah and possibly Tyler, if he hadn't already lost interest in our exchange, which wouldn't be a surprise. He hated our family drama to the point that he couldn't spend more than two consecutive days in California with us. And he had the perfect excuse not to come. He lived in Boston now and the travel just wasn't worth it, as he repeatedly reminded us during his short and rare visits.

I grabbed the shoe box from under my bed, and I emptied it. I didn't trust my mother. She could come snooping around again. I didn't want to have to explain the two thousand dollars I had hidden. But I didn't want to walk around with that amount of cash in my pocket either.

I got downstairs and walked past Sylvia, who as I thought, was sleeping on the sofa. Apparently, she had finished another bottle of wine last night because there were now two empties by the speaker. The disturbing thing was that the whole living room was covered in candles. She arranged all of them all over the place. No wonder the house smelled so much worse than last night.

She's losing it.

The phone started ringing in my hand. I looked at the screen.

Dad.

I took the pillow of the armchair and unzipped it. I figured anything I was hiding right in front of her eyes would be better protected than if it was in my room. I put the money inside, zipped back the pillow, and I glanced at my mother again. She was snoring.

My phone was still vibrating in my hand. I knew I had to tell dad about her. It was the right thing to do.

I got out, marching quickly to my car as I answered my father's call.

"Hey, Dad," I murmured.

"Hey, honey. Is everything OK?" he asked. I paused, hyper-aware that the woman I just left inside was getting worse and that this was the perfect timing to come clean and share that beauty with the family.

And then he started talking.

"Are you mad at me? You didn't like your present, did you? I knew you wouldn't like it, but Adina kept repeating it was awesome."

Adina was his new, twenty-two-year-old girlfriend. My sister Madison was twenty-five, not that he was interested in that fact. And the present was a cashmere sweater that I didn't need because... duh... Southern California. Also, it was something I would never wear.

"I loved it," I lied and took a deep breath. "Listen, dad..."

"Great!" he shouted in my ear with relief. "Sorry, honey, I just wanted to clear the air. I have an early meeting. I'll call you later this week, okay?"

The decision was made in my mind that split second. I wasn't going to parent them, since they hadn't ever really parented me.

"Sure, dad. Don't worry about it".

CHAPTER TWO

Lucas

It was the first day of school for everyone except the football team. My team. Coach Howard was retiring at the end of the year, and he wanted to win the championship so badly, he made us come all summer long. I didn't mind. We both wanted the same thing. To be the best.

I got out of my car in the school parking lot and heads started turning. I felt people's gazes on me. It went with the territory. Being watched and admired was something I was used to and enjoyed most of the time. I accepted the role I had to play, and I didn't half-ass it. I was an all-or-nothing kind of a guy.

"Cole! We're going to annihilate them on Friday, man," a jackass I had English Lit with last year yelled from fifty feet away. He obviously had an intellectual disability, because *we* weren't going to do that on

Friday. My team was. He was no part of that. He was just the typical asshole who wanted all the perks that came with being a jock but lacked the discipline and the talent to actually do the work.

I knew I couldn't say that. So I did what was expected of me. I glanced in his direction, and I answered with a smile.

"We are."

I noticed a girl was standing next to him. She looked like a sophomore, and he probably tried to impress her by talking to me.

I looked around, and I saw Chase. He was surrounded by girls who I had no doubt were ready to suck him off right there and then if he decided to ask. One of those jock perks I mentioned.

I strolled in his direction. A familiar voice came from behind a second before the fingers of its owner ran through my hair.

"Hey there, Prince Charming."

"Hey, Amy." I suppressed my annoyance, took her hand, which was now lingering on my neck, and returned it next to her body where it belonged.

Amy was beautiful. No one could argue that. She had long, blond hair that felt like silk, which I knew because she found ways to pin her tight body to mine on a regular basis. She had great tits, a fine ass, and the attitude of a *Playboy* Bunny whenever her twin brother, who also happened to be my best friend, wasn't around.

But she seemed determined to get me to fuck her no matter what, which always made me hold back. I was sometimes rude in my attempts to show her we were never happening. I ignored her and publicly made out with other girls in front of her. She just smiled as if I gave her a compliment and tried again the next time we were in the same room. And that, unfortunately for me, was pretty often.

We stopped next to Chase and the group of wannabe cheerleaders.

"Do you have to act like a slut all the time?" Amy asked her brother. I couldn't say she was a bitch, but I definitely understood why most people thought she was. And the horrified look on those girls' faces made me change the subject fast.

"That's it, man. One last season." I pretended I didn't notice the tension.

"For you maybe," Chase grinned and played along. "I'm going pro, Cole. You will watch me on Super Bowl Sunday and will tell your average-looking hookups that you once were touched by my greatness."

I laughed. He was good, but I was better. The thing was I didn't want to do the professional football player thing and he did. So much so that I really thought he had a chance to be one.

"That's if you cut back on the bullshit on the field," I said. I knew he hated when I commented on his wacky behavior, but I had two reasons to do it. First, he was my best friend, and it was my obligation to tell him when he acted like a dumbass and, second, I was the captain of the team. Everything that happened on that field during a game was my responsibility. And most of the time Chase was a liability.

"I like it when you're acting crazy on the field, babe, it's really funny," the chick under Chase's arm meddled in our conversation. She was the perfect example of the girls Chase liked – fuckable and agreeable. He hated pussy drama more than anything and avoided it at all costs.

"He acts like an ass," I snarled. "And has more confidence than skill, which does not equal a one-way ticket to the NFL. If you want one day to be able to brag in front of your friends you banged this moron in high school, you shouldn't encourage him."

Me snapping at people like that was unusual, but I was under a lot of pressure. It was my senior year. Coach had ridden my ass all summer long, and I didn't need some random chick to inspire an even more rebellious behavior from Chase.

The girl, whose name I didn't actually know, narrowed her eyes at me as if she was about to come after my ass, but she knew better. I was this school's golden boy.

Seriously. There were people using that nickname for me.

"Leave it, babe," Chase said to the girl. His eyes were concentrated on something behind my back. The frown on his face made me turn and look around. It took me a few seconds to recognize the person I was seeing.

The. Fuck?

I heard Amy explaining the scene that was unfolding in front of my eyes.

"Oh, yeah," the smirk in her voice was obvious. "He's back. And not to visit. His parents got divorced, and he moved here with his mother. He'll graduate with us."

"Who is he?" the girl that defended Chase asked.

"Dylan Williams," Amy answered. "He's a childhood friend."

"I wouldn't say that," Chase snorted. "He visited his grandparents every now and again. We just happened to hang out with him."

"Anyway," Amy dragged. "A few years ago, he spent New Year's with us and that was the last time we saw him."

A few? She knew exactly how many. And Chase's explanation that we just *happened* to hang out with him? There was a particular reason for that, and her name was Hannah Spencer. Head cheerleader, a pain in everyone's ass, and Clementine Hartley's only friend.

"It was a weird party." Amy shook her head with a smile, not tearing her eyes away from Dylan.

The mere mention of that party made my skin prickle. The fact that the motherfucker was standing just a few feet away from me and was talking to *her* made me see red.

How. The. Fuck. Did. That. Shit. Happen?

Again.

The son of a bitch saw me. He smiled at me and nodded as if we were buddies. He was changed. The last time I saw him he was a tall, thin, and funny-looking fourteen-year-old. Now he looked like that dude from the vampire series girls were wetting their panties for, but with blond hair. Still thin, but he had added some muscles over his bones.

He was still looking at me when he offered Clementine his hand. We were both waiting for her reaction. She shook her head, explained something, then turned to see who he was looking at.

The color of her face went from a snow white tan to fucking corpse-pale one when she realized it was me.

Our eyes locked. A rare event.

It lasted no more than three seconds and she looked away. No surprise there. After all, she spent her days and nights avoiding me.

She tried to convince herself and me she wasn't aware of my existence. The pathetic little soul obviously had no idea I knew she hid behind the curtains in her room like an idiot. I also knew she would spend hours sitting in her car in front of her house just so that she wouldn't have to face me. I checked that theory once or twice over the last couple of years when I was feeling bored and had nothing better to do.

It took me a while, but I learned to control myself and ignore the urges to observe her over the years. I had to. Looking at her was a torture back then. The images that came to my mind when I allowed myself to look at her pissed me off to the point I wasn't functioning like a normal human being for days.

Later on, I found ways to get back at her, and I started to feel better.

Hannah Spencer popped out of nowhere, got between Dylan and Clementine, and the three of them got inside the school building. I finally tore my gaze away from them.

The news about Dylan's presence hunted me the entire day. I found out that Hannah was supposed to show him around and make him feel welcomed. She was the person to do shit like that around here. She started an anti-bullying club two years ago. She helped everyone with everything and did it with a smile. That girl's need to please other people was probably exhausting.

That information only made me think about all the time Clementine would spend around Dylan now that he would become Hannah Spencer's charity project one more fucking time.

People were trying to figure out the last time Dylan Williams was here.

I knew exactly how many years had passed. Almost four.

Almost one thousand five hundred days that I wasn't talking to Clementine Hartley.

The exact same number of days I spent hating her.

This town was not immune to gossip. I was sure someone would soon revive the story.

By the time football practice started, I was already coming to terms with the fact we were all going to be in each other's faces this year. And I had a lot to lose. I wouldn't let someone as insignificant as Dylan Williams ruin it for me.

I was warming up when I noticed my team gathering around someone by the bleachers. I had a gut feeling who that someone was, so I approached them.

"Cole," the coach started. "This is…"

"We've met, coach," I cut him off, not wanting to hear Dylan's name yet again that day.

"Great," the coach shoved his hands in his pockets. "No need for introductions then. Show us what you've got, Williams."

Everyone spread around the field, including Dylan, who was in full gear.

Chase was walking beside me.

"I'm not letting him on the team," I murmured.

"Oh, man," he groaned and rubbed the top of his head nervously. "Just don't break any of his bones, okay? They'll kick you off the team."

I didn't want to make that promise, but I didn't want to risk my position either. So, I nodded. Reluctantly.

I spent the first twenty minutes of our practice tackling Dylan to the ground. His smirk told me he knew what I was doing, but he didn't draw back. Under different circumstances, I could be impressed.

"Cole!" Coach Howard shouted.

I ran to him, feeling my body tense, every muscle in it clenched with contained and controlled anger.

"What the hell are you doing?".

"Playing football, coach."

"Like a savage, I could add. Are you trying to break someone's limb? Get back there and watch it," he warned.

I could feel my nostrils burning with every breath I exhaled. Dylan's stubbornness irritated me. Chase ran to me and pushed me hard.

"Pull yourself together, dickhead."

I pushed him back, knowing the coach did not appreciate aggressive behavior between his players. He wanted us to save all that shit for the night of the game to take it out on the other team. I couldn't wait until Friday, though.

"You're ruining the practice," Chase growled in my face. "He's spending the entire year here. Are you going to be PMS-ing until graduation?"

"Shut up," I took my helmet off, tugged on my hair, and inhaled deeply. I used every drop of self-control I had to try to avoid an outburst.

"I hope they finally fuck each other. That will get her out of your system."

I pushed Chase down on the grass.

"That's it," I heard Coach Howard yell. "Cole, get your ass off my field. Now!"

I felt hands pulling me away from Chase's body, and I was guided to the locker room. I took the coldest and longest shower in my life, trying to prevent myself from exploding. I wasn't counting on it, but it helped. It took the edge off. When the rage evaporated, I started thinking clearly again.

This fucking school was my kingdom. No one caused me any trouble. Not the students nor the teachers. I could probably fuck the principal's wife in front of the entire administration and then take a dump on his desk and he would still think I am the best thing that happened to his football team. Well, second-best at least, as people reminded me from time to time.

Clementine knew all that. Dylan Williams was about to figure it out too. I would make sure of that.

I decided to watch the rest of the practice and analyze that asshole, so I sneaked under the bleachers. He was good. But I wasn't letting him on my team. Coach Howard paced back and forth, speaking on the phone.

"Yes, I know, Principal Smith. Believe me. No one wants us to win this year more than me," he laughed and snorted like a pig.

He paused, listening to what was coming out of Principal Smith's mouth. Bullshit, no doubt. He was an old prick who tolerated everything the jocks were doing. Bad grades, fights, skipping classes, everything was forgiven and forgotten when it came to us. As long as we won games.

"Well, sir, he's good, but he's no Tyler Hartley," Howard continued.

No news there. Clementine's brother was out-of-this-world good, and Howard was still mourning the fact he switched sports after graduation. I bet he lay awake at night, fantasizing about Tyler playing in the NFL and reporters coming to interview his old ass.

I knew I was given the title of second-best, which was a huge hit on my ego. I didn't do second best. That was the reason I still couldn't stomach what Clementine did to me.

I tuned out the conversation these two were having, and I heard the annoying voice of Hannah, saying goodbye to the cheerleaders. They just finished their practice. I looked at them, and I spotted Clementine waiting for her friend.

I allowed myself to look at her.

She was still the most beautiful girl I had ever seen. She wore jeans and a simple tee as always, and it made her stand out in the crowd of our overdressed classmates, who preferred short skirts and dresses. Her hazel brown hair was down, flying below her shoulders. It made my fingers twitch with the need to run them through it. Her full pink lips were pressed together just like when we occasionally ran into each other in the hallway. Her huge, coffee-colored eyes were fixed on the cheerleaders. Her body barely moved. It seemed like she was deliberately trying not to look at the football practice. How long had she been there?

I had to remind myself why I couldn't know the answer to that question and that it didn't matter anyway. She might have looked like a goddess, but on the inside, she was dark and screwed up. She didn't live by the meaning of the name she hated so much.

"It means mild and merciful," she told me once when we were ten.

There was nothing mild about her and I knew it even then. She was wild, weird, and twisted in the most fascinating way possible. And she was as merciless as one could be.

I saw the girls from cheer surrounding Clem. I knew why. They all wore her handmade jewelry. I sometimes found myself in a situation when a girl was sucking my dick and I was wondering if the earring dangling from her ear into my lap was one of Clem's.

I often touched the trinkets. I thought of it as revenge. Touching something she had touched while another girl kneeled down in front of me.

The only girl who ignored Clementine and went straight to the locker room was Amy.

I could hear Chase's voice in my head.

"Pussy drama."

Chapter Three

Clementine

Twelve years ago

"Come on, Clem, I'm going to be late," my sister said over her shoulder, trying to make me walk faster. I dragged my feet on purpose even more.

"Where is Mom?" I asked and, even though I was only six, I knew what the correct answer would be.

Anywhere but with you.

"Home," Maddie answered, looking ahead while I was still walking three steps behind her.

"Why didn't she pick me up then?"

"It was Dad's turn to pick you up, but he has a meeting."

"Why do they have to take turns if Mom is always home and Dad is always working?"

I asked that question a lot for the past few months and no one was answering me. Madison exhaled loudly, turned around mid-step, and kneeled down. Our faces were at the same level now.

"Don't think about that, okay? I can pick you up. Just not on Tuesdays and Thursdays."

She had ballet on those days. Mom took me once two years ago, when I was four. I didn't like it. She yelled at me for three days because I refused to go. Then she yelled at Dad for defending me.

Madison took my hand in hers and we started walking again. I thought about her ballet lessons.

"Maddie?"

"Mm?"

"You hate ballet. Why do you keep going?"

My sister's head snapped in my direction. She was thirteen, and she was almost as tall as Mom, so I had to look up to see her face. She had long blond hair and green eyes, and she looked exactly like Mom when she was Madison's age. Or so everyone kept repeating. My brother Tyler also took my mother's features, while I looked like dad. No one ever admired my simple brown hair and ordinary brown eyes.

"Why do you think I hate it?" she asked.

"I heard you say it. You were talking on the phone."

Madison tried to hide a smile but failed.

"Clem, you know that eavesdropping is bad."

"But you never tell me anything!" I pouted, but I knew she was really in a hurry and didn't have time for this.

I loved Maddie. She took me shopping for clothes and shoes when I needed new ones, she made me breakfast on the weekends, and she always came to pick me up when Mom and Dad didn't. I felt bad she would get in trouble because of me so I quickened my pace.

"Come on, Maddie. I'll be faster."

"Thank you," she squeezed my hand.

A minute later, a car slowed down and stopped right next to us. I recognized it immediately.

"Hey, girls," our neighbor Elizabeth Cole smiled at us. "Do you need a ride?"

I wanted to hop in her car the second she asked. I loved Elizabeth. Sometimes I thought I loved her more than Maddie, but I knew I shouldn't say that.

Elizabeth was not only our neighbor, but also my friend Lucas's mother.

I didn't remember a day when Lucas and I weren't living across from each other, even though Elizabeth once told me the story of the first time Lucas and I had met. She was always the person to talk to me and tell me all kinds of stories.

Lucas and I were still in diapers. We smiled, wobbled towards each other, and hugged.

"It was like you already knew one another."

"Could you take Clem home, Mrs. Cole?" Madison asked and looked down at me. "I have to be there on time, Clem. I'm sorry."

I wasn't. I got to spend time with Lucas and his mom. Besides I knew that Madison's ballet teacher would call mom if Maddie got there late again. And Mom wouldn't be happy about it. Or understanding.

"And where are you going?" Elizabeth asked my sister while Maddie was helping me climb in the SUV. "We could drop you off if you want?"

Madison shot her a look, then proceeded with my seat belt. She kissed my forehead, slammed the door, and moved to the open window of the front passenger seat.

"I have a ballet lesson in ten minutes."

"Hop in."

That entire year, Elizabeth picked me up on Tuesdays and Thursdays. She always repeated it wasn't a big deal. Lucas and I were at the same school. We were living next to each other.

"No trouble at all," she kept saying to everyone.

But it was a big deal to me.

I started staying at the Coles' until Maddie came back from her ballet lessons. We played in the backyard. Elizabeth joined us every time we asked her to. She always had home-baked cookies, a smile on her face, and some fun ideas for the couple of hours I was spending there with them.

The grim look on Lucas's face every time I had to go home was an exact image of the one I thought was on my face. But we sucked it up, sneaked upstairs to our rooms, and continued talking through the windows, mouthing words and using signs until his father made him go to bed.

No one made me go to bed on time. My brother Tyler, who was ten at the time, sometimes read me a bedtime story that was actually a comic book about superheroes. I didn't listen to the words he read. I was just enjoying the fact he spent half an hour with me.

Maddie always came to check on me before she went to bed. She promised to braid my hair the next morning or take me out on the weekend for chocolate waffles. Dad came in too, late at night. He always woke me up when he did, but I pretended to be asleep. He kissed me, rearranged my blanket, and left without a word.

Only one person never came to my room. My mother.

CHAPTER FOUR

Clementine

The present

The first two days of the school year passed with a lot of Dylan Williams talk.

There were people who asked who he was. There were people who remembered who he was but forgot the last time they saw him. And there were a few people who knew who he was, what he did the last time he was here, and who he did it with. I dreaded those people.

I couldn't bear the possibility of someone bringing that into the light. I was already the weird chick with the weird hobby, and I didn't need that scandal blowing up in my face, considering I had no idea if I could trust Dylan not to reveal the only thing I managed to keep under wraps for so long. He was the only one who knew the whole story, except my best friend Hannah, and I wanted to keep it that way.

The football team seemed to train all the time these days, so I wasn't surprised to find them all on the field when I got outside on Wednesday. I was on the track team. It fit perfectly, given the fact I was always running away from someone or something in my life.

I was stretching alone a few steps away from the others when a finger poked my shoulder. I almost jumped out of my skin. I turned around. Dylan lifted his hands in the air as if he was trying to show me he was harmless, which I knew he wasn't. But I wasn't either, and he knew that about me too.

"I didn't mean to scare you. I just wanted to say hi."

"Hi then," I replied with the intention of turning my back on him, when I realized his outfit was more fitting for my track team than football practice. "I thought you were playing football?" I asked, confused.

"Yeah," Dylan smiled. "That didn't work out."

"Why?"

"The team's captain has a fragile ego."

My heart dropped to the ground. My worst nightmares were coming to life. Everything that happened that New Year's Eve four years ago would come out, and I had zero control over it.

"Are you okay?" Dylan frowned at me. "You look...horrified."

"What happened?" I managed to ask under my breath.

"With Lucas? Nothing really," he sounded disinterested. "He just made it clear he wasn't having me on his team. It's fine. There is a better company here anyway," he flashed me a grin.

I didn't answer. First of all, I was trying to regulate my heartbeat and, second of all, I didn't want to give him any indications I approved of his flirtatious comment.

I continued my stretch as if he wasn't there, doing my best to hide the mini breakdown I just had.

"Can we talk?" he asked.

"No."

"Why?" I heard the smile in his voice, and I glanced at him. He really looked amused.

"Because I don't enjoy talking while running. I prefer to be able to breathe."

His smile got even bigger.

"You weren't so grumpy the last time I saw you."

"People change."

"My point exactly," he took a step closer to me. "I know what I did the last time we saw each other was bad."

"Which part?" I mocked him, thinking he wouldn't continue. He surprised me.

"All of it. That whole evening was a mistake. I had my reasons for my behavior, but I had no right ..."

"Yeah, yeah. I got it," I cut him off. Some of the people around us were watching with open interest. Boys didn't usually come to me for a conversation. Not that I never went on a date. I just never went on a *second* date. And the girls had already labeled Dylan as the new hot guy. Me getting attention from him was not a desired outcome for the female part of the students. Which made them stare.

"No need to apologize," I added in my attempt to shut him up before someone heard the end of his story.

"Really? Because you looked like you could stab me to death for just coming over to say hi."

"Don't take it personally. I look at most people that way."

"But not Hannah. She's still your friend?"

I knew what the real question behind those words was: was Lucas still my friend?

I figured two days here were enough for him to find out on his own, but I decided to answer like a normal human, and not start an argument.

"Yes. Hannah is my friend. I know she's the one to show you around, and it's fine. That's her thing. She always takes the new people under her wing."

The new ones, the harassed ones, the wallflowers... She just couldn't bear to see people get hurt.

"I remember."

Of course he did. That's how he got into our group in the first place. Hannah brought him.

Dylan was still looking at me, even though I expected that conversation to be enough for him to move on.

"Is there something else?" I asked.

"No," he bit his lower lips with his perfect white teeth to suppress a smile. He really was handsome.

"Why are you still here then?"

"Honestly?" he took a step closer to me. "I feel connected to you somehow. You probably already heard why I'm here. My parents got divorced."

I heard. He had been the number one topic since he showed up. From the reason he was here to the number of dimples he had when he smiled, which was exactly two, one on each cheek, to the question that concerned my female classmates the most: did he have a girlfriend back home?

"Yes, I'm sorry about that," I said, and I meant it. At least I didn't have to move when my parents got divorced. Dylan left his whole life. I really felt sorry for him. He waved me off and shrugged.

"Are we good?" he asked and offered me his hand again like he did the first day at the parking lot. I didn't take it then. I was so overwhelmed by his sudden appearance after so many years that I didn't know how to react or what to expect. Now that he apologized, even though I interrupted him, I felt uncomfortable refusing him again.

His parents got divorced, he had to leave his whole life and move and, on top of that, he had to spend his senior year with complete strangers and a group of people who weren't exactly fond of him.

So, I took his hand and smiled.

"We're good."

Two days later, on Friday I was sitting on Hannah's bed, waiting for her to get ready for a party I wasn't invited to.

"I'm really sorry, Clem. But if I don't go, they'll cut my head off," Hannah apologized for a millionth time.

I got it. Lucas was the captain of the football team, and she was the captain of the cheerleaders. She had to go.

"It's fine," I shrugged, even though I felt awful and *not* because she was going.

Lucas's birthday party had been a big deal ever since his sixteenth one. People talked on and on about it for days. Not to mention it was held in his house, which was right in front of my window. Everyone was invited by default. Everyone except me. Not that he ever told me not to go. It was just common knowledge. No one even thought about it.

He was turning eighteen. I bet his football buddies would organize some kind of a special orgy to go with the theme of being allowed to fuck in every country around the globe. Not that any of them were refraining from sexual activity anyway. The stories about their parties sounded almost made-up, but Hannah had seen things with her own eyes. Stories were true, there was no doubt about that.

"No, it's not fine," she argued. "I really don't want to do this anymore. The new girls are so bad, I think at least one, but more likely two, will break a leg by the end of the season. The only thing that's keeping me from quitting is the joy it would bring to that bitch. And the fact that she will probably take my place."

There was bad blood between Hannah and Amy mostly because of me. Up until four years ago, we were all part of the same group. Now we were split into two. The rivalry between Amy and Hannah escalated because of cheerleading, and it became clear they would have hated each other anyway. They were somewhat alike. They both always got what they wanted, just in a different way and for different reasons.

Hannah was a force of nature. Smart and fearless, but nice and caring. No one could deny her anything if she decided to get it. She was all in and could draw you out from your cold, dark internal cave like a warm sunny day.

Amy was also smart and fearless, but in a selfish way. In the last few years she became sneaky, cunning, and vile. She used people to get what she wanted. Girls didn't really like her. She was hanging out a lot with the jocks. From what I was hearing, in a lot of places and in lots of different positions.

I sometimes wondered if she had slept with Lucas already. She always followed him around. I had a mental list of names of the girls he fucked as far as I knew from numerous stories I had heard over the last couple of years, but Amy's name was never mentioned. It was only a matter of time, considering they would be the perfect couple.

"Yeah, don't do this to the poor girls," I produced a fake laugh. "She will crush their souls."

Hannah read me like a book. She sat on the bed and took my hand in hers.

"I know in a way it sucks that Dylan's here. Bringing all the memories back," she paused. "But on the other hand, you have to admit. He apologized. He's acting nice so far. He ignores Lucas and the twins, so he's not trying to cause problems. And...He. Is. Hot." Hannah looked at me with caution, then she continued. "Too bad I don't date guys in high school anymore." I knew what was coming next before she said it. "But even if I was... he looks at you like he wants you to be his next meal."

I rolled my eyes at her sexual innuendo. She always tried to fix me up with someone. And yet everyone I went out with lost interest before we even went on a second date, which was pretty embarrassing and didn't actually help me get more dates.

"Let's go back to the part about you not dating guys in high school," I tried to change the subject. Hannah stood up and went to her jewelry box that was almost exclusively filled with my pieces. She started looking for something to wear with the short, hot pink dress she chose for the party. We looked so different. I sometimes wanted to wear a dress. But I was always wearing jeans. Ripped jeans, Daisy Dukes. Whatever. Sylvia hated jeans, but she considered ripped ones a personal insult. She was a model before she married Dad and she still dressed like she was going to a fashion show in five minutes.

"You should stop," I continued. "You know I say it because I love you. My brother *will* eat you for his next meal if presented with the possibility, and not in a pleasurable way."

Hannah had had a crush on my brother since we were twelve. At least at the beginning, I thought of it as a crush. Six years later it was more of an obsession. An unhealthy, risky, and dangerous obsession.

"I love my brother, but he is a dog," I added, and I meant it. He was the definition of a playboy. Unreliable, unpredictable, and also reckless. He wasn't dating material at all. He would break her heart into million pieces and then joyfully scatter them around the world, so that she would never be able to puzzle it back together.

"Clem, I know your brother has a dark side. But I think I see in him something you will never be able to because you're his sister," Hannah explained calmly.

"And what is that?" I asked with more disbelief than I intended to show.

"His soul. It's a broken one, yes, but still."

I sat silently for a couple of seconds. I didn't want to pressure her and make her feel bad. After all, my brother was thousands of miles away, and he came here so rarely, it would be a miracle if they saw each other more than once a year after graduation. And it wasn't like she was just sitting around, waiting for him to show up. She dated other guys. She would fall in love eventually.

"Can we go back to you fucking Dylan already?" she cut my thoughts. "'Cause we really have to go," Hannah asked with a smile. "I can't believe you're not sensing the sex vibes he's sending you".

"Oh, I am, believe me. I just don't trust him. Yet."

He was acting way too charming way too soon. There had to be something not quite right.

"You don't trust anyone, Clem," Hannah frowned. "That's your problem. You just assume everyone's all bad, and that's it."

I shook my head and smiled.

"Not true. I trust you."

"Anyone else?" Hannah asked with a pitiful look on her face.

I swallowed hard. We both knew the answer to that. She took my face in her palms.

"You should stop with the destructive behavior. Stop lying. Stop with all the secrets. You should call your father, tell him what's going on with Sylvia, and let him deal with it. And then... you should do something good for you. You should do Dylan. I'm not saying you should marry the guy. Just have some fun. He's new. He's hot. He's into you. It's perfect! That's if you bring yourself to stop hating your parents and mentally separate from them," Hannah tried to convince me.

"You should stop watching those self-help videos," I murmured, purposefully not engaging in discussing any of the problems she had listed, especially the lying parts, since she was one of the people I was currently lying to.

"Just think about it, Clem. Now get the fuck up. You have to drive me to that stupid party."

***

A few hours later, my walls vibrated with the voice of Lil Wayne bouncing off them. I was sketching. I tried reading, but I couldn't concentrate with the freaking noise that came from the Coles' house. Or at least I was convincing myself it was the noise and not the irrational anger that coursed through my body.

I was irritated, anxious, and had the urge to do something nasty to someone. Well, not someone. Lucas Cole would be my first target.

I even knew what to do to him. Yesterday, while I was running from my car to my front door, Elizabeth Cole showed up out of nowhere. It was almost like she was hiding behind a tree or something. She asked me to call her if her son's birthday party got out of hand. It was so bizarre. Asking me to do that, given the fact we hadn't really spoken for about the same amount of time I hadn't spoken to her son. We occasionally waved at each other. She tried to start a conversation with me every now and again, but I cut her off pretty fast.

I dismissed her request with a raised eyebrow and a snort. She pretended she didn't understand my reaction and smiled at me like I was an angel.

But now, hearing girls laughing in their backyard, under my window? I felt the urge to call her. I even grabbed my phone twice.

I didn't follow through. It would mean a war. A war between me and Lucas. A war between me and his football buddies. A war between me and every half-naked girl at that party. My curtains were closed like every other night, but I could imagine what they looked like. It seemed like there was a dress code for these parties. If your ass or tits weren't about to pop out, you were not dressed accordingly.

Everyone would be pissed at me for ruining the social event of the year and that didn't fit with my attempts to stay out of everyone's sight.

A loud thud mixed with Sylvia's scream came from downstairs and cut my dreams about ruining Lucas's party. Usually, I wouldn't even think of checking up on her, but with all those people so close to our family mess, I couldn't risk it for her to do something that would embarrass me. It was embarrassing enough that I was the only one not attending, if you're not counting Dylan. He was in the same boat with me when it came to Lucas's disdain.

I got up and went down. I found my mother on the kitchen floor. A chair was next to the counter. She must have fallen trying to take something from the open cabinet. I helped her get up without a word. She was silent too. No explanation, no gratitude. She seemed fine, nothing broken. Just drunk, as usual.

"What do you need?" I asked with the nagging feeling inside that told me she didn't deserve my help. But I wasn't stupid enough to let her fall again and crack her head open. That would mean countless hours with her in the hospital. They would start asking questions about her obvious alcohol abuse. I was still seventeen. They would call the police. The police would call my dad... No, thank you.

"The wedding china..." she hiccupped. "Throw it out."

"Seriously?" I took a deep, calming breath before I opened my mouth to speak again. It didn't help. "You want to throw out the wedding china, and you decided to do it now? In the middle of the night? Drunk as a skunk?" I asked, my irritation rising to new levels.

"Just do it, Clementine," she ordered, and it made me see red.

I swallowed all the accusations that tried to come out of my mouth. Nothing would change even if I allowed myself to vent. I would just give her the satisfaction of knowing she pushed my buttons. I stepped on the chair and stretched my arms so that I could find the fucking china that just had to be thrown out that very second. The cabinet was filled with old dishes no one had used in years.

"Why the hell are you keeping things you're not using?" I asked.

And why the hell am I still trying to talk to you?

Hannah must have gotten into my head with her be a do-gooder speech earlier.

Then I saw it. A very, very, very old and ugly mug. My sister Madison made it. I remembered the day she brought it home and gave it to mother. She had spent a week at some camp. I must have been four.

"Mom, look what I made for you!" Madison squealed with excitement and pulled the mug out of her backpack.

Sylvia took it and looked at it from all angles and simply said, "You could have done better."

Madison looked so sad and broken. She cried for half an hour while my mother cooked dinner and ignored her sobs. While I reacted to these kinds of insults from my mother with a violent refusal to live by her standards, Madison took the other path. She spent her entire childhood, trying to be the perfect daughter and please Sylvia in every possible way. She was a straight A student, captain of the cheerleaders, always composed and behaved. Not that mother appreciated it. She was cruel every time she thought Madison had failed in anything.

As a result, my sister was now a younger version of Sylvia. Cold. Heartless. But everything she did was flawless. She was always perfect. Just like Mom wanted all her children to be.

I turned to face my mother with Madison's old mug in my hands.

"I thought you hated this. You said it was ugly at least a thousand times over the years. Why do you keep it?" I asked, tears filling up my eyes. It was like a souvenir she kept to reminisce about the good old days when she was torturing us mentally.

"Your sister made it. You and your brother never bothered to give me anything. Madison was the only one who was grateful for everything I did for you. She's the only one who did something for me," she answered as if it was obvious.

"Then why the hell did you make her feel like shit about it?" I felt like I was about to scream.

"It's garbage. I did what I had to do so that she learns from her mistakes and stops making them."

"Are you fucking crazy?" I screamed at her. "She cried her eyes out! Your eleven-year-old daughter who wanted to give you something she made for you."

Sylvia snorted.

"Well, I'm sorry then, I should have kept every shitty thing you three ever made, put it on a shelf, and bragged about it."

Yes, you should have. At least while we were children.

"Your sister is a grown person now and understands. If you ask her, she would also tell you she thinks it's ugly and one should not be praised for something that's not..."

"Perfect?" I snapped, not being able to wait for her to finish the sentence.

She just exhaled like I was annoying her, which I knew I did ever since she gave birth to me. She waved me off and moved towards the living room. "Take the china down, Clementine."

I smashed the mug on the floor with a hysterical scream, and my mother turned to face me. Silence fell between us for a few seconds.

"You broke it beyond repair," Sylvia hissed as she looked at the pieces all over the kitchen floor.

"You broke your children beyond repair," I said, my throat hurting from the scream I had let out. I was now grateful there was a party next door, otherwise the neighbors would have heard me.

"You made Tyler and Madison run so far away that they have an excuse not to come back here. Guess what will happen when I graduate?" I smirked. I was in full bitch mode now. "You spent my entire life reminding me you never wanted me, and yet you pushed me to fulfill your expectations," I paused and got down from the chair. A piece of the mug pierced my foot, but I refused to let her see me in pain, so I went to her, not even bothering looking down to avoid other cuts.

I stopped one step away from her and shook my head still with a smirk on my face.

"Three children and you're gonna die alone. Probably covered in booze and your own vomit," I cocked my head to the side and wondered. "Do you think all three of us would make it to the funeral?"

Sylvia's eyes narrowed and her lips were so tightly pursed, it almost looked like she didn't have any.

"You are the biggest mistake I ever made," she said as if she hadn't already said that a thousand times. I shrugged.

"I don't care what you think of me. I'm not Madison."

Chapter Five

Lucas

Eight years ago

I was sitting on the grass in my backyard, looking at the new boy Hannah brought with her for the last couple of days. Everyone was already here, except Clem. We were going to play hide and seek. Amy was pushing us to start without her, but I wanted to wait. The others didn't care about the game anyway. Chase was inside, stuffing his face with my mother's home-baked cherry pie and making my two-year-old brother laugh, and Hannah was asking the new boy every question on planet Earth.

He was visiting his grandparents, who lived right next to Hannah. That was enough for her to start bringing him everywhere she went.

I didn't mind, but I didn't pay much attention to him either. He was only visiting for a few weeks this summer, so what was the point? But it was nice to have a third boy in the group. I was getting tired of playing girls' games most of the time just because there were two of us and three of them. The girls won every time we voted. Dylan, being here, didn't help us win, but it made the girls negotiate instead of just order us around.

I was glancing at the door leading to our kitchen for the fifteenth time, wondering if I should go get Clem, when she finally arrived. I jumped on my feet and smiled at her. She walked over to me first. We both did that whenever we entered a room. We immediately found one another. Mom said we were like magnets from the moment we met.

Clem stopped right in front of me with her red nose and puffy eyes; her gaze moved from her shoes to mine. I felt something in my chest every time she cried. I didn't know that it was, but it was painful, and it made me want to make her laugh no matter what.

"Can we play now?" Amy asked with irritation.

I ignored her and focused on Clem.

"Are you okay?"

She nodded and a smile I learned to recognize as a fake one formed on her lips.

"What are we playing?" her voice sounded different from the crying.

"Hide and seek?" I asked. We had already voted, but I didn't care. I would kick everyone else out and stare at the wall for the rest of the day if she wanted me to.

"Inside?" she wanted to know.

I nodded with pride. I had already convinced Mom to let us hide inside the house. We had a pretty big backyard but there were no good hiding places for six people.

While we played the first two games, I noticed Dylan was staring at Clem every time he had the chance. It annoyed me in a weird way. While seeing her cry weighted on my chest like someone was sitting on top of me, this felt more like something rising in my stomach, slowly but surely spreading all over my body all the way to my hands, making them clench into fists. And instead of feeling pushed down, I felt like I was able to demolish every wall around me.

She was my best friend, and I already shared her with Hannah. There was no way I was sharing her with him too.

"Do you want to go outside?" Clem suggested, then without waiting for anyone's answer pushed my shoulder, giggled, and started running. Had she felt the tension building inside me? Or she just wanted me to chase her? I wasn't sure, but I ran after her like I always did.

I heard the others teasing each other behind us. Soon we were all running away from the others, trying to avoid being caught. At some point the twins were both trying to catch me. I stood still for a moment, figuring out which way to go. I decided I had a better chance of escaping Amy than her brother, so I ran towards her and glanced around to check on Clem.

My eyes found her a second before it happened. She was running two steps ahead of Dylan, his hand was reaching out in the space between them, trying to catch her. And he did catch her. His fingers grabbed her ponytail while it was flying left and right over her shoulders, and he pulled.

It looked playful rather than harmful.

But she screamed.

Two seconds later I was next to them.

I knew she could handle anything on her own. I had seen her defend herself in school. She also held her own with her mother, who was the scariest woman alive, but I couldn't help myself. I punched him anyway. Straight in the chin, just like Dad taught me to.

It was my first real punch. I hurt my knuckles more than I expected, but I was proud of it anyway. My mother, who was always keeping an eye on us, materialized out of nowhere. She didn't scold me in front of my friends. Instead, she helped Dylan, but I knew I wasn't getting out of this one. She hated everything that could be qualified as violence.

Half an hour later, Dylan and Hannah left with his grandmother. Amy and Chase went home too. Clem was still hanging around. She was more than just a friend in my mother's eyes, so she explained to us both her ideas for my punishment.

"You're staying home for two weeks. No TV, no video games."

I was so pleased with myself for what I did, I didn't even try to feign remorse. And that punch was worth it. I wouldn't mind adding two more weeks if someone gave me permission to make his eye blue too.

My mother noticed my smug face and that provoked her to add a little something.

"And no visitors," she looked at Clem. "You'll have to go, honey. I'm sorry."

Clem's eyes were huge at that moment. Neither of us could believe it. She started walking away, but then ran back to me, grabbed me in a bear hug, and squeezed hard. I hugged her back and whispered in her ear a single word, but I knew she would get it.

She left, and I immediately got upstairs to my room and glued myself to the windows, waiting. Two minutes later, I saw her doing the same in her own room. Smiles formed on both our faces while we looked at each other.

Not seeing Clem felt unmanageable the moment my mother uttered it aloud, but those two weeks turned out to be the best time I had ever spent up until then. We both stayed in our rooms every single day.

We read the same book; played the same games. We wrote each other notes on big pieces of paper and pressed them against our windows.

One day, her brother Tyler walked in her room and saw me looking at them from my house. He pointed at me and asked her something. I saw her shrug while she answered him back. I waited for Mom to come and move me to a different room. She didn't. The next day Tyler installed a TV in Clementine's room with the screen facing my windows.

By the time the punishment ended, Clementine had gone out zero times. Just like me. She had had zero visitors. Just like me.

And when my mother finally allowed me to invite my friends over and Hannah brought Dylan along with her, I didn't mind him staring at Clem. Because now I knew she would choose me over him.

CHAPTER SIX

Lucas

The present

My birthday party was wild. Good-looking people doing ugly-ass stuff. Except me. Not this time, anyway. I promised myself to stay away from girls and alcohol during the season. Nothing was more important than football, and I never let anything compromise my performance. And I also had a nagging feeling related to my neighbor and the new guy that prevented me from having a good time. I saw them on the field the other day. She was stretching and he was ogling her ass. He was in the track team now, and it crossed my mind that I might have done him a favor by refusing to accept him in my team.

I could have tortured him during practice and kept him away from Clementine. But now they had something in common. Something that would bring them closer.

Good work, Cole. Why don't you offer him a condom with her name on it the next time you see him?

I scanned the room. Two girls were staring at me from different corners. Amy had been sending me inviting looks ever since she got here, and I ignored them all, as usual. Even if she wasn't my best friend's sister, I would still avoid her. I didn't do relationships, and I had the feeling Amy would want one from me.

Hannah Spencer, on the other hand, was sending me hateful looks, as she had for the past four years, and I was so used to it, I ignored them all too. She was the captain of the cheerleaders and the most popular girl in the fucking school, but still no match for me. She was in no position to put me down. It was exactly the other way around and she knew it. She just didn't care. She was so loyal to that liar.

The fact I wasn't fucking anyone tonight, or any night in the foreseeable future, wasn't going to stop me from fantasizing about it. I was imagining a girl a few steps away from me, in a very compromising position, trying like my life depended on it not to compare her with the brunette next door, when someone smacked my back.

"It's official," Chase declared. "You're becoming a cunt, aren't you? Do you know you're pouting? What happened? Someone has prettier nails?".

I might agree his stunts during games were funny if you're not the captain of his team, but the drunk Chase was a fucking asshole and pissed everyone off. The good thing was he didn't hold a grudge if you punched him in the drunken face. I knew that from personal experience.

"Go take a nap, man," I didn't pay attention to his attempts to irritate me. "Would you like me to entertain your girlfriend while you do?" I purposefully used the word *girlfriend*. I knew it could make him break sweat and, possibly, vomit.

"Have at it, birthday boy! But you could wait a minute and put your now-adult dick in..." Chase paused and stared at the front door, "...that.". At the door stood a not-so-sexy stripper. Or at least that was my first thought. Then I replayed Chase's words in my head again and finally got the occupation right.

"Are you out of your fucking mind?" I hissed as the crowd around us spotted the new face at the door and started whistling. "You called a hooker? There is a ton of underage drinking happening feet away from suburban moms who will speed-dial 911 the second they see her. And the more important question. What am I? A fucking virgin? A forty-year-old divorced dentist?" I wasn't raising my voice yet, but I was getting there. I just needed to get rid of that walking gonorrhea on a stick first.

"Relax, it's just a joke. Because of your celibacy, you know?" Chase slurred. "Why are you so touchy lately?"

"My celibacy?"

I pretended I didn't hear his last sentence, because we both knew why. There was no point in stating something that was already known by everyone involved in the conversation.

I left him standing and marched through the living room. Guys started howling and tapping my shoulders as if there was some sort of accomplishment in banging someone who got paid for it. I saw Hannah's disgusted look as I passed her by. I was never going to admit it out loud, but the thought of Clementine hearing about this made my skin crawl.

"Hi," I cleared my throat. "There has been a misunderstanding. Your services won't be needed. You can leave." I pulled cash from the back pocket of my jeans. She put her hand on mine, preventing me from giving her a generous undeserved tip.

"It's already paid," she purred. "Are you sure you don't want to see what the fuss is all about, honey?" Her voice was no doubt deliberately sweet and inviting. She didn't know she was just a part of a joke. She thought I was a virgin.

"I know exactly what the fuss is all about, *honey*. My friend is a moron. Let me give you something extra for the ride ho... wherever you're going".

She motioned closer to me, her hand sliding from my wrist up in an attempt to... what? Seduce me? Change my mind? Shouldn't she be happy that she got paid for nothing?

"I'm sure the girl you slept with is no match for me, handsome." She removed her hand from my shoulder and aimed for my crotch. I caught it midair and held it inches away from my very, very soft dick as I examined her face. Maybe she was pretty when she started doing tricks, but who could say for sure. She looked forty, tired as fuck, and repulsively motivated to make me fuck her.

"Listen, lady," I tried to emphasize the age difference between us, "If I decide to, my pussy count this week alone will exceed your number of prepaying dicks for the whole month. I don't need your services. If you need to get laid, you're free to take with you the jackass who found you in the first place. I'm sure he wouldn't mind. Now, turn around and get the fuck out."

I turned my back on her and went back to Chase, who was frowning at me. I pushed him into the laundry room. I needed a minute away from all those assholes in my house anyway.

Chase was looking at me like he knew something I didn't.

"What?" I snapped.

"You'll regret it, man," he shook his head.

"Regret what? Avoiding a burning sensation every time I take a leak? Or not spending the night in the police station after someone already pissed off about the noise we're making decides a hooker in the neighborhood is a bit too much?"

My mother would burn my mattress along with my ass if she knew a hooker was dripping juices on it. And Elizabeth Cole was nice, delicate, and had a cheerful spirit. Sylvia Hartley, for example, was our street's version of a cartoon character that skinned puppies to make herself a coat. She would skin *me* alive and wear me with a smirk. I had no doubt the two women next door would call the cops and guide them directly to my ass.

"I'm not talking about the hooker. She'll walk all over you, man. *Again*," Chase cut my thoughts who were already spiraling in Clementine's direction anyway. "Besides, I heard her and Dylan are getting cozy."

"No way," I snorted. "She can't be into him."

But I knew she could, and Chase spoke the words that were already forming in my head.

"She liked him once," he mumbled. "And no offense, but every girl in school likes him. Ever since he came back, you can't stop yourself from looking at her. Why do you think that is?" he asked sarcastically. "You're looking for clues. Admit it."

It was true. Despite my every intention, my eyes drifted in her direction every time she was near. I knew there was no point in trying to hide it, so I decided not to even try.

"I don't want her," I said and crossed my arms over my chest. "I just don't want *him* to have her either".

"Yeah, I know. Him *and* anyone else," Chase pressed.

A knock on the door saved me from that embarrassing conversation. Every fucker in school knew he had to stay away from Clementine if he wanted to walk around on his feet instead of rolling in a wheelchair in the hallways. I issued a personal warning to every asshole that asked her out. Chase and I just never talked about it, although I'd seen his opinion on his face. It screamed that I was pathetic.

"Are you boys decent?" Amy asked from the other side of the door, trying to be funny and failing.

I opened it and she scanned our faces. She was aware something was happening. She was probably eavesdropping.

"Bradley's dad texted him. Someone called the station and complained about the music. An officer is coming. Everyone's leaving," Amy paused and looked me in the eye. "I could stay," she licked her lips and swallowed. "Help you clean up".

"No, thank you. I'm good."

An hour later, I was enjoying the silence and looked for empty bottles or other garbage tossed in my front lawn. I didn't want a used condom to stick to my mother's fancy shoes. It would make me look bad and cut my credibility in half for other future parties.

I heard a noise coming from Clementine's front lawn, and I turned my head in that direction. Sylvia was dragging a box. I looked at my phone. It was almost two in the morning. What the hell were those two witches doing in the middle of the night?

Sylvia fell on her ass, and the knight in shining armor in me almost jumped out of my body to go help her. I had to stuff him back in. I wasn't helping them. Not with their trash, not with their heavy boxes.

My mother would be disappointed in me, but I left Sylvia Hartley sitting on the grass next to her box and went back inside. I got upstairs to my room and flipped the switch. My gaze fell on Clementine's window. Her curtains were closed, as always. I knew she must have heard some of the noises we were making tonight. At least the music. I wondered what she thought about the fact she was the only person who wasn't welcome. Well, her and her new BFF.

I turned the lights off again and approached the window.

Why was she trying to make herself invisible? It made no sense. And yet she rarely made any sense. That was part of her charm.

***

Days rolled on as they did every year. A whole month had passed since the beginning of the season, and we were killing it so far. Coach Howard looked so pleased with our performance he could piss in his pants like a dog, but he kept pushing us. Me in particular. It wasn't so bad, because it was a distraction from the two lovebirds everyone in school talked about.

Girls were wondering if Dylan and Clementine were together. I tried not to ask myself the same question every five minutes like a normal, sane person wouldn't. I mostly failed. I observed the situation closely.

Was he coming to visit her at home? He wasn't.

Were they going out on dates? They weren't.

I checked. Multiple sources.Not that the lack of official dates meant anything, I knew that better than anyone, but the fact no one ever saw them making out was a good sign.

A good sign? You hate her, remember? The only sign you should be thinking about when it comes to her is the middle finger.

"What the hell does he see in her? It's just not right," Chase's girl for the day supplied, her shoulder on my locker.

"Oh, yeah? How so?" I asked her, itching to pick up a fight with someone. I was feeling restless, and every time Clementine passed me by with Dylan walking next to her, I wanted to grab him by the fucking neck. Not that I was jealous or anything. They just didn't deserve to be together, to be happy. And it pissed me off they might eventually be.

In order to prevent a very public strangulation from happening, I needed to take my fury out on someone else.

"She only hangs out with Hannah," the girl started counting on her fingers. "She doesn't really like people. And can you imagine how many hours she puts in in order to make that jewelry? How sad is her life exactly?" she chuckled. "And he's hot. Like a Hemsworth brother hot. It's weird he's into her."

"Don't you think it's weird you sucked every dick on the football team and now you have to start from the beginning?" I asked, and her face went blank for a second, then her gaze fell on my crotch.

"If I'm starting from the beginning..." She made a show of licking her lips.

"No," I roared. "Also get the fuck off my locker."

She moved without saying a word and dragged Chase to class. I had one with Clementine. For the past four years I never had a problem having classes with her. I pretended she was air. Now it was a completely different story. I felt her presence in the room with every fucking cell of my body.

I stepped into the classroom ten minutes late. Clementine was standing in front of everybody. She looked my way only for a moment. Her whole face reddened.

She is still uncomfortable around me.

A satisfaction coursed through me. I loved moments like this one. I had a reason to look right at her. She was standing in front of the whole class.

"Sorry I'm late, Miss Brown. Coach How..."

"It's fine, Lucas, take a seat. Clementine, please continue."

I chuckled. I once promised I would never call her by her full name. Today I would do it over and over again. I would scream it from a roof, on the field, from my fucking bedroom window, just to cause her pain.

If I talked to her, that is, which I didn't plan on doing. If her presence could do all this shit to me, I didn't want to find out what a fucking conversation would.

"Thank you, Miss Brown." I smiled and took a seat in the back of the classroom. I looked at Clementine's face again. She was irritated, uneasy. She was looking around, probably trying to figure out how to prevent this from happening.

"Clementine, go on," Miss Brown pushed her with frustration.

I grinned. At that exact moment, Clementine's gaze searched for mine. A single second felt like eternity. We hadn't looked at each other so openly in ages. Her eyes narrowed when her doubts were confirmed. I was taking pleasure in this.

She returned to whatever the hell she was reading, and I didn't hear a fucking word. All I did was stare at her. She, however, didn't look at me again for the rest of the class.

For the rest of the week, to be exact. I tried to do the same.

On Friday I watched them warm up for their track workout during my practice. They were laughing. A sixteen-year-old knocked me down and pushed the air out of my lungs like I was a ragdoll. Chase just shook his head, not saying a word.

I spent that same evening on his couch. Amy was there too. She tried to glue her thigh to mine. Chase noticed she was too close, but he just rolled his eyes. I knew his official position was he didn't care what was happening between us.

"My sister is a big girl. If she wants you to break her heart, that's her choice," he told me once.

We watched some stupid horror flick but even that amount of screams, blood, and gore didn't distract my mind enough for it to stop showing me images of Clementine's face smiling at Dylan.

It was 1 a.m. when I finally left. I was almost at home when something caught my attention in Clementine's house. A weird light inside their living room. I stopped on the sidewalk, giving a few seconds to my preoccupied brain to understand what was happening.

A fire.

My heart dropped. I ran to the front door and started ringing the doorbell so I could wake them up. Then I broke the nearest window and got inside. And I froze by the staircase, looking at their living room.

It was covered in candles. All of them lit. It looked insane. The window curtains were burning, and the fire was spreading fast. There was a lot of smoke already. Footsteps thundered from the second floor down the stairs. I saw the shock on Clementine's face when she saw me. I also saw the fear written all over it. Then she passed right beside me and sprinted into the living room. I grabbed her by the elbow and jerked her back.

I was about to scream at her crazy ass when she pulled her hand away from mine.

"My mother!" she screamed in my face.

I hadn't noticed Sylvia was there. Clementine ran to their sofa and started shaking her mother pretty hard. She looked as if she had passed out.

"Move," I barked, and Clementine stopped her hand midair just before she bitch-slapped Sylvia. I kneeled next to the unconscious woman and took her in my arms, honeymoon style.

"Is there anyone else in the house?" I asked between coughs as we got out on their front lawn.

"No," she said, her voice all husky from the smoke.

We crossed the street, and I put her mother down on the ground and tried to find her pulse. I really thought she was dead, but she wasn't. And yet, the way Clementine shook her would have woken up a person who was alive.

Maybe she's taking sleeping pills. Isn't that a thing with old people?

"Call 911," I said, tossing my phone behind my back, still focused on Sylvia.

Silence. I looked behind my shoulder. Clementine just sat there on the grass, half naked and barefoot, looking at her home. I could already hear the fire crackling behind me. All of a sudden, she jumped on her feet and ran Usain Bolt-style back to her house.

I left Sylvia without even thinking and went after Clementine. I grabbed her by the waist and pinned her to my chest. I pressed her back to me as hard as I could without hurting her. She was fighting me. She wanted to get back inside.

"Are you fucking crazy?" I yelled, as I stumbled back with her body still pressed against mine. She produced something resembling a roar as she tried to escape me. I felt amused, which was really sick I had to admit. Who took pleasure in anything at a moment like that?

Me. I did. The guy who felt like his entire body exploded the minute her back hit my chest.

The neighbors started coming out of their houses, they have probably heard me screaming at her. Gasps and shouting surrounded us.

All I could focus on were her moans as she tried to free herself from me.

"Did anyone call 911?" a woman asked. My mother actually. Her voice was alert but still sounded pretty normal. Something I couldn't say about some other female residents of our street who were piercing my ears with their howls.

"Stop fighting me," my lips touched her ear and she quivered. "I won't let you go back in there."

I allowed myself to think for a second it was my touch that made her tremble, but it was in the middle of the night, and she was almost naked. She was wearing a t-shirt that barely covered her ass.

The ass that was now pressed against my groin, by the way.

Besides, she was probably in shock and obviously NOT into me as she has proven over and over again for years.

Much to my surprise, she did what she was told. She stopped fighting. She was breathing heavily, her eyes never leaving the sight of her burning home.

I took my hands off her, and I expected her to give me shit about what I did. She didn't even turn to look at me. She just stared at the fire. I took a step back to give her some space, but not enough for her to be able to flee.

My father mouthed *Are you okay?* and I nodded. Troy, my little brother, was glued to his side and looked terrified. Fuck, that fire looked terrifying to me, and I wasn't a child anymore.

Clementine, on the other hand, didn't look scared at all. Or unhappy. She looked... mesmerized?

Weirdo.

I looked at Sylvia. She was surrounded by people. I only saw her feet. She looked like a corpse, and I was glad Clementine wasn't looking in that direction.

I heard sirens and, a minute later, paramedics were examining Sylvia, and firefighters were trying to put out the fire. From the outside it looked like it had consumed everything inside the house. Clem literally had only that old t-shirt she was wearing and nothing else. Her mother was unconscious, and there was no one here for her.

I didn't want to be the one consoling her.

"Do you want me to call someone?" I asked.

"Hannah," she mouthed more than vocalized.

Of course. Hannah. I could have figured that out on my own.

As I dialed, I saw a scratch that started from my wrist and ended almost at my elbow. I had felt Clementine scratching me while I was pulling her away from her house, but I didn't think she could actually leave me bleeding. I was amused and impressed. I looked at her and grinned.

Freak.

Ten minutes later, Hannah arrived. She jumped out of her car in pajamas and socks. No shoes. No jacket.

Sylvia had already been taken to the hospital, and a police officer was questioning Clementine, or at least he was trying, and I was standing nearby, feeling oddly protective of her. She had a hard time forming a coherent sentence, and it didn't feel right to leave her alone. But now that Hannah was here, I could.

I should.

I didn't.

That guy was an asshole who tormented her while she clearly wasn't fit to answer his stupid questions.

"Officer, maybe I could be of use, since I'm the one who woke them up?" I asked, and Clementine turned her head in my direction. Her confused look rattled me.

She was a mess. Her hair was tangled, and her face was covered in soot. If I lined her up in row right now with every other girl from school in their tight dresses with their perfect hairdos, she would still be the most beautiful.

I pushed that thought aside.

"I mean, she's in shock or something, and her house just burned down."

"Are you teaching me how to do my job, son?" The cop used his stern voice, trying to intimidate me. Before I could answer, he barked at me. "Name and address."

Then he pointed at Clem with his pen, "You can go. But I want you in the station first thing in the morning. Is this the friend you're staying with?"

"Yes, she's staying with me," Hannah answered for Clem. "My father is Harry Spencer." She used her father's name to scare him off. I smiled.

"Oh. OK then," the cop changed his attitude immediately. "Will Mr. Spencer be coming to the station too?"

Harry Spencer was the meanest criminal defense attorney in a thousand-mile radius. He represented real criminals quite often, and his success rate was astronomical. The police and every normal person in town hated his guts.

But no one dared to say so to his face. So everyone just kept licking his ass.

"Sure," Hannah said and pulled Clementine away from us. Before she got in her car, she looked at me and mouthed a thank you. I nodded and dared to look one more time at Clem, who was sitting on the passenger seat. Her eyes were pinned on me.

CHAPTER SEVEN

Clementine

I spent the days after the fire at Hannah's place. My father showed up the first afternoon for about five minutes. He told me he had to do something, gave me a new phone and a credit card, and left.

"I'll come back later," he said.

That was three days ago.

He texted me once to order me not to go to school until he came back and that was it. So, I was lying around all day long at the Spencers', waiting for him and thinking about my current situation. Everything pointed in one direction.

I was screwed.

The money was gone. Burnt to ashes along with my dreams of freedom. I didn't have a backup plan. Every penny I had was lost in that stupid fire. Unfortunately, the second floor was also damaged, as

Hannah's father informed me, which meant my drawings were gone too.

"You sound depressed. Do you want me to come?" Tyler asked when he called a few hours after dad left me the phone.

"No, I'm fine," I answered immediately. I didn't need my irresponsible brother here. I needed my money back. But at least he offered. Madison didn't even bother calling. I knew she was somewhere in Europe now, organizing glamorous events with her fashionable boss, but I would call if she was almost baked to death in her sleep.

And I really was fine. I wasn't depressed. I was mad at myself for forgetting to take the money out of that pillow when I had the chance. Or my sketches that were spread all over my desk in my room, I could have snatched them.

My anger started mixing with boredom by day three. I had one constant source of entertainment, though.

I played over and over again in my head the moment Lucas grabbed me, preventing me from going back inside the house. I had remembered the money and I wanted to get it. When Lucas squeezed me and pulled me back, it pissed me off so much. I wanted to take his skin off with my nails. I dug them in his arms and pressed, and dragged until I felt his warm blood on my fingertips.

And yet it felt good, being so close to him.

I didn't even want to begin to think about the fact we spoke to each other. Like exchanging actual words. Were we talking now?

Another thing I couldn't get over was my absent mother. Everyone assured me she was fine and nothing scary happened to her and yet she didn't call. Just like her pretty little Madison. I wouldn't be surprised if the two of them coordinated the act of ignoring me.

The Spencers refused to tell me where she was. They only told me that my father was with her, and she was no longer in the hospital.

I wondered if she was badly burnt, and they moved her to another medical center, although I was sure the fire hadn't reached the sofa at all while she was still lying on it.

Hannah's parents knew my mother was drinking. I had broken into tears once in their house after a fight with her, and they refused to let me go without explaining what was wrong. But I sensed my mother's alcohol abuse made them uncomfortable, so I was avoiding the subject. I knew they must have figured out that my mother was drunk, and even suspected she was responsible, which she was. There was no doubt about that. And yet I didn't say a word about it, and as I noticed by now, neither did they. They were hiding something. On day four of my visit at their house, I found out what.

My father arrived that Tuesday and was looking bad. His clothes were wrinkled, which never happened to him. He looked sleep-deprived and nervous. He had a beard that was a few days old and huge dark spots under his eyes.

It wasn't his usual look. He was always charming, cracking jokes. His normal behavior was more suitable for a teenager than a fifty-year-old divorced architect, but at least it answered the one-million-dollar question: what did his numerous twenty-year-old girlfriends find in him?

Answer: Richard Hartley was as fun as a frat boy and had the wallet of a... well, a fifty-year-old architect.

I assumed this was the reason his young PA fell for him after their brief affair while my parents were still married. One day she came knocking on our door to inform my mother she was sleeping with dad and to make a scene, both of which lead to their divorce six months later.

My father squinted and cleared his throat. He looked frustrated.

"We have to talk."

Was he holding me responsible for not telling him about mom? I braced myself for the blow. He rubbed his cheek.

"Your mother is in rehab."

Pause.

"She caused the fire."

Pause.

"Well, not on purpose," he reached for my hand. I let him squeeze it. My heart was sinking into a huge pond of guilt. "She swears it was an accident. I can't imagine how hard it must have been for you. To watch her fall apart like that and to have no clue what to do to help her."

There were two problems with that statement. I knew exactly what I had to do; I just didn't want to do it. And I definitely thought she didn't deserve any help. Not from me anyway. But I knew better and kept these thoughts to myself.

"Where is she?" I asked, avoiding the conversation he obviously wanted us to have.

"She's close. There is a great center in Nevada. I drove her there and settled her in."

"How did you know?" I asked.

"Doctors figured it out. She cried the whole drive to the center. She can't believe you almost died because of her."

Oh wow. Mother of the year.

"I don't want to rush you," he continued. "We could talk about this if you need to, but we have a bigger problem," my father said hesitantly.

I forced myself to stay calm.

"Our house burnt down; we could have been dead. How is there a bigger problem?"

"I know. I know," he sighed and held his head between his palms. "God, I know. I can't even imagine getting that call. It was nerve-wracking when I knew you were safe."

"What's the big problem then?" I cut his drama performance short. I had to know what was wrong.

"The program your mother will have to complete is... long." He watched me like I was about to burst, which I was, mostly because I already sensed where this was going.

"I'm not moving," I said nonchalantly.

"Clem..."

"I. Am. Not. Moving."

"I think it's the healthiest option for you. I already talked with a great therapist in Seattle. You could start seeing him this week."

"A therapist now?" A dark chuckle escaped my lips. "No."

"Clem," he warned.

"Dad," I mimicked his voice.

I knew he didn't have it in him to get angry with me. He had no trouble putting his foot down when it came to Madison or Tyler. But I was his soft spot. I had always been.

"I can just stay here. It makes sense," I smiled. I had just lost my childhood home and every single possession I had, and I still preferred to live with strangers than my own father. I had to try to soften my rejection.

"No," he said, a little more determined than I expected.

"Oh, come on, Dad. The Spencers are great. It's my last year. Besides, Mom will be back in a month or so, right?"

He shook his head. "Three. She'll be back in January."

"Fine, three. It's not that big of a deal."

Except it was. It was way too long for them to leave me without a parent at the age of seventeen.

"The Spencers wouldn't mind, Dad. Please. Don't make me move."

"I don't want you staying in their house. They told me they knew about your mother. They should have called me. This might have never happened."

I'm the one who should have called you.

"You're not staying here. I don't trust their judgment." He sounded determined. Panic waves were washing over me. My stupid feud with my mother led to this.

"You could rent me an apartment?" I said without thinking, and yet the moment I said it, I realized it made perfect sense. "We will have to rebuild the house, right? And I will be eighteen soon. I could live on my own."

"Are you crazy?" he looked at me as if I really was out of my mind. "You almost died because of your irresponsible mother. I'm not going to be the other parent that lets you down. You're not living alone. This is your senior year. You have to finish school. I'm not letting you play games pretending to be an adult."

Ouch.

"Well, Dad, you won't let me live alone, you don't trust the Spencers, and I won't come to Seattle. Any other ideas?" I was pretty sure I was winning the argument. He would agree to leave me with the Spencers. He had to. It was the safest house in the state. Criminals would never target their home. Harry Spencer was their BFF.

"Ideas? No." My father grinned and my stomach turned. "I have a whole plan."

***

Twenty minutes later, we were standing on our street, eyes glued to what was left of our house. I hoped my mother really suffered. I knew it meant a lot to her. All the fancy furniture, the designer clothes, the pictures from her modeling days.

My father put a hand over my shoulders.

"I'm sorry, Clem, we have to speed things up. I really need to go back to Seattle. My plane is in three hours."

"What?" my head snapped in his direction.

"I have to go to the airport," he repeated softly. He was scared I would make a scene. He hated scenes. Especially those created by women. No doubt my mother's constant hysterics had something to do with it.

I suppressed a ton of insults I could use about him and her that were flying inside my head.

"You haven't even told me the plan. What if I don't like it?"

He shrugged. "You could always come to Seattle. Although you'll have to get on another plane because my flight is fully booked. I got the last seat. My assistant really deserves a bonus," he chuckled.

I bet I know what kind of bonus you want to give her.

"I'm not moving to Seattle. And I don't like this. It feels like you're cornering me," I sulked.

"I think you'll like it. Come on."

He shook me with his hand still over my shoulders and pulled me in a direction I would never ever consider as a place to stay overnight, let alone spend the next three months.

My mouth stopped working. I couldn't make a sound. I just walked next to him. Dad rang the doorbell and seconds later, Elizabeth Cole opened the door with a welcoming smile on her face.

"Oh my God, Clem," she dragged me into an awkward hug. "I'm really sorry. I can't even imagine the horror... I'm happy we can help." She squeezed me harder.

Behind her back I saw Troy, Lucas's little brother. He was the only member of their household I didn't know what to expect from. He was so little when I stopped coming here, I practically didn't know him.

He was looking at me and seemed impatient. I wondered if he had the attitude of his brother. If he was going to hate me like Lucas. I couldn't believe I was scared of a ten-year-old now, but he had the same piercing blue eyes the older Cole son had, and at that moment they were dissecting me.

"Umm...," my father cleared his throat. "I really have to go catch my flight. Thank you, Elizabeth. You're a life-saver." Then he kissed my hair, put his hand on my back, and pushed me inside. "Call me if you need anything. Love you!"

And he just left. My mouth fell open, and I sensed my eyes trying to pop out of their sockets while I looked at his back. Did my parents go to some class on how to be the shittiest parents in the world? Because they could definitely teach it.

The only thing that was good about my current situation was that it looked like only Elizabeth and Troy were home. It made sense. It was a Tuesday afternoon. The football team had practice. But I still had to leave. Fast.

"Clem," Elizabeth was looking at me as if I was a puppy. A blind, three-legged, left-by-the-fucking-road, dying puppy. The saddest part was I got it. Every normal human being wouldn't approve of what just happened. And I knew Elizabeth was a good person. A good mother. There was no way she approved of this. "I'll cut to the chase. I got the feeling your father doesn't know that you and Lucas... you know."

"That we don't talk or look at each other? I told him years ago. Obviously, it slipped his mind."

Elizabeth narrowed her eyes at me and cocked her head. Her eyes moved from me to Troy only for a second, but I saw it. The hesitation. She didn't like my negativity and wasn't appreciating the dark vibe I brought with me to their perfect home.

Don't worry, Elizabeth, having a broken family is not contagious.

"Look, I don't know why this is happening, but obviously I won't stay. I'll go back to the Spencers' house and I'll call my dad."

"Don't," she almost yelled when I turned to open the front door. "Please, Clem, stay. I know it must be weird for you because of Lucas. But I promise you, he will be on his best behavior."

I shook my head. He may have saved my life, but there was no way he would be okay with me living in his house. I was not okay with it either, and I was basically homeless.

I faced her again, full of suspicion.

"Why do you want me to stay here? He won't be happy about it."

That was an understatement. He was going to be furious.

"I talked to your father a few days ago. He came to see your house... you know," she waved her hand dismissively. "He said he was sure you won't go to Seattle, and he didn't want to leave you with the Spencers. He didn't know what to do." She paused, looking attentively at my face. "You can't live on the street, Clem."

"And?" I asked, knowing there was something more important to her than my well-being.

"And Mom thinks Lucas is a selfish little prick, and he needs to get down to earth," the little man behind her answered my question.

"Troy!" Elizabeth gasped.

"That's what you said to Dad," he shrugged.

A smile tried to form on my lips, but I suppressed it. They were a cute picture together, but I had to get out of here.

"I'm sorry. I don't see how all this is related to me." I started walking backwards, moving closer to the front door.

Elizabeth took a deep breath. "Please, spend the next three months here. I swear you will be treated like a member of this family by *everyone*. I'll make sure of that."

Yeah, good luck with that.

"You can go to school, be with your friends, and maintain your usual life. I won't try to parent you outside of the rules your parents want you to follow."

"In exchange?" I asked sharply.

She shook her head. "Nothing. I don't want you to do anything. Just live your life under our roof while your house is being repaired."

I had mixed feelings about her agenda and, luckily, Troy meddled in the conversation again.

"Mom thinks you being here will help Lucas become normal again. I think he's a lost cause."

Elizabeth turned towards her son, "He went into a burning house because of her."

So that's what this was all about. I laughed. Elizabeth looked confused.

"I'm sorry, Elizabeth, but you got it all wrong. Me staying here would be a disaster."

"OK, then. No worries," Elizabeth smiled. "Thank you for listening anyway." She grabbed her phone. "I'll book you a seat on the next flight to Seattle."

"No." I shook my head and smiled. I could be nice if I wanted to. And right now, I wanted to. I needed her to let me go without resistance. "I'm not going to Seattle."

"Sorry, sweetheart. Your father was very clear about it." She grinned. "If you refuse to stay here, I have to buy you a ticket for the next plane and make sure you board it. And I always keep my promises."

An hour and a half later, I was lying on the floor in Elizabeth Cole's guest room, looking at the ugliest chandelier I had ever seen in my life. The carpet was comfy though.

It was a typical guest room. Definitely designed for grown-ups. There was a big double bed, two nightstands, a big closet that I couldn't fill in, since the clothes I currently had, a pair of jeans and two shirts, were borrowed. I got my phone out of my pocket and wrote Hannah a message:

Me: We have to go shopping. I want my own clothes.

I ignored her one thousand messages concerning my whereabouts. I still wasn't sure that I would stay. Or that we would go shopping together for that matter. I couldn't bring myself to lie on the bed. I considered it a decision-making act. The decision to stay here and accept what others had planned for me. My father's rules for me staying in California. Elizabeth Cole's agenda for me staying at her home.

These plans weren't what I wanted for myself. I had no desire whatsoever to please my father. I'd had enough of his hands-off parenting approach. And I had no desire to let Elizabeth Cole exploit on my family drama. I already had a controlling birth mother.

A thought was circling my mind. I could run away. I could go to Boston and stay with Tyler. He was irresponsible enough not to care about me graduating or that I was underaged. I could wait until everyone was asleep and write a note where I was going. By the time they found it, I would already be far away enough for them not to be able to bring me back.

A gentle knock on the door startled me.

"Clem? Can I come in?"

I sat up and invited her. Elizabeth's smile dropped when she saw me on the floor.

"What are you... Is there a problem with the bed?" she asked and looked sincerely perturbed.

I didn't buy it though. Why would she be worried about me? I hurt her son.

"Yes, there is. It's not mine. And not to sound offensive, but it's unnatural you suggested I stay here. You must have known your son hates me. Are you trying to get back at me or something?"

She froze for a few seconds. Then she sighed and sat on the floor next to me.

"Sometimes people do things that seem unreasonable, but actually make a lot of sense. If you really think about it."

"You want me to *heal* him," I said mockingly. "Not that I know what that even means. But that's why you invited me here."

"No," she shook her head. "I invited you here because your father had no idea what to do. After I talked to him, I just couldn't get you out of my head. I wanted to help you. At some point I saw something I could benefit from, if you stay here. Is that so bad?"

Her voice was calm and soothing. That was the reason I often imagined Elizabeth was my mother when I was a kid. She was compassionate and caring.

"I can't do what you need me to do for him," I said honestly. "I have no idea how."

"I don't want you to do anything. I swear." She paused and then continued. "He doesn't want to fall in love, you know? And he's leaving soon. I can't send him off to college knowing he will continue with these meaningless relationships he has with girls. I want him to be happy. He can't be happy if he's scared to love. He needs to forgive you."

I was the worst possible person for the job. Forgiveness wasn't even in my vocabulary. But I couldn't say it to her. That would require me to open up to someone.

No-fucking-thanks.

"I know it's a lot to ask, but I think I could do something for you. Compensate you for your efforts." She smiled impatiently. She was excited. I rolled my eyes. "Just look at it this way. You need something, I need something. I'm offering you a bonus for your cooperation. I'm no idiot. I know my son can be difficult."

"What's your offer?" I dropped my gaze to the carpet. Difficult didn't even scratch the surface, but even I realized I kind of deserved it. The karma of me being here.

"You know I worked as a photographer in Europe when I met Garret, right?" she asked. I nodded.

"If you're about to offer me a professional photo shoot for the prom, I will have to stop you right there. Not my thing."

She laughed. It was so easy to talk to her. I couldn't help but compare her to Sylvia. I envied Lucas for the mother he got. No wonder he was a good person, if you put aside the fact he was apparently hate-banging the female population because he couldn't punish me.

"I've seen some of the jewelry you're making. You could use some guidance. I think I know the right person."

I shook my head. "I don't have my sketches. Harry Spencer checked. The second floor is also damaged," I explained.

"So? Draw new sketches. Think about it." She shrugged as if it didn't matter. But it did. No one ever helped me with this.

"Who is that person?" I asked, trying to sound indifferent.

"An ex-boyfriend. He's a jewelry designer. He works with Prada, Valentino, Dior. You name it. I could ask him to help you. See your pieces. Give you some advice."

I wanted to scream my lungs out in excitement. Of course, that was out of the question. I never let people see they had something I wanted. A person like that could help me immensely. He could help me get better and answer the gazillion questions I had about making this a steady income for me.

"How do you even know a person who works with Dior?" I was amazed. "I'll have to think about it."

Elizabeth bit her lips to suppress a smile. She knew I was hooked. She also knew she shouldn't push me. She got up and looked at me with amusement.

"Clem?"

"Yes?"

"Please don't sleep on the floor just to prove a point, okay?"

I rolled my eyes. "I'll sleep on the bed, don't worry about it."

"Great." She smiled and headed out. She placed her hand on the door handle and added, "Oh, and would you please try not to run away tonight?" Her body leaned forward a little bit as if she was about to share a secret with me, "I was wild once too."

CHAPTER EIGHT

Lucas

When I parked my car in front of my house on Tuesday evening, all I wanted to do was eat and go to sleep. The sight of Clementine's ruined home next to our recently painted house was still something that drew my eyes. I wondered how she felt, knowing everything she ever had was lost forever. That night, when I was watching her and she was watching the fire, I got the feeling she was somehow pleased. It was another twisted inexplicable thing about her.

I went inside my house and the smell of what I hoped was my favorite lasagna made my stomach growl. My mother rarely missed a chance to cook us dinner. I think she did it because of me and Troy. I was pretty sure she hated cooking, and the minute we got out of this house, she would just stop and make my father eat takeout for the rest of his life. Cooking for three men was a challenge. But Elizabeth Cole was up to it. She was up to anything when it came to her family.

"Mom, tell me dinner is ready!" I yelled from the front door and went towards the kitchen.

The answer? Complete silence.

"I'm kidding," I explained, thinking I was annoying her. "I can wait, and I can even help."

As I entered the kitchen area that was separated from the living room only by a short and narrow hallway, my smile died. I lost my appetite and probably my sleep for the night.

No amount of home cooked lasagna could make up for that particular surprise.

In my fucking house.

I was sure this was my mom's doing. My father would never even think of it.

Clementine Hartley was sitting on our kitchen island. Her gorgeous long hair down, her eyes dead on mine, her lips parted. It looked like she was holding her breath, waiting for my reaction. I had none.

I could probably yell my lungs out right there and then, but just didn't. There had to be a good reason for her to be here. Correction. My mother must have had a good reason for inviting her. Clementine, though? What the fuck was she thinking?

My brother murmured some sort of a greeting and continued talking. He was looking at her as if she was a fucking goddess. I knew that look and the feeling that went with it.

"Lucas," my mother's voice was about a thousand octaves higher than usual. She knew I would be pissed, which only made me even more pissed. "Dinner is almost ready. We're having company."

"No shit," I mocked her, my eyes still glued to Clem's beautiful face.

"Language!" my mother scolded me with a laugh.

Guilty conscience, huh?

She usually gave me a massive hard time for any bad words that came out of my mouth, especially in front of Troy. He was ten and didn't have my *attitude*. Her word, not mine. Elizabeth Cole was delicate and well-mannered, so it really bothered her when I acted like a *caveman*. Again, her word, not mine.

She was also everyone's favorite neighbor around here. She joined a few DIY home repairs around the neighborhood, drove old people wherever the hell they were going at their age, who knew, as if she got paid for it, and she constantly brought homeless animals in.

That's exactly what Clementine Hartley was these days. A homeless animal. I still had a scratch on my arm and a view from my bedroom window that proved I was right and not at all offensive.

"Do you mind coming with me upstairs? I have... a thing." Mom literally pushed me out of the kitchen.

"I hope you have a good reason for this," I hissed in the hallway. "And I mean *really* good. She-was-dying kinda good."

"Yeah? Just like you then. Four nights ago," she said in an angry whisper.

We went upstairs and into the guest room. My mother started pulling clean towels out of a drawer. A sudden headache appeared. I waited until she placed them on the bed, just to be sure. A bed that looked like someone had lain on it. I couldn't hold it anymore.

"You've got to be kidding me." I shook my head in disbelief.

"Come on, Lucas. Holding a grudge over a childhood crush? You're better than this."

"Umm, no. No, I'm not." I crossed my arms in front of my chest.

She looked at me as if she couldn't believe my words. So, I made it perfectly clear.

"I'm sticking with the grudge. She's leaving."

"Who told you you're the one making the decisions around here?"

"I'm the one making the decisions when it comes to Clementine Hartley invading my personal space. It's bad enough I have to see her face every single day at school."

My mother smiled. "Well, you're going to see her face at home too. Because she's staying."

I wanted to strangle them both.

"This is not a joke!" My voice was now bouncing off the walls. "Kick her out!"

"Stop yelling right now." She pointed at me as if I was a toddler. "You're being selfish. The girl lost everything. She was your best friend. How can you be so cruel?"

I knew this meant a lot to her. Not being cruel to others. I knew she was disappointed in me. But I ignored her words, even though she was right.

"I don't care. I want her out! You know, you're not the only one living in this house! Did you even think to ask the rest of us before inviting her here?" I was still screaming at her, well aware that my voice was probably reaching everyone's ears downstairs.

"I asked the reasonable part of our household. Your father and Troy didn't have any objections." Her voice cracked at the end of her sentence. She was lying. My mother was such a bad liar.

"By the look on Troy's face, I would guess that Dad was the one with the objections," I smirked. She didn't even bother to answer me. I knew the fight was over, and she had kicked my ass. I decided to go seek parental support downstairs.

But the moment I reentered the kitchen and saw the look on my father's face, I knew I wasn't getting any. He was looking at me like I disappointed him. I knew they heard my not-so-delicate conversation with Mom. I couldn't care less. Clementine could crawl and sleep under a bridge for all I cared.

And yet you saved her ass not so long ago, you, miserable piece of sh...

"Do you want to see my Lego collection?" my brother tried to save the awkward situation from exploding in my face.

He probably thought the sweet, beautiful Clementine was hurt. He had no idea she was the one who was doing the hurting in our twisted... thing.

I wasn't crazy enough to call it a relationship. We never even kissed. We didn't even talk. And even though I didn't have girlfriends, I knew enough on the subject to know you have to at least tolerate the other person to the point of listening to their blabber. So, no. This thing between us couldn't be called a relationship.

"Later, Troy," my father stopped them from going to his room. "Let's wait for your mother and discuss the changes."

Dad stared at me, and I could see his disapproval of my jackass move, yelling at my mother and insulting our guest. If Clementine knew what I really thought about her, she wouldn't be insulted. She would be terrified of the thought of spending the night here.

I saw some understanding in Dad's eyes. He knew why I hated her so much. I presumed this was his objection. He put himself in my shoes, unlike my mother. I finally got the balls to look at Clementine. I wanted to see what my words have done to her. Her face was... infuriating.

She was calm, collected and... sort of at peace.

What a freak...

My mother appeared a minute later. Fresh as a daisy. Like she didn't have a care in the world.

"Lucas, sit down, please," she sang.

"I'm good," I replied, pressing my back to the wall.

Mom sent me a warning look and started talking.

"Richard was here the other day. We were talking, and he said that Clem can't stay at the Spencers', and that she wouldn't want to go to Seattle with him."

My mother paused. She looked uncomfortable. To be honest, I didn't do anything to make her feel better. My eyes, my whole face and body were sending the same message: I'm about to go on a killing spree.

"I couldn't get this idea out of my head," she continued. "So, I called him and offered our home until hers is rebuilt. Or her mother comes back. But even if you stayed here until graduation, we wouldn't mind," she told Clementine and squeezed her hand.

"Comes back from where?" I asked. Not that I cared where Sylvia was, but shouldn't she be here picking up her daughter and dragging her, I don't know... to the other side of town.

"Sylvia is in a rehab center," my father said, and his eyes were warning me to watch it.

I suspected Sylvia Hartley was an addict and, unwillingly, or at least I hoped so, started a fire with both her and her daughter inside their house. I didn't understand it when I saw her on that sofa, unconscious and obviously mental, judging by the number of burning candles surrounding her. But I put it all together a few days later.

Clementine knew her mother was sleeping on the sofa. She immediately started pushing her around to wake her up. As if she knew she won't wake up easily. And I was pretty sure I saw an empty bottle of wine on the coffee table and some pills spilt next to it.

My guess was Clementine had a very good idea of what was happening downstairs.

"When?" I asked, and dad understood my question immediately.

"Sylvia is coming back in January. Richard thinks the walls and floors could be ready by then too," he answered, then turned to Clem. "It won't be finished, but you could sleep there if you want to. But as Lizzie said, you're welcome to stay as long as you want."

Three fucking months. I had to live with the girl who crushed my soul for three whole months?

Troy cut my thoughts with his happy squeal.

"That's so cool. I mean, not that your mom's not coming home for three months, but that you're going to be here the entire time. Do you like board games?"

Clementine chuckled and messed with his hair. "Depends on the company," she winked. She winked at my ten-year-old brother, chill as fuck. She didn't look lost, homeless, or even sad.

I couldn't stand her anymore.

"Nice chat. Let me know when dinner's ready."

I left them in the kitchen without commenting on the big announcement. I wasn't confident enough in my abilities to control the words that came out of my mouth at this level of rage, coursing through my body.

I was already going up the stairs when I heard my mother's steps behind me. "Not in a mood for a talk, mom. Just let it go."

Then a small, thin body jumped in front of me and stood in my way. Clementine's, not my mother's. I started doing everything my father made me do to calm myself down when I was a little kid who got angry and out of control.

I inhaled deeply and exhaled slowly. I started counting to a hundred. We had established that counting to ten wasn't doing the trick for me. This time I would probably need to use my pillow as a punching bag or wait until practice to get it out of my system. Or better yet, find Dylan Williams and smash his nose inwards. That should do it.

"Can I help you?" I snapped at her when I realized she wasn't about to speak first. She opened her mouth to answer me, but I cut her off, "Oh, wait. I already did. I saved your miserable life. So, what the fuck do you want?"

"Lucas...," my name came out as a moan out of annoyance, but it still made my heart flip inside my chest. And that made me hate her even more.

I shook my head to make her stop talking. She did.

"Nothing's changed. I don't want to talk to you, I don't want to look at you. I still hate you. You don't exist."

She lifted an eyebrow and cocked her head, "Is that a thing? Hating someone who doesn't exist?"

She was mocking me. A defiance I hadn't seen in her for years poured out of her entire body. It made me want to crush her like a cockroach. To intimidate her. She was on my territory. That should be easy, right?

"I could make your life even more miserable than it already is. Your room for the next three months is three steps away from mine. Don't provoke me, *Clementine*," I deliberately called her that. I wanted to hurt her. Show her we were no longer the kids we used to be. That the promises I gave her wouldn't be kept. "And I'm not even going to begin explaining the damage I could do to you in school."

I took one step towards her and erased the space between us. Our bodies almost touched.

"Or to your boyfriend."

"He's not my boyfriend," she said breathlessly and licked her lips, her eyes glued to my mouth. Mine were examining the little gold dots in hers.

I forgot she had those.

"I don't care," I snarled. "Stay out of my way. I'll stay out of yours."
I paused. "I can't promise anything about that creeper, though."

She rolled her eyes, showing me she wasn't impressed with my moody attitude. It was fine. I had time to torture her. Three whole months. I leaned forward and my nose almost touched hers. She took a sharp breath.

"Now get the fuck out of my way."

CHAPTER NINE

Clementine

My first dinner at the Coles' home was a disaster. Lucas was so pissed I thought smoke would start coming out of his nostrils every time he exhaled loudly through his nose. His lips were tightly pressed together most of the time. He was cutting his meal with such anger I wouldn't be surprised if he imagined he was cutting me into miniscule pieces.

There was an awkward silence. The only one talking was Troy. He was blabbing about one of his video games. I nodded the whole time, barely listening to him. The hate that Lucas radiated from across the table was affecting not only my hearing, but also my sense of taste. I was sure that Elizabeth's lasagna was good enough even for people who were used to home-cooked meals, but it was tasteless to me.

I felt so out of place, I didn't dare to move.

Lucas finished his meal at what I believed was a record time and stormed off upstairs. He closed his door with a thud. All eyes, even Troy's, darted at me.

Elizabeth exhaled as if she was holding her breath for hours.

"He'll get used to it," she half-smiled at me. Lucas's father, Garret, snorted, but said nothing. She pretended she didn't hear him. "Tomorrow will be better."

I wasn't sure if she was convincing us or herself. Troy looked confused. I could bet that there were not many conflicts between his parents, but obviously Garret wasn't on board with my being here. He probably thought my presence will cause more problems than solve any. I thought that too.

I had a few more bites and went to my room upstairs as quickly as I could. I was afraid Lucas would pop in the hallway. I definitely had no desire to cross him. I had spent the last four years avoiding him. Why would I piss him off when I was so close to leaving this fucking town forever?

Except I wasn't anymore. I had zero cash. No supplies for making new pieces to sell. Even my sketches were gone. That dude Elizabeth told me about, her ex-boyfriend, was my best shot. I had to stay here. At least for now.

I got almost zero sleep that night. The next morning, my head was pounding, reminding me of that tossing and turning in my new temporary bed. I went to school for the first time since the fire, and I was looking and feeling like shit.

"You're not listening," Dylan said with a smile and not at all irritated.

I enjoyed the fact that he was the one doing the talking, since everyone else grilled me about the fire and my mother's breakdown.

Hannah warned me there were rumors about drugs and a suicide attempt, but I didn't expect that much attention.

"I'm sorry. I'm so tired," I rested my head on his arm only for a second while we were walking slowly towards my locker. "I didn't sleep last night. And all these questions people ask are torturing my barely functioning brain."

"Why?" Dylan removed a lock of hair that was falling in front of my eyes and tucked it behind my ear, while I was digging in my backpack. He was leaning on shoulder on the locker next to mine.

"I don't like explaining myself to people," I shrugged, and he chuckled.

"Not that," he leaned closer to me. "Why didn't you sleep?"

I was so tired. I didn't move away even an inch. I bet this kind of leaning into one another was the reason Lucas called Dylan my boyfriend. I knew he was asking about Lucas. Was he the one keeping me awake last night, considering we were now living together? It was another hot topic in school. The weird chick that hated people, living with the man-whore who couldn't live without other people's adoration. Not that anyone would dare to call Lucas a whore. That was only in my head.

Apparently no one remembered we were once friends. I couldn't judge them. It was hard for me to remember it too. And painful.

Dylan, on the other hand, was anything but painful. He was nice and thoughtful. And he really was handsome. Sexy. Hannah was right. His blond, slightly curly hair, friendly smile, and eyes that never looked away from me when I was near could actually be a good thing for me. If I had any desire to date him, which I didn't. Not that he had asked me out anyway. We were just two friends, sharing a four-year-old secret.

"Oh, my God, your brain is really not functioning," he teased, and I remembered I forgot to answer his question about my sleeping problems. I was about to laugh, but, as I moved away from my locker, I bumped into someone and lost my balance.

A pair of strong, veiny hands helped me stay on my feet. It turned out my brain was functioning just enough to recognize Lucas's scent of pine, wood, and my next nervous breakdown before I even saw his face. I got a sniff of it last night when he told me he would stay away from me if I stayed away from him. His fingers left a trail of goosebumps from my elbows to my wrists before he removed them from my skin.

"A word?" he asked, looking down at me. I was tall for a woman, but he still soared five inches above me. I frowned. I wanted to tell him to beat it, but I was also curious. I cocked my head sideways and placed a hand over my chest theatrically.

"Are you bipolar?" I pretended to be shocked, paused, then returned to my normal self again. "I thought we're not talking to each other."

Maybe Elizabeth was right, and he could really forgive me.

"I'm not talking to you, nemesis," Lucas scowled and leaned forward.

Nemesis? Seriously?

"I'm talking to your boyfriend," he added.

He spat the word *boyfriend* like it was an insult. I blushed both from anger and embarrassment. Oh, and his closeness. Somehow it got on my nerves even though we were surrounded by people and he couldn't say or do anything to me. It would hurt his good guy status.

I got the feeling my friendship with Dylan got on Lucas's nerves, so I decided to use this against him and neither deny nor confirm a relationship between us.

"Oh, my bad," I smiled and batted my eyelashes. I could swear I saw his lips trying to smile against his will. "He's all yours," I added with a buttery tone that suggested this exchange was the ultimate pleasure for me, but I actually wanted to smash his balls with my knee.

I left Dylan and Lucas in the hallway, pretending I wasn't interested in their conversation. I tried to stay calm. This couldn't be related to me; I did nothing to provoke it.

They were probably talking about football. Maybe Lucas needed him to join the team. I tried to convince myself that was a real possibility, even though deep down I knew Lucas would ask literally anyone on planet Earth before he asked Dylan for any favor whatsoever.

Two hours later, I was sitting under the bleachers, still trying to figure out reasons for Lucas and Dylan to be talking that didn't include me.

"I can't believe these assholes," Hannah murmured for the fiftieth time that day. She meant our classmates who made this first day back at school extra crappy.

"Fuck them," I rubbed my temple. I was so tired. "They will stop, or they won't. Either way I don't care," I released a sigh. "I'm sorry about my father's reaction. Are your parents mad?"

"What? No! They feel guilty as hell. They think he's right," she paused. "God, Clem, I think he's right. They knew, *I* knew all along, and I never really helped you. You could have died."

Tears rolled down her face, and I whipped them with my thumbs.

"It's neither your fault nor your responsibility. And he's not right at all. He's never visiting. He sees my mother at weddings and funerals. They don't even talk on the phone. He's the one who should be feeling guilty."

The fact that my very-concerned-for-my-safety father hadn't bothered to call me since he left me at my new temporary home to check on me only made me blame him even more. Not to mention Madison, who lived three thousand miles away when she wasn't abroad and who talked to Sylvia more than I did. She must have noticed something, right? Why hadn't she tipped dad about mom? Why was I other people's responsibility?

Of course, I knew Madison didn't care enough about me to even text to see for herself that I was alive, let alone call me, but it was still painful to be neglected by every single one of your parents and siblings. Tyler was no good either. They all deserted me with the woman who broke us apart.

"Are we going shopping after school?" Hannah cut my thoughts. "I need the distraction".

"What's wrong?" I hadn't even noticed she was feeling down. Now that I had really looked at her, she was actually pretty miserable. And I was a shitty friend.

"I got carried away," she shook her head. "After the fire, I really hoped Tyler would come see you."

That sounded like my brother. He managed to hurt her without even showing his face.

"I really hate that you're into my brother. He's a dick. You deserve way better".

"Maybe he just needs to be loved," Hannah argued.

"Or maybe you should face the music. His childhood home burned down. His mother is in rehab. His underaged sister is living with the neighbors. And he's a no-show."

Hannah rested her head on my shoulder. A few seconds later she looked at me.

"Speaking of disappointing love stories... When are you going on a date with Dylan?"

"Mm," I wondered for a moment. "Probably never. Too complicated. Too much history."

"The history you're referring to is between you and your new roommate. You and Dylan have a clean slate. And as I probably said once or twice, he is hot."

I tried to imagine me and Dylan, and I instantly knew I had no desire to go out with him.

"Can we go back to your depressed self, please?" I teased.

"Nope. Your miserable love life distracts me from my own," she smiled.

"I don't have a love life," I protested.

"Exactly," she winked at me. "We have to change that."

Deep down, I knew this was the worst idea Hannah ever had.

"Me dating Dylan while I'm living with Lucas?" I asked her with an are-you-out-of-your-fucking-mind look? I knew I shouldn't judge Dylan for what happened. He apologized. And even though he gave me a manipulative asshole vibe four years ago, this was no longer the case. He was actually pretty nice.

But something was shifting between me and Lucas, and it scared me. It was not a good time to start dating anyone. And my mission in the Coles residence was to help him forgive me, not get on his bad side while he obviously had issues with both me and Dylan.

"Lucas has fucked the whole town since the shit between you two blew in your faces," Hannah said.

"Thanks for the reminder," I frowned.

"Dylan's not going to fuck you on their dinner table while they're eating. He's just going to get your ass out of their house and then bring it back. I think Lucas will live."

I had a hard time confessing to my best friend about Lucas's threat. She had a wild imagination and a big mouth. Dangerous combination.

"You're right. But I'm not into Dylan anyway."

"Jeez. I'll have to return that maid-of-honor dress I got last week," she said sarcastically.

"Who made you a maid of honor?" I was kidding of course. If I was ever to be married, she would no doubt be exactly that.

"Please," she dragged. "I'm your only option."

A whistle startled me. Football practice was over. Coach Howard was yelling at someone. Lucas was talking to Chase. They had their helmets on, and I couldn't see his face. But it wasn't a big deal. I was now living with the guy. His face would be there when I wake up in the morning and when I go to sleep at night. If I managed to fall asleep in that house.

"Let's go buy some clothes," Hannah said, leaving the Dylan conversation unfinished.

Two hours later, I got back to my new home, carrying too many shopping bags. I was feeling restless, so I overspent. Not that my father would care. While paying for a pair of jeans my mother wouldn't like with my father's credit card, a thought of withdrawing his money to replace my now-gone savings crossed my mind. Maybe not all at once, but I had to buy everything a person needed. Everything. All he got me was a new phone. I needed clothes, underwear, shoes, new books for school, for fuck's sake, I didn't even have a toothbrush that wasn't gifted to me. How could he ever figure it out? It would be so easy.

But I hated the thought of using his money. I wanted to do it on my own. Prove everyone I could live without them. And even though they might never figure out I used his money, I would know, and that would not help me feel free or capable.

"Do you need help?" Elizabeth rushed to my side and took some of the bags.

"I think I overdid it," I laughed nervously. I didn't think what it would look like in her eyes. Yesterday, I wanted to leave, and, today, I came back with personal belongings to fill up my entire room.

We went upstairs, and Elizabeth looked way too excited while peeking in the shopping bags.

"God, you really are bored, aren't you?" I smiled.

"For you I must be like a thousand-year-old, but I'm still a woman. The only girl clothes I'm buying are my own and they're nothing like these...," she pulled what I called a piss-your-mother-off dress. First of all, it was black, and my mother hated black. She only wore it to funerals just because she cared what other people thought of her. Second of all, it was barely covering my ass and breasts.

I didn't really care so much about the clothes, but I cared deeply about disturbing my mother. Was it weird I tried doing that even when she was not around to see my rebellion?

"Just don't make me try them," I pleaded. "Hannah pushed all my buttons and I have zero patience left in me."

Elizabeth went through the bags, and I noticed a laptop on my bed. It was turned on.

"What is this?"

"Oh, I wanted to show you my friend, the one I told you about. The designer. Check him out and tell me what you think."

I sat on the bed and took the laptop in my lap. Ten minutes later, I knew I wanted to be mentored by this guy. He was the real deal. I had no other connections in the industry. This could be my only shot of ever knowing someone that successful. I could really become someone with his guidance.

I placed the laptop back on the bed and stared at Elizabeth, "Do you think he will agree to help me?"

"Do you want him to help you?" she asked, surprised. She thought I was going to say no. And I probably should have.

"Yes," I decided to be honest.

"Then I'll call him."

And that was it. Lucas came back home later that evening and acted as if I wasn't even there. Just like he promised. He talked, and laughed, and was his regular self. Or at least what I thought he was normally like. It made me think we could pull it off. Living under the same roof without killing each other. Without bringing painful memories back. But as I was looking at his smile from across the table and felt butterflies every time I heard his throaty laughter, I had the gut feeling it wasn't going to be that easy.

CHAPTER TEN

Lucas

A week had passed since my mother brought Clementine Hartley home, and I had to admit to myself I had a new form of entertainment, and I was loving it. Clementine rolled eyes, lifted eyebrows, huffed, and shook her head All.The.Time. I also noticed she crossed her arms in front of her chest quite often. Mostly when I was talking. I was doing a good job of intimidating her, and I wasn't even trying.

I also got to notice exactly what triggered those other gestures. Our family routines. Oh, and every general sense of happiness.

I heard Clementine arguing with my mother on her first morning home. She wanted to skip breakfast. I was sure it had everything to do with me and my outburst the previous day, but I didn't really care. I was surprised, however, that Mom won the argument, and Clem was now reluctantly eating her breakfast with the family every single morning.

"Does anyone have suggestions about the fun day this week?" Mom asked, then looked at Clem and explained. "Every Sunday we all do something together."

"Shocker," Clem whispered sarcastically and looked like she wished she choked to death with the orange juice she was drinking. I saw it on her face, and I chuckled inside. I just couldn't resist it. She was there. Sulking. It was a no-brainer. I had to make it even worse for her.

"I think we should let our guest come up with something."

I was aware I was breaking my word. I basically just stopped pretending she didn't exist. But it wasn't a big deal. It was obvious we couldn't avoid speaking to each other any longer. We spent too much time in the same room on a daily basis. I wasn't at all feeling bad that I was the first to break the silence between us. The way I saw it, I controlled the narrative; she was complying.

Mom and Dad shared a look, but they didn't say a word. I continued.

"We have to make her feel welcomed. A part of this household. Your words, mom," I winked at my mother, provoking her to contradict herself. She didn't. "She spent her first weekend at Hannah Spencer's home, but if she is really going to be a part of our family, she should be participating in family events."

Clementine slowly put her glass on the table without making eye contact with anyone in the room.

"No."

Her voice was firm, and she sounded bored. She looked disengaged, but I knew she was squirming inside. I just needed to see it on the outside. Break her spirit and shit.

"I'm sure you'll plan something nice, nemesis."

Her whole face screamed contempt and I was on the receiving end. That didn't stop me though. I kept looking straight at her face, even though she avoided my gaze. I wanted to make her feel uncomfortable. See her deepest layer of insecurities displayed for me to poke and play with it. She deserved it.

"We should let Clem decide if she wants to join us, and not make her do it," my father said calmly, but his eyes sent me a warning. *Don't be a dick.*

I ignored the warning.

"Hey, I'm just following Mom's rules. If I have to treat her like family, she might as well act like it."

I was also not very pleased with the double standard. My mother obviously twisted her arm about breakfast. Why couldn't I do the same with the fun day? Clementine's fingers twitched, and she immediately hid her hand under the table. She lifted her gaze and looked at me like I was a cow shit on her favorite shoe. But there was something else too.

Mischief.

She knew what I was doing, and she was up for the challenge. I felt strangely excited.

One of the most maddening things of high school girls? They talked all the fucking time. I hated listening to their constant blabbing. But for some masochistic reason, I wanted to hear Clementine's words.

"When was the last time *you* planned something?" she cocked her head sideways.

I opened my mouth to answer with a lie, but Troy made her case and ratted me out.

"He never does."

A slow, smug smile spread on her face. Mine never faltered, even though the little traitor sort of killed my whole act with one sentence.

I was aware my parents, especially my mother, acted like they were deaf and mute. It rang a bell in my head. A bell I decided to analyze later, since I was enjoying Clementine's attention. It was probably nostalgia. She hadn't changed that much. She was still a hurricane on the inside, but this time I had no intentions to try to tame her. Quite the opposite. I intended to release the storm and let her ruin her own life. While I watched from the front row.

"Fine," Clementine leaned forward. "I'll do it. But next week it's your turn." She didn't even let me answer, like I was supposed to do it, just because she said so. "Anything goes?" she asked Mom.

"Yes," Mom nodded, but her voice sounded uncertain. "Well, within reasonable limits of course."

Oh, Mom, you finally got it. The girl is a nutcase.

Upon closer inspection I noticed my mother looked like she was about to do a happy dance and cry her eyes out at the same time. That woman was a serious case of a softy. I suspected she would project her unfulfilled dreams of having a daughter on Clementine, but crying over this stupid shit was too much even for Elizabeth Cole.

We finished our breakfast in silence. Ten minutes later, Dad left for work and Mom was getting ready to drive Troy to school. She had repeated the same Q&A every morning since Clementine came here.

"I really don't understand why you need to go with two separate cars. You're going to the same place."

Mom was a lot of things, but she was not dumb. She knew exactly why. Me and Clementine in a small, confined space? Alone? It seemed unnatural. Every nerve in my body protested. By the way Clementine's shoulders stiffened, I could say the same for her.

Fortunately, she picked up the conversation before I did. I had had nothing else to add since yesterday morning, and I really hated repeating myself.

"Elizabeth, don't get me wrong, but I don't have to explain myself to you. I have a car and I intend to use it."

I found it really funny that Clem was all over my mother every time she pushed her buttons but said nothing to me when I cornered her to organize a fun day. It made me feel good. Like I had some power over her.

Of course, I knew this wasn't true. No one had power over that nutter.

The two of us got out at the same time. Her car was parked in front of her house. We didn't speak a word to each other now when we were alone. Clementine had almost reached her car, when she did a one-eighty and bolted straight towards me. A rush went through my body as I watched her approaching me.

"You...you...," her fists were clenched. She was fighting the urge to punch me. Adorable.

I leaned on my car and yawned. I wanted to make her feel insignificant. Something similar to what she made me feel when I was still in love with her.

"You're unbelievable," she spat.

That's it? Unbelievable? How disappointing.

"So they say. Usually with their clothes off."

She blushed, and I smirked. Around the others, she acted like a person that had no opinions, no feelings, and no fucking needs to be met. She couldn't hide from me, though.

I observed her the other day. She received a package. At first, she seemed confused. But then she read a note. Her hand began to shake, and when she looked up, I saw her eyes. They were shining with tears.

"You said that nothing's changed," she ignored my sexual innuendo. "You told me you'd stay out of my way. Why, the hell, are you doing this?"

"Why, the hell, did you move in with me?" I shrugged. I just wanted to irritate her some more. I didn't really care about that at that moment. I was having too much fun with her around.

"I didn't move in with you," she growled. "And I had no choice!"

"I don't believe that, nemesis."

"Stop calling me that!" she raised her voice.

"Why?" I pushed myself off the car and took a step towards her. "You're exactly that. My downfall. I can't escape you no matter how much I try. Your fucking face haunts me everywhere."

Clementine didn't seem to realize it, but we were so close, our bodies almost touched. She looked fascinated and confused. Like a thousand questions were flying inside her pretty head.

I could smell her shampoo. Pink grapefruit. I might or might have not deliberately taken showers after her for the past few days just to be able to inhale that smell because, let's face it, burying my nose in her hair was not an option. I might have also rubbed one out every time I was in the bathroom, picturing her spreading soap all over her naked body.

Maybe I was overwhelmed by her closeness or that smell had already created a shortcut in my brain, signaling my dick to wake up, but I surprised myself with the idea that came to me and the fact that I didn't even try to suppress the urge of telling her.

"I could play nice," I started. "But you have to give me something in return."

"And what the fuck is that?" she snapped at me, completely unaware where I was going with this.

"Well, you don't have much to offer, do you? I mean, what do you even have left?" I pretended to wonder. I lifted my hand slowly enough for her to be able to stop me, but she didn't move. I ran my thumb over her bottom lip. "Except this."

"You want me to kiss you?" her voice showed she doubted it, but she was also not moving an inch away from me.

"I wanted you to kiss me when we were fourteen," I dropped my fingertips down and followed the line of her neck. She shivered. "I want more than that. I want *everything*."

She wasn't pushing me away, but still it was a dick move. Black-mailing a girl for sex was a low I never thought I would go to, but hey, I never thought I would be living with Clementine Hartley either. Things changed every now and again.

It's the celibacy thing. You wouldn't be so attracted to her if you had sex on a regular basis.

"I also want to break your neck quite often," I continued. But I'm sure you know that. You're pretty consistent when it comes to provoking me. I doubt it's not deliberate."

"It's not," she said.

My fingers lingered on her collarbone when she suddenly snapped out of our moment and took a few steps back. Her chest was lifting up and down with every breath. It took me a few seconds to realize why she ran away from my touch. Mom and Troy were going out.

"What are you two doing here?" mom nagged. "You're going to be late."

"So? That's her problem," I said without looking at Clementine. "No one cares if I'm late. People love me."

"You," mom pointed at me with her finger. "You should care. I don't have time for this. We'll talk later."

"Why? Are you *late*?" I pretended to be shocked.

Mom shook her head and rushed with Troy to her car. "Go to school!"

I smiled and turned my back to them. I wanted to continue my conversation with Clementine. She obviously didn't want that, as she was already opening the door of her car. I chuckled. We were living together now, and she still tried to hide from me.

"Running away from a difficult conversation? That tells a lot about your character, Hartley!"

She hit the gas and left me standing there without a word. I caught up with her at the first traffic light, and I drove behind her the whole time. When we arrived at the parking lot, she passed by two empty spaces next to each other and continued forward. It made me laugh. She knew I was messing around with her and tried not to give me more opportunities. I respected that.

I parked my car and got out. My eyes found her. She was walking towards the building, looking frustrated and one step away from an outburst. I felt a warm, happy feeling of satisfaction.

That was until Clementine saw that dipshit Dylan and her face changed from a state of torment to relief. It twisted my insides. The fact he was the one to make her feel better.

Dylan was strolling in her direction, smiling like a decent human being, not grinning at her like I did. And yet, I couldn't understand how that piece of shit managed to win over the most self-isolating girl in town. He hugged her enthusiastically; she half-hugged him. People looked at them with curiosity, talked behind their back for weeks now.

I was intrigued. It was the first time I saw them together and didn't have the urge to break his spine. Because I had a very vivid, very recent image of her enjoying my hands on her and a front-row view of the *I-don't-want-you-but-I'll-use-you* hug she just gave him.

"The point is to go to college next year, not jail, you creep," Chase smacked my back, mocking my weird stalking situation. "Still obsessed, I see."

I ignored him, thinking about Dylan. He seemed to be into Clementine for real. I was contemplating a picture in my head.

Me. Using Clementine to get back at Dylan.

Also me. Screwing her until I got her out of my system.

Two birds with one stone.

I wouldn't be violating the celibacy rule. Sex with Clementine wouldn't be about pleasure. It would be about revenge.

"Asshole!" Chase tried to get my attention. "They went inside. What the fuck are you still staring at?"

"My payback."

CHAPTER ELEVEN

Clementine

Living with Lucas Cole was a disturbing experience. He kept me on my toes, playing a sick game of push and pull with me. The same day he bullied me into planning their family fun day, he came home and told everyone he would do it. No explanation whatsoever.

Not knowing what he was thinking was so nerve-wracking, I declined the one thousand verbal invitations from Elizabeth to join them and made plans to spend the weekend with Hannah. Again. Nothing special, just me bitching about my stay at the Coles, and Hannah daydreaming about Tyler. But everything was better than spending hours with the asshole not knowing if I would become his target for the day or not.

The two of us had a routine. Well, he was the one establishing it. He pushed my limits one day, then ignored me the next two. He loved making me feel anxious and uneasy.

He also never touched me again like he did that morning before school, but he found ways to brush me with his arm or squeeze me between his perfect hard body and the kitchen counter while trying to grab something.

I knew these were no random actions, but I couldn't force myself to get angry. On the contrary, it made me warm in all the right ways. Or in our case, in all the wrong ones, since we hated each other.

The next Friday night I was left alone in the Cole residence. Lucas had a game. I never got the football bug. It just wasn't my thing, but sitting there in his house, while his whole family went cheering for him, felt stupid. I could have gone with them. It wasn't like he was going to sit with us. But I also felt an excitement of some sort. An anticipation. Was he winning?

An hour later I was still alone. I knew he would probably stay with his friends after the game. But his parents and Troy should have been home already. I took my phone to check with Hannah when I received a notification about a video. It was posted by one of our classmates. I clicked on it, and I started the video. It was from that night's game. The front door flew open, and I stopped the video.

Elizabeth was the first to enter. She was pale; locks of hair had escaped her up-do. She mumbled a quick hello and went into the kitchen. Garret was explaining something to Troy. The two of them didn't look as disturbed as Elizabeth.

"That's why what Chase did was not acceptable."

"But everyone laughed," Troy argued.

"No, everyone supporting our team laughed," Garret explained. "The others were not."

I followed Elizabeth in the kitchen. She was pouring herself a glass of wine. My gaze stayed a little too long on the bottle.

"Oh," Elizabeth gasped. "I'm so sorry, Clem. I forgot," she left the glass in the sink. "I promised myself I wouldn't drink while you're here, but it just slipped my mind. Did you hear what happened?"

"No," I shook my head. "I was about to watch a video, but you came home. And you can drink, you know. I don't mind."

I really didn't. It just surprised me. Everything was so different here. I sometimes forgot about my mother's alcohol abuse and that I was living at the Coles' house because of it. Elizabeth looked at me intensely.

"Lucas says you lie a lot. Are you lying now?"

Why the hell would he say that to his mother?

"No, I'm not. You can drink in front of me," I reassured her.

"Good," she let out a breath. "Because I need it. Lucas scared the shit out of me."

The word *shit* coming out of her mouth was a first. I sat at one of the barstools next to the kitchen island. I wanted to know everything.

"What happened? Did they win?"

"Yes," she picked up her glass from the sink and took a sip. "But Chase crossed a line and he went so far beyond it that I can't even... Maybe I'm old, and I forgot what it's like to be a teenager, but he just looks for trouble, that kid." Elizabeth leaned forward, and her face was now on the same level as mine. She was looking me in the eyes, and it all felt so sincere. Like she was confiding in me. Like we were friends. "He kissed the head cheerleader."

"He kissed Hannah?" I frowned.

It didn't make sense. They had already made out once last year at a party. Another one I wasn't invited to. They barely spoke to one another. Why would he kiss her?

"No. The other one. Just seconds after the game ended. He just went for it."

"So? Chase kisses a lot of girls. Your son does it too, you know."

I did not like how that sounded. Like I was bitter about it. Elizabeth tried to hide her amusement and continued with her story.

"The girl has a boyfriend. The quarterback and captain of the other team."

I laughed loudly. I didn't like football, but I knew enough about football players to know Chase didn't receive only a verbal backlash.

"The two of them got into a fist fight. Seconds later, everyone was fighting right there on the football field. You should see Lucas's face. He was covered in blood."

Elizabeth put a hand over her stomach and her voice cracked. I sat up straight, alert.

"Is he okay? Where is he?"

"He's fine," Garret walked in. "It's just a cracked brow. It bleeds a lot. He's at a party. No one's hurt. Not even Chase."

"Can you imagine? They just went to a party." Elizabeth was outraged.

I shrugged. "If they're fine...," I started, but her facial expression stopped me from finishing my sentence.

"Oh, honey," Garret intervened. "I have to warn you. Tomorrow his face will look even worse. So don't panic, okay?"

He patted her back, wished me good night and went upstairs. I followed him soon after because Elizabeth's dread was getting on my nerves. I wrote about five hundred texts to Hannah, and I sent zero of them. I wasn't sure how to explain my eagerness to find out what was happening.

I tried to sleep, but hours later, I was still awake. Everyone else was sleeping. I didn't know if Lucas was even coming home tonight. Maybe he had plans crashing somewhere else.

At some point, I got thirsty and went downstairs. It was two in the morning and, unfortunately, I was wide awake. It wasn't exactly worry that kept me up. If Garret said everything was fine, I had no doubt it was. But I still felt the need to see him with my own eyes.

I was sipping water, looking at the Coles' backyard from the kitchen windows, when a big warm hand covered my mouth from behind, and I screamed.

"It's me, nemesis. Don't freak out."

Lucas slowly removed his hand from me, and I turned aggressively towards him. Even in the dark, I could clearly see his swollen cracked lip. He had a band aid on one of his brows and some uncleaned blood here and there on his face.

"Why the hell didn't you just say something, asshole? Did you have to grab me like a rapist?" I immediately started bickering. I couldn't risk showing him I cared about his beautiful, scarred face.

"Yes, I did. I would have scared the shit out of you if I just *said* something."

"You scared the shit out of me anyway."

"Yeah, but you didn't wake up the whole neighborhood."

He took a bottle of water from the fridge but, instead of drinking it, he placed it on his cheek.

"Your mother was worried," I started hesitantly.

"My mother's always worried," he answered, but seemed disconnected.

"Does it hurt?" I couldn't hold that question in me anymore.

"Do you really care?" he asked, staring at the kitchen counter. His eyes were empty.

"Are you drunk?" I honestly couldn't tell. I didn't remember ever seeing him drunk. It was understandable. I never attended their parties.

He slowly turned his head in my direction and looked at me with a frown.

"You're asking a lot of questions tonight. Why is that?" he hissed.

I swallowed hard. My hands began to shake. I lifted them up and started gathering my hair as I was about to make a ponytail. I wasn't. I just wanted to hide the trembling. His gaze dropped to my legs. I was wearing a football t-shirt with my brother's old number on it. Tyler sent it to me last week with the following note.

"I don't have anything of yours to give back to you, but you should have something old, used, and smelly.

P.S. If you tell anyone I did that, I will harass every boyfriend you have for the rest of your life.

Ty"

The tee was huge, and I looked ridiculous, but I had worn it to bed every night ever since it arrived, even though I had perfectly good brand-new pajamas that were my size. It covered most of my thighs if I didn't put my hands in the air. Which was what I did when I made my improvised ponytail. So now my legs were on full display. I was glad it was completely covering my underwear.

Lucas slowly lifted his gaze up and looked at my face. I was embarrassed. Not because he saw my naked legs. I used to have skirts no longer than that. But the atmosphere between us changed. We weren't in a crowded school hallway, trying to avoid each other. We were alone in the middle of the night in a dark room. The last time we were in a similar situation we had a sleepover. We were eleven, and the air around us wasn't sizzling.

Lucas took a step closer to me.

"Why are you wearing this?" his voice was lower than usual. He tugged the end of Tyler's t-shirt. "And where the fuck did you get it?" His fingertips brushed my bare thigh where my t-shirt ended. Shivers went through my body. I let down my hair, and he smiled. He enjoyed making me uncomfortable.

"It's Tyler's," I murmured.

"I know." His tone suggested it was obvious. "Why are you wearing it?"

"What kind of question is that?" I was getting annoyed.

"A simple one."

"He sent it to me," I said, not even sure why I felt obligated to give him an answer.

"So? If I give you a t-shirt with my number, would you wear it?" He pressed. I didn't understand where this was going.

"I would burn it," I said with a smile on my face.

His head tilted back with a quiet laughter. I hated how he laughed at me. It made me sober up.

"What?" I snapped at him. He looked at me like he was seeing everything inside me. The thoughts, the feelings, my confusion.

"Go to bed, Clementine," he turned away and placed the bottle of water to his cheek again.

"Don't call me that," I roared.

"That's your name, isn't it?"

"You know I hate it."

"You hate a lot of things. I can't keep track of them all. And I don't have to. Point your expectations at Dylan. I hear you two are really hitting it off this time around."

"Asshole," I said and stormed towards the narrow hallway leading to the living room, but Lucas cut me off. He looked angry all of a sudden.

"I told you what you have to do if you want me to be nice."

"You're crazy if you think I want to sleep with you," I tried to look repulsed by the idea. He placed his hands on my neck and used his thumbs to lift my chin up, trying to make me look at him. I did without saying a word, my pulse hammering in my veins. I wondered if he felt it on my neck.

"I see you. Maybe it won't be tonight, but I can see it in your eyes. Your mask is cracking. You won't be able to hide. Save us a couple of days."

I pursed my lips infuriated and pushed his hands off my face.

"I will never sleep with you," I growled. "Never."

"I doubt it, but even if you manage to control yourself, I know it won't be because you don't want me." He leaned forward. His lips an inch away from mine as he whispered. "It will be because you're a coward."

Then he stepped away, and I left him alone in the kitchen.

***

Lucas spent that weekend without producing one smile. Fun day was canceled. No one was in the mood. His phone was constantly buzzing, but he ignored it every time. He just flipped it with the screen down or put a pillow over it. I was curious but couldn't ask. So when he left his phone on the couch, I fought the urge to pick it up and check who was calling so much. Luckily for me, the phone started ringing. All I had to do was lean in and flip it only for a second. So I did.

"Isn't that a thing for girlfriends only?" Lucas' firm voice filled my ears. I put on an innocent look and turned to face him.

"The curiosity? No, I think all girls are equal when it comes to learning things."

"How about invading a guy's personal space and going through his phone?" His eyes lacked the usual spark that blinded me every time we argued. What was wrong with him? I ignored his question simply because he was right, and I had no excuse.

"Is Chase the one calling all the time? Why are you not answering him?"

"Seriously?" he looked frustrated. "You're not even going to apologize?"

"I didn't go through your phone." I rolled my eyes. "I just flipped it. It was innocent."

"Nothing about you is innocent, nemesis."

I both hated and loved my nickname. I hated it, because he picked it up to point out we were never going back to being normal around each other. We would always be enemies. But I loved how the word rolled off his mouth. It had a meaning, a deep feeling behind it. And I heard it every single time he called me that.

"Maybe if you tell someone what happened, you would feel better?"

I heard the irony. I sounded like Hannah when she was talking to me. But again, I was curious. I was allowed to use every trick to find out what was happening. A dark, painful chuckle escaped his lips.

"You're one to talk," he murmured, and I was thinking he would just shut down, but he surprised me. "You want to know what's wrong? Take a wild guess." His words were like a whip. It sounded like he was mad at me too. But what could I have in common with Chase?

Then it hit me. The kiss.

"You're mad at him because he kissed the girl in front of her boyfriend."

"Ding, ding, ding."

For a moment, we both just stood like statues, looking away from each other.

"Are you still mad at me?" I heard myself asking.

"What's your guess? You're obviously good at this game. Would I spend the last four years pretending you didn't exist if I wasn't mad at you?"

"Are you going to forgive him?"

Are you going to forgive me?

He looked at me like he heard my second question as well. For a second, I felt like I was about to cry. Ask him to forgive me. I knew he would. He was good. Not like me. And that was the reason I stopped myself from asking him. I didn't deserve his forgiveness. But my inner demons couldn't just leave me alone and made me say the stupidest thing.

"We weren't together, you know. You have no right to be mad at me. And I don't need your forgiveness."

His disappointed look was like a knife to my chest. He needed my apology. Why couldn't I just say the fucking words?

"I'm not mad at you because you owe me something, you fool. I'm mad at you because you didn't even like him. I know you didn't. You blew it all up for nothing. And you never even tried to explain what happened."

He took a step closer to me. I lifted my hand in the air to stop him.

"Don't do this," I pleaded.

"Why? Everything is already fucked up anyway. Just tell me why you did it."

I couldn't. I was ashamed. Ashamed of what I did and why I did it. He was right. I never wanted Dylan. Never liked him like that. Lucas hated me because of what I did, but at least he didn't know the reason. I couldn't come clean. It was too much for me to bear. So I did what I always did. I lied.

"You're wrong. I liked him then. And I like him now."

CHAPTER TWELVE

Clementine

Three weeks of my mother's rehab program had passed, and we hadn't spoken once. I felt great being away from her, and I could only imagine how happy she was, now that she didn't have to deal with me.

I had one pressing issue. It was with Elizabeth, and it was related to my birthday.

She wanted to throw me a big party. I wanted to be left alone. She wanted to bake me my favorite cake. I wanted to go out with Hannah and eat waffles, drowned in chocolate, like we did on both our birthdays ever since we were nine.

"But you're turning eighteen, that's huge," Elizabeth protested after my tenth refusal. "You have to have a party."

I rolled my eyes, which had become like breathing to me these days. It was necessary for my existence. This place was like a never-ending shrink session. Elizabeth was always trying to make all of us talk about our freaking feelings. I needed something to unwind.

"I don't want a party," I tapped my foot under the table as the whole family was having dinner. Together. Again. *Mental eye roll.*

"Well, you're having one. So, you might as well tell me how many of your friends are coming."

"That should be about..." Lucas pretended to count. "One."

After our not-so-honest conversation about what happened between us, or more specifically between me and Dylan, Lucas and I got back to the usual snarky comments here and there. Nothing too engaging. It felt better. Familiar. At school we continued to ignore each other. I often saw him in the hallways with a girl all over him. I was grateful he wasn't inviting them to dinner, but it still tortured me.

I examined his face. He looked nervous. Pressed. It took me a few seconds, but I figured it out why. It was my turn to push his buttons.

"Hannah, of course. Like Lucas suggested," I started calmly looking down at my meal. "But I guess if I *have* to have a party, I could invite another friend of mine," I poked my potatoes as if I was trying to find something under them. "Is that okay?" I lifted my gaze from my plate to look Lucas in the eye. "*He*," I deliberately made a pause to get his attention, "...is very nice. You'll like him."

Lucas's eyes narrowed at me. He knew who I was referring to, but I guess he didn't think I would have the nerve to actually follow through and invite him here. If he had the nerve to question me about Dylan, ask me to be his fuck buddy, and then just let girls suck his neck in front me, then I certainly could invite a friend to my birthday party.

"Oh, is that a boyfriend?" Elizabeth was trying to sound excited, but her voice cracked.

My secret agreement with his mother was making me restless. Even though we didn't do anything in particular except me showing up in this house and in his face all the time, I knew Lucas wouldn't take it easy if he knew Elizabeth's agenda. I tried to communicate as little as possible with her in front of him out of fear he would figure us out.

"Mmm? Oh, no. Just a friend," I looked at her. "For now."

The conversation at the table died completely. Everyone looked at Lucas like he was about to explode. To be honest, he really had that look. His jaws were so tightly clenched, I imagined him breaking a tooth. I couldn't hold my smile anymore, because of that picture in my head. I giggled. Lucas dropped his fork in his plate like I was a misbehaved child and he was my outraged grandmother.

I didn't roll my eyes for the rest of the dinner. I didn't have to. No one was talking and at least one person was pissed off. This was what I was used to. It really cheered me up.

My good mood turned out to be brief.

Later that evening, I went back to my room after I got out of the shower. As I was closing the door of my bedroom, a hand pushed it open, and Lucas stormed in. He slammed it behind his back, not caring that his parents could hear his tantrum. He walked in and stood in the center of the room while I stepped backwards, closer to the door. Not that I thought I would need to run away from him, but it was comforting to have the option to do so.

"Can I help you?" I crossed my arms in front of my chest. I felt naked. Not because of Ty's tee that I was once again wearing, but because of him being in my room. It was too intimate.

"You can't do it," his voice was firm and husky.

And hot.

I knew what he was talking about, and I wasn't going to pretend otherwise.

"Why?" I asked. It was all I managed to say without exposing all the feeling he stirred in me. The jealousy I felt when I saw him with other girls. In just a second, he was only a step away from me.

"Because this is my fucking house and because I say so."

He looked emotionally detached. His hair was a mess. It looked like he had run his fingers through it a thousand times. I felt the urge to defy him just to make him lose it. Something I suspected he did to me on a regular basis.

"No," I said nonchalantly.

His reaction was instant. Like he knew I was going to say that. Like he knew what he would do. Like he knew *I* wanted him to do it.

He grabbed me by the waist and my back landed on the door with a thud. I could feel his body everywhere on mine. It was intoxicating.

"Don't provoke me, Clementine," he warned. "I don't care if it's your birthday; he won't go out of here standing on his feet."

I laughed. Not because it was funny, or because I thought he wouldn't do it. I laughed because he cared. Solid proof I was deranged.

My laughter made him frown. His gaze scanned my face like I was a crazy person, dropped to my lips, and stayed there while he spoke. "This act of yours," his voice was low and it melted my insides. "You're too sassy and defiant to pull it off."

"What act?" I narrowed my eyes.

"This thing you do. When you pretend you don't have feelings and people can't affect you." He leaned in, his lips almost touching mine. "Say you won't do it," he whispered.

My breathing was out of control, my chest was moving up and down against his. He didn't wait for me to speak. He clashed his mouth on top of mine, and we both moaned. Our first kiss was wild. Angry. Like us. And it felt so good.

His tongue parted my lips and invaded my mouth. My whole body went on fire. My skin was burning. I grabbed his shirt in my fist and pulled him even closer to me, even though I knew it was a mistake. He grinned, his mouth still on mine, and his hand reached down. He lifted the end of my tee, and his fingertips caressed my naked thigh.

"Did you think about it?" he broke off our kiss. He was smiling. I pouted. I needed more of him.

"Think about what?" I sounded like a moody child.

He huffed annoyed, and I felt like an idiot.

"About your brother's t-shirt, my darling Clementine."

I pushed him in the chest. Hard. He immediately withdrew. The thing was I was already kind of used to him calling me Clementine. I hated that it wasn't irritating me so much anymore. And I hated that he did it just to piss me off.

"I swear, Lucas, if you start singing *that* song..." I warned him.

He laughed at my attempt to intimidate him. I wanted to punch him in the smug face. When I was little, everyone sang that stupid song to me. It was maddening.

"You try so hard to make people believe you're this badass that doesn't feel anything and doesn't need anyone, and yet you sleep in your brother's old t-shirt. I saw you almost cried when you received it."

"Get out," I roared and stepped away from the door.

I felt my cheeks burning with humiliation. I needed to fight back. To hurt him, humiliate him back. The audacity he had. Coming to my room. Analyzing me.

"Are you sure?" he smirked and his gaze scanned my body. I was trembling with rage, but arousal too, and I could see on his face he knew it. "You look on edge. I think you need an orgasm, nemesis. I could deliver. But I'm sure you already know that. Girls talk."

"God," I growled. "I hate you."

"Oh," he placed his hand on his chest. "You finally got my name right. I thought I would have to put in more effort than that," he pointed at the door which I wouldn't be able to look at ever again. "But I don't have a lot of experience with virgins, you know. No judgment."

And then the bastard yawned.

Not that I wanted to draw his attention to it, but his assumption pushed me over the edge of sanity, and I couldn't stop myself.

"Just because I haven't slept with *you* and your dumbass friends, it doesn't mean I'm a virgin, Cole."

Lucas waved me off. "No one in this town is stupid enough to fuck you, Clem."

Well, that hurt. Because it was actually true. I couldn't make a guy ask me out on a second date, let alone have sex with me. But it was also true I wasn't a virgin.

"Good for me my father doesn't live here then," I said, and I saw his jaw dropping. "I visit him every summer, you know. I guess there are stupid enough guys in Seattle."

His eyes searched mine for the truth. I recognized the moment he realized I wasn't lying. He looked disappointed. In what? Me? He had no problems fucking around and then brag about it.

"I didn't see that one coming, but I guess I should have," he paused. "Did you fuck Dylan too?" he asked out of nowhere.

I was too into an inflicting-pain mode to even consider telling the truth.

"Yes. Repeatedly."

He scanned my face again for a few seconds, then shook his head, and walked past me. He knew I was lying about Dylan.

"You're a fucking mess, Clem," I turned around to face him, but he was looking at the door, holding the handle. "And you're a bad liar. Don't use *him* to piss me off. He'll get hurt in the process."

***

My birthday came with a huge dark cloud over my head. My father pushed me to talk to my mother.

"Come on, Clem. She's trying. You're turning eighteen, and she gave birth to you, after all. You could at least let her wish you something."

He, of all people, should understand I had nothing to say to her and didn't want to hear her voice.

"Maybe I'll call her on Christmas," I said, even though I had no intentions of doing so.

"It's your birthday, Clem. And Christmas is in six weeks."

"Speaking of Christmas..." I started. He didn't let me finish.

"Madison and Tyler are coming, and so are you. I'm not letting you spend Christmas alone."

Except I wouldn't be alone. But I didn't want to admit to myself that I preferred the company of Elizabeth Cole and the men in this house. And I certainly couldn't tell my father that. But I already had a picture in my head what Christmas would be like here. And it was a nicer picture than the one in which I would participate in Seattle.

My father wasn't the only reason for my sour birthday mood. Elizabeth's English ex-boyfriend, aka my *mentor*, turned out to be a pretentious, snarky, middle-aged creep that I just couldn't imagine with the sweet soccer mom that was determined to throw me the best birthday party ever.

He used a lot of words to qualify my pieces. The first few pictures I sent him were evaluated as *boring*. I got that. He had been working in this industry for decades with some of the biggest international brands. I could accept the word *boring*, even though I had the gut feeling he was just genuinely disappointed in my work. After all, the point was to get some advice, and he obviously was as direct as one could be.

But the more we texted back and forth, the more he got annoyed with me. Boring became awful, dreadful, rubbish. I even got a whole sentence once.

"You should quit."

I had sent him a photo of the best necklace I ever made. That was his response.

You should quit.

At first it pissed me off. If he were here and not in London, I would probably go find him and say a few things and then end my speech with the middle finger. But this was not an option. And I could never embarrass Elizabeth like that anyway.

But I was walking around, asking the girls in school to let me take pictures of their necks and ears so I could show him my work. And he wasn't even mentoring me. He was just insulting me.

Eventually the thought stuck with me. What if I wasn't good enough? What if I really should quit? The logical part of my brain told me that he was just a mean old jerk, and I should ignore his nasty remarks. The emotional one, however, wanted to crawl under a rock if possible, with all the *rubbish* I made, and stay there until everyone I knew forgot I ever made jewelry.

I felt the pressure of making this thing work. I had to stick it to my mother. I didn't want to be like Madison. Depending on my parents for years to come until I found a job they approved of just to start answering their other demands. I assumed my big sister was about to be pressured with a marriage-mortgage-children plan about her life, since she was mommy's perfect little princess who never failed to deliver on anyone's expectations.

So, I sent this Duncan dude a picture of a new necklace I was still only sketching. It wasn't ready. But it was different from all I've sent him so far. He had seen the photo for hours now and replied nothing. I hated the fact I was checking my phone every five minutes, but I still did it throughout the day.

When I got home from school, I was already thinking about calling the whole birthday party off. I felt guilty, because I was sure Elizabeth went all in for this one, but I pushed the feeling aside as I did with guilt in general, and figured she would get over it.

And then I got inside the house.

The ceiling of the living room was covered in pink and white balloons. There was a huge Happy Birthday banner hanging on the wall and the number eighteen made out of, yes, balloons. It would probably reach my shoulder. The room looked awesome. And I felt warmth inside my chest. To have someone doing that for me.

I heard Elizabeth's laughter from the kitchen. She sounded even more excited and happy than usual.

I can do this for her. She did all that for me.

I walked towards the kitchen, and I heard a familiar voice. One that I haven't heard in person in months. My eyes and nose started burning.

Five seconds later, I was already squeezing the hell out of my brother, who was half-laughing, half-trying to get away from my hug.

"What the hell have you done with my sister?" he asked Elizabeth while he was pealing me off of him. "Are you a hugger now, little monster?" He frowned, but I knew he was joking.

"Are you here for my birthday?" I grinned.

"Shit! It's your birthday?" he tried to look shocked. "Don't make a big deal out of it," he belittled it.

"Are dad and Madison..." I started, but he didn't let me finish my question.

"No," he shook his head. "They're not coming. I'm all you got. Sorry about that." Tyler smiled and I did the same.

"I don't care. You're my favorite, anyway."

Elizabeth looked at me. She was surprised I could actually show affection to someone.

"Let's go," Tyler pushed himself off the kitchen island and grabbed my wrist.

"Where?"

"Who cares?" he waved me off.

"Do you need any help?" I yelled to Elizabeth while Tyler was dragging me out of the house. She just laughed.

Half an hour later, we were sitting on a bench in the park, and Tyler was opening a second beer.

"Dad said I make him look bad," he murmured. "By coming to your birthday."

"I don't care about the stupid birthday. In a way, I'm glad no one came," I pouted. He shot me a look.

"I mean, I'm glad you did," I said. And I really was, but I was also worried how it would play out tonight. I had a best friend that was crazy in love with him, a roommate that hated me and was *not* afraid to show it, and a boy that had had an odd fascination with me since the day he came to school this fall, all coming to a party that I didn't exactly want in the beginning, but was sort of anticipating now.

"Okay," he chuckled, not believing me.

I placed my palm over his hand and repeated myself.

"I really am. I'm glad you're here. Thank you."

"Well, I didn't want to leave you alone with the Coles. Dad thinks you'll cut his head off the moment you see him for the way he left you here." He kicked my foot with his, signaling me he wanted an answer on that one.

"Is that his excuse for not coming?" I asked, outraged. "He just dumped me there with no warning. Did he tell you that?"

"Yes, he told me. You don't need to yell." Tyler looked at me amused. "God... Living alone with Mom made you really violent, huh?"

"You're the one to talk. I know what you do in Boston," I crossed my legs and arms with a victorious look on my face. Like I knew everything while I only heard snippets.

"I do it for the fun of it," he shrugged, and I realized that part of the conversation was over.

But while we were sitting in silence, a thought came to my mind.

I was the only one angry at mom. Tyler and dad had basically the same hedonistic nature, and pleasure was their prime objective. Tyler was into boxing now, and he was beating the shit out of people for fun, apparently. Dad was screwing twenty-year-old after twenty-year-old. Madison seemed to like her life of a cold-hearted bitch, chasing a glamorous career in New York and wherever her job led her these days. She put to real use her unnatural perfectionism and did great for herself. They all found a way to deal with their emotions. Even mom was in a better place than me. She was getting mental help for her addiction and I... I was just stuck.

Stuck in all the hatred and negativity I had been feeling for years.

"Why did you come?" I asked Tyler. "Dad didn't. Madison sent me a happy birthday text she would probably send to the person doing her nails."

I didn't want to talk about the thirty missed calls from an unknown number. It was my mother calling from the clinic; I was sure of it.

"I felt bad you were alone," he shrugged. "Not today. The whole time while Mom was drinking. Was it bad? Did she abuse you?"

Ahh. Guilt. If I allowed myself to roll in that feeling from time to time, maybe I would have recognized it without having to ask.

Tyler wanted to calm his conscience. Not that I had a reason to expect anything but a selfish motive from him. He was never big on leaving behind his needs for the sake of others.

"Honestly?" I looked at my feet. "Lately she barely even noticed I was there."

"Was that a good or a bad thing?" Tyler hesitated how to interpret my tone.

"Still debating," I smiled, not daring to look him in the eyes. Coming clean about mom and how I deliberately let her get worse just to get back at her, wasn't a desired topic for either of us.

My phone buzzed in my pocket. I got a new message.

Duncan: It's not good enough yet, but it's better than the crap you've been sending me so far. Finish it.

I gawked at my phone like the mediocre idiot Duncan Walsh already thought I was. I got a whole proper sentence. Two actually.

Tyler got his face in my phone and read the text.

"Who's this Duncan guy?" he asked suggestively.

"Oh, this fifty-year-old guy I've been talking to online," I said nonchalantly.

Tyler's eyes almost popped out and I laughed.

"Elizabeth knows him. He's a designer and he's helping me. Or at least he thinks he is. I'm not so sure. He's trying to be my mentor."

"Your mentor?" Ty cocked his head. He had no idea what I was talking about.

"I have a... hobby," I cringed. "I'm making jewelry. Girls at school are buying them. It's stupid."

Tyler was confused and looked at me like he knew that wasn't everything I had to say on the subject. I could see the decision-making process behind his eyes. His never-ending need to escape the complications in life overcame the small part of his mind that wanted to know if I was doing something stupid.

"If that's your thing," he seemed eager to change the subject. So was I. "How is school? Is Principal Smith still preaching against short skirts and normal human needs?"

"You mean like the need to have a threesome on the football field? Yeah, he's still not a fan." We both laughed. In his senior year, my brother was caught with two cheerleaders with their clothes off right in the middle of the field. There was no real punishment for anyone involved, but Principal Smith had had strict rules about PDA ever since.

Tyler and I managed to escape all topics that would potentially get one of us in an awkward position for the next couple of hours. On our walk back, I sent a text to Hannah to tell her that she would after all see my brother like she hoped a few weeks ago, and I went back *home* almost happy.

Chapter Thirteen

Clementine

I opened the door to the Coles' home and after a few steps inside, I got a view to their living room and the tall, handsome smiling guy sitting on their couch, playing around with the pink balloons. He smiled, and I had to bite my lip to hide my own grin. He looked so good, I had to remind myself all the time that he was actually tormenting me. Well, that one was a bit of a stretch. All he wanted from me was to speak my truth, explain, and admit to every shameful decision I made. I preferred to wait until graduation and bury my secrets once and for all.

Lucas stood up and shook Tyler's hand, ignoring me.

"Haven't seen you around in a long time."

"I've been busy," Ty supplied and landed on the couch. Lucas followed him and turned his back on me like I wasn't even there.

I was hurt that he didn't even say happy birthday to me. Not in the morning, when Troy and his parents sang for me, hugged me, and made me blow out a candle on a miniature cupcake. Not at school, where we bumped into each other a few times. And not now, when we were pretty much alone if you don't count the other self-absorbed quarterback in the room.

"How's Coach Howard doing? Clem told me he's retiring," Tyler started, and I huffed. They both shot me a surprised look.

"I'll go change. I can't stand *that* talk." I dragged my feet up the stairs. The last thing I wanted was to listen to a conversation about football between two quarterbacks with egos the size of the state.

"What talk?" my brother yelled after me.

"Never mind," I shouted back.

I went to my room, and I pulled out the dress. I had a few. They were more appropriate for a night out, looking for someone to undress you, than a birthday girl just becoming an adult, partying with her forty-year-old neighbors.

I picked the long-sleeved one that covered everything from my neck to my mid-thigh. Everything except my back, which was completely bare. But I figured I could always stand by the wall like a fucking statue.

I went downstairs and straight to the kitchen, passing by the dinner table already set up by Elizabeth. I loved everything she cooked, but I was a total sucker for her baked goodies. I devoured those. I refused to acknowledge Lucas and Tyler while I passed them. I was scared of their possible disapproval of my outfit.

Elizabeth was helping Troy with his homework on the kitchen island. They both looked frustrated, but no one acted out. It was so different from what I'd been used to. The funny thing was that I was starting to really enjoy everything that irritated me in this household in the beginning.

I looked at them for a while. Elizabeth lifted her gaze and smiled at me but continued talking to Troy. She really loved being a mom.

I approached her, and I planted a kiss on her cheek. She looked surprised.

"Thank you," I said. "Everything is amazing. I love it."

She dragged me into a hug and squeezed me hard but didn't say a thing.

I started to feel anxious about the whole Dylan invitation thing. Elizabeth made everything perfect, and all I thought about up until now was to get back at Lucas for parading his numerous flings in front of me. If he followed through on his threat and beat Dylan up, that would ruin everything.

But it was already too late to cancel. The doorbell rang. Garret never did that. I knew Hannah and Dylan were coming together. So, if my father hadn't decided to make a surprise appearance, which I doubted, my friends were at the door.

I froze partly because I realized I didn't want to be in a room with both Dylan and Lucas. Then the doorbell rang again, and Lucas showed up in the kitchen, looking straight at me.

"Birthday girl, go greet your guests," he smiled wolfishly. The bastard knew I was deliberately delaying the inevitable and took pleasure in my agony. His eyes were daring me to finish what I started. To follow through.

My palms were sweating when I walked out of the kitchen. Lucas followed me in the short corridor, leading to the living room. He placed his hand on my lower back, my *naked* lower back, and whispered in my ear.

"I like this dress," he slid his fingers up my spine and then slowly down again.

"What are you doing?" I hissed. I wasn't protesting against his touch. I was worried there were too many people around, and someone might see us. Not to mention the person who was waiting at the doorstep.

"I just like this kind of provocation more than inviting your boyfriend in my house," his fingers twitched before he removed his hand from me as we were entering the living room.

I felt my face turning red and warm while I was walking to the front door. The first thing I heard when I opened it was Hannah's gasp.

"You're gorgeous," she wrapped her hands around me. "You'll drive him crazy with that dress," she whispered in my ear.

I had no idea if she was talking about Dylan or Lucas and that made my heart race. I had to point my attention to something else, and I did.

"So are you," I cocked my head suggestively. She was wearing a very tight black V-neck dress and her blond hair was gathered in a messy bun. She looked older. No doubt she wanted to break the image of the little girl my brother associated her with.

That was the reason she refused to date high school students now. In July, I paid my dad my annual visit in Seattle, and Hannah's parents let her come with me for a week. Tyler also came for about a day and a half. It was more than enough for him to make her cry. Hannah overheard him explaining himself on the phone to someone and jealousy made her eavesdrop.

"What girls? It's only my dad's girlfriend and I'm not into that kink. The other one is my sister's best friend. She's a fucking child."

"How do I look?" Dylan chimed in, not at all aware Hannah and I were having a silent conversation about her trying to impress my brother. I finally dared to turn my focus to him. Hannah answered for me.

"You're a man. No one cares what you're wearing."

We laughed. Dylan grabbed and squeezed me in a bear hug. It wasn't as intimate as Lucas's touch a minute ago, but it felt too much. He usually wasn't physical with me. We shared an awkward hug every now and again. He brushed me with a shoulder or patted my hand when he wanted me to pay attention. But it was my birthday, he had a reason to hug and kiss me, and no one would think it was too much. No one but me apparently. I suspected Lucas would share the sentiment.

"Happy birthday," Dylan said cheerfully.

"Thank you," I patted his back as a sign to let me go. I wanted to prevent his spine being broken before he even had the chance to step inside the house. He loosened his grip, and I moved away from him. I tried to make it look like I was ushering them in, but I needed some space between us.

Tyler was standing next to me, looking at Hannah with wide eyes. It was like witnessing a crash. It's horrifying when you realize what you're looking at, but you just can't stop.

"Little Spencer...," he said in a husky voice. The look he gave her made me uncomfortable, so I moved my gaze towards Lucas. He was staring at me, but he looked surprisingly calm. The silence between my brother and my best friend was deafening. Then Tyler cleared his throat and broke it. "How's school?"

"Good," Hannah sounded disappointed. To be honest I was also expecting a compliment by the way he was eyeing her. "You know. Graduation. Colleges. Kid's stuff."

Of course, he didn't catch the provocation behind her words. He had no idea she was into him and that she knew he considered her a child. In fact, I was certain he had forgotten about that statement coming out of his mouth the moment he said it.

"Where do you want to go?" he asked and sounded interested. He was good in feigning feelings. That's what our childhood taught us.

"New York," Hannah answered. I used the just mentioned ability and pretended to be invested in their exchange just to avoid talking to Dylan in front of Lucas. "Or Boston."

Wait. What now?

Dylan passed us by and went inside. I had to point my attention to him, even though this new information made me worried about Hannah's mental health. Would she go to Boston because of my brother? Was she really that obsessed?

"Cole," Dylan greeted joyfully. It was clear he was enjoying being here. Maybe he knew it pushed Lucas's buttons.

"Williams," Lucas sounded bored.

Elizabeth and Troy barged in. She shook Dylan's hand and went straight to Hannah and Tyler.

"How's track team?" Lucas's hands were in his front pockets. His posture was relaxed and nothing about his appearance showed he hated Dylan's presence here. It scared the bejesus out of me.

"Love it," Dylan smirked, and I squirmed.

"I'm sure you do."

The three of us were standing a few steps away from each other with me sort of in the middle. I felt like I was in between sliding doors but couldn't decide if I was going in or out, so I just stayed there, waiting to be smashed.

I had no idea what Lucas was up to, but I knew he wasn't trying to be nice or have a chitchat.

"Football eats too much of your time and there is something else I realized is worth pursuing. So, you actually did me a favor," Dylan snickered. My heart was beating so fast, I thought everyone could hear it hammering inside my chest.

"Should we go eat?" I asked in a high pitch that was completely unusual for me. Every head in the room turned towards me except one. Lucas's gaze was pinned on Dylan's face.

Tonight is going to be bad.

Hannah came to us and almost pushed Dylan to the dinner table.

"Troy, honey, could you bring me my phone? I want to check on your dad." Elizabeth brushed his hair backwards with her hand. She was also nervous.

Troy rolled his eyes but marched to the kitchen. I turned to Lucas.

"Seriously?" I started nagging, trying to keep my voice low, so that no one else could hear us. I didn't mean to sound like I was begging, but I realized I did sound just like that. For a moment, I thought I saw a hint of understanding on his face. Like he felt my worry and wanted to comfort me. But then his expression went blank.

"What?" he played dumb for a second with an innocent look on his face, then he continued. "It would be in my favor to have an excuse to reshape his face."

"Please," I snorted. "Since when do you need an excuse to do anything?"

Lucas grinned.

"So you're saying that I don't need an excuse? Should I just go for it? Can I do it now or do you want me to wait until after the cake? It's a *perfectly good* cake. I'm the one who told my mother you would love it."

That was like a slap in my face.

For my twelfth birthday, Sylvia bought me a raspberry cake. It was Madison's favorite cake. I hated raspberries. She didn't even apologize. She said it was a *perfectly good* cake and screamed at my father that he was spoiling me with his constant need to please me. Lucas was there, sitting beside me, while I sobbed for an hour in my room.

Was he that cruel? To pick a painful childhood memory to repeat it on my eighteenth birthday when I was already homeless and living with my *nemesis* as he loved to call us.

I figured he was. After all, he knew all too well I hated my name and vowed he would never call me *Clementine*, and yet he did. All the time.

Troy returned with Elizabeth's phone, and my brother joined Hannah and Dylan at the table. Lucas leaned closer to me, changing the subject as if it was insignificant.

"Do you know Hannah wants to bang your brother?"

"Excuse me?" I squealed.

"I said..."

"Stop," I roared. "He could hear you."

"You did know then. You're just full of secrets, aren't you, nemesis?"

"If we were friends, you would have known my secrets. And would you please not call me *that* in front of other people?"

"Hannah's your friend, and she knows shit. Well, she knows some of it, maybe. But deep down you're not capable of telling the truth. Even to yourself. That's why that clown is here." He pointed at Dylan. "Oh, and I'm pretty sure you love it when I call you *that*."

"You are unbelievable," I shook my head and left him standing alone in the middle of the room. His laughter filled the open space.

I pulled a chair and sat at the table. Everyone did the same. Dylan picked the spot next to me. Tyler sat next to Dylan. Hannah was probably mad at my brother, because she chose the furthest spot from him. She was sitting across from me.

The members of the Cole family that were currently present joined us a few seconds later.

"Garret will be late." Elizabeth looked on edge. "It's weird being the only adult here. Except you, Tyler," she smiled at my brother.

"I can't say I'm a good influence, but I could chaperone with your guidance," he mocked us all.

Hannah frowned, obviously offended. He deserved to be ignored by her for the rest of his life in my opinion, but, apparently, she planned to move across the country to follow him around.

Conversation was pretty much nonexistent. Elizabeth checked the time every five minutes, no doubt wishing for her husband to come back sooner and help her with this mess. The mess that I created. It wouldn't be so intense if Dylan wasn't here. Why couldn't I just keep my mouth shut every now and again?

"Why so grim, birthday girl?" Dylan bumped his shoulder into mine. I half-smiled.

"I...umm...I...," I was sounding like a moron. I could barely breathe and swallow, let alone think of a lie. I couldn't tell him that I regretted inviting him, that I was hurt about my family not showing up for my eighteenth birthday, that I felt homeless long before my house burnt down, and that my stay with the perfect Coles was a constant reminder of that. I didn't even want to begin to dig into my feelings towards Lucas and the fact he had told his mother to get me a raspberry cake because he knew it would cut my heart into pieces.

"You should be excited. Have fun. Are you turning eighteen or eighty?" He tried to be goofy and funny, but I just wasn't in the mood.

I glanced at Hannah for moral support. She seemed as worried as I felt. I caught Lucas eyeing me and Dylan, but I avoided looking back at him. Tyler was occupied with his phone and paid no attention to us. Elizabeth and Troy were arguing about some sleepover he wanted to attend over the weekend. I thought she might be deliberately distancing herself from the four of us. She was maybe even reconsidering my stay here.

"Honestly," Dylan continued, without any indication from me that I was participating in that conversation. "I have never seen anyone more miserable on their birthday." His tone was starting to feel judgmental.

Lucas started talking, and I was pretty sure he meant to start his sentence with the word *dickhead*, but Hannah cut him off with a suggestion.

"Maybe we could play a game?"

Lucas wasn't having it and said what he had in mind anyway.

"She's living here against her will and three out of four of her family members didn't even bother coming for her birthday. I think she's doing pretty great."

Tears started filling up my eyes. My whole body shook. I pushed my chair back and darted up.

"A game it is. Should we go outside?"

I didn't have anything particular in mind. I just didn't want Lucas and Dylan to ruin the house while they tried to kill each other.

"Great idea." Hannah was the only one to speak. "Truth or dare?"

She glanced at my brother, and I could already see her brain going through hundreds of questions she would ask him if presented with the possibility.

"How about Never have I ever?" Dylan asked with a wicked grin on his face, looking straight at Lucas.

"As a chaperone I have to remind you that you are not allowed to drink," Tyler said, then leaned over to Elizabeth and put his charm in action. "Am I doing it right? Rules are not my strong suit. Breaking them is more my thing."

"You're doing fine, Tyler, but since it's a party, I think we could allow a glass of wine each."

My head snapped in her direction. That was something that this party didn't need for sure.

Tyler rubbed his hands together.

"In that case, I'm voting for Never Have I Ever."

"You're playing?" I was surprised.

"Sure. It's a fun game and drinking is allowed," he lifted both his brows in a playful gesture. "Vote," he pointed at me.

"Never Have I Ever." I wasn't going to play a game that implied I had to tell the truth with Lucas and my older brother present. Not that I had a problem lying. I did that all the time, but why risk getting caught in a lie, when there was another possibility.

"Cole? Little Spencer?" Ty asked them to vote.

"Whatever the birthday girl decides," Lucas said with a grim look on his face. He wasn't in the mood for a game, but he would play anyway.

"Does it matter what we think, considering you already have three votes and there are only two of us?" Hannah cocked her head sideways.

"I suppose not." Tyler stood up and waved to the kitchen. "Go outside then. I'll bring the wine."

Ten minutes later, Hannah and I were each holding a glass of wine, Lucas and Dylan a beer, and my brother was having a scotch. The bottle was on the ground, next to his leg.

"Never have I ever broken a bone," Tyler said.

The guys drank; Hannah and I didn't. I looked behind my shoulder. I could see Elizabeth and Troy through the kitchen windows. It calmed my nerves a little.

"Never have I ever sexted," Dylan teased.

We all drank. Tyler made a disgusted face.

"Dude, that's my sister over there. Watch it with the questions, okay?"

"Never have I ever had a threesome," Hannah challenged Tyler.

Lucas and I laughed. Dylan had no clue why, but when my brother gulped his scotch in one go without tearing his eyes from Hannah's face, he figured out it was directed to him somehow. He leaned forward, and they fist bumped.

Men.

"Never have I ever stolen something." Tyler looked at my best friend, and, when she lifted her glass to her lips, I found out I was missing something here.

"Never have I ever lied to my best friend," Lucas said. I didn't move. He lifted an eyebrow, suggesting I was cheating by not drinking. I closed my eyes in actual physical pain. The tears I managed to swallow back at the dinner table were now burning my eyes.

"Excuse me," I somehow managed to say through my clenched throat, and I ran inside and straight upstairs to my room as fast as I could. I heard Hannah's heels as she was following me. I just wanted to calm myself down before I lost it in front of everybody.

Just as I entered my room, I heard Lucas's voice behind me.

"Keep him downstairs or he'll be flying out the window." He slammed the door in Hannah's horrified face.

"Why did you do that? You humiliated me," I pointed at him going round in circles, trying to calm myself down. My tears were falling down my face.

"Are you fucking kidding me?" he roared at me. "The reason we played that stupid game was because he acted like an ass at the dinner table. You told him nothing."

"You have no right," I cried. "You treat me like shit and then you pretend to be concerned about someone else hurting my feelings?"

He didn't answer. He was just staring at me. Jaw clenched. I was furious.

"I don't need you. I don't need your attention and I certainly don't need your protection. Especially from Dylan. Back off."

"He's an asshole, Clem. I can't believe you don't see it."

"You don't know him," I argued just for the sake of arguing. I cared about my fingernails more than I cared about Dylan.

"Neither do you. You've known him for five minutes. You've known me your whole life."

He was barely moving. The exact opposite of my behavior. I was circling the room like a wild animal he was trying to catch, and it made me want to escape him even more.

"Don't settle. You deserve better," he tried reasoning with me.

"Oh yeah? Like who?" I stopped and dared him to say it.

He didn't.

CHAPTER FOURTEEN

Lucas

Clementine looked at me defiantly, and it made me want to tear her to pieces.

She was crazy if she thought I would say the thing that would erase any rationality and caution I had when it came to her. But there was one thing that made her stop pretending she felt nothing for me. So I went for it.

I grabbed her by the back of her neck, and I covered her mouth with mine. Her defiance melted immediately. She ran her fingers through my hair and pulled it hard. I pressed my palms on her bare back, and we both moaned. I paused for a second and I looked at her.

"Happy birthday, nemesis," I smiled. Her face was red and wet from tears, but she grinned back at me.

I lifted her in the air, and she wrapped her legs around my waist. I pinned her to the closest wall. Her smooth skin was burning hot everywhere I touched. I broke the kiss and sucked her neck. Her throat bobbed.

The sounds she made drove me insane. I knew there were people downstairs who would come up any second now to see if we had killed each other, but I couldn't bring myself to stop. I squeezed her thighs. I wanted to push into her right that moment. To make her mine.

A knock on the door made her freeze in my arms. I let her go immediately. I didn't want to be another person who was trying to cage her when she was feeling vulnerable.

"Come..." she tried to invite the person on the other side of the door with a shaky voice, but I grabbed her hand and I made her look at me. She looked miserable. Maybe I was getting it all wrong. Maybe she had feelings for him.

Too bad because I wasn't ready to let her go yet.

"We can't be what we used to be, Clem."

She nodded. She had already accepted that a long time ago. I was the one who had not completely dealt with the reality of her, me, and Dylan. I wasn't exactly ready for that revelation, so I released her hand from mine and left her standing there alone.

Hannah was on the other side of the door. She opened her mouth to insult me probably but saw something on my face that made her just pat my shoulder. I left her to pick up the pieces of what I just did and went downstairs.

Tyler looked like he was waiting for me. I decided to get it over with.

"I presume you want to warn me not to mess around with your little sister."

He grinned like an idiot.

"Not my style. You, kiddos, are on your own. I'm not getting in the middle of that shit."

I wish I could get out of that shit.

The next hour passed like a decade. Dad came home. No one was leaving, but everyone wanted to. Even the people who actually lived in this house. The birthday girl looked so burdened I couldn't stand it. It was no surprise that my outburst and her hiding upstairs ruined the mood. I had promised my mother that I wouldn't fuck up the party. I tried to tolerate the presence of Dylan, and I was fighting the impulse to throw him out days before he stepped inside my house.

The day I interrupted their conversation in the school hallway after her first night here was the first sign I wasn't handling her closeness all too well. I had no intention of talking to him. But I saw them walking together, her head was on his shoulder, and I just lost it. I told him what I told every guy that showed interest in her. Leave her alone. I never actually had to explain myself. Everyone in school just agreed with everything I wanted them to do.

Dylan said no. He didn't care. I could see it in his eyes. The satisfaction that he was the reason we never got together in the first place. I remember he treated her differently compared with Hannah and Amy when we were kids, but I was now figuring out that he liked her then, and he probably liked her now.

Hannah was killing herself trying to make everything look normal. Dylan looked amused. I bet he loved it. It looked like Clem and I had the fight of the century, and not like we dry humped against the wall while everyone else was waiting for us.

Mom finally announced the cake. Troy was singing happy birthday, and Clem smiled at him. It was at the wrong brother in my opinion, but I could still turn things around. In fact, I was sure I was already turning them. The cake was part of the plan. I just felt like the goal was changing. I no longer wanted just to fuck Clem and get back at Dylan. It wasn't about revenge. I wanted to get the girl.

"Make a wish," Troy reminded Clem when mom put the cake in front of her. She was just staring at it. It was not a raspberry cake as I deliberately made her think. It was a chocolate waffle cake.

The entire week mom grilled Clementine with questions about the birthday, and I got so tired of listening to that shit every day, I told her about the waffles. I wanted to spare Clementine more questions from mom and try to make her happy. Even if it was just a stupid cake she didn't even want.

Chase was right. I was a goner.

Clem closed her eyes and blew the candles. Everyone clapped. Except me.

I was having an epiphany. The days I spent wanting revenge were gone. The thought of her suffering because of me didn't please me anymore. It tore up my insides.

I wanted to know what she wished for, but I couldn't ask. Luckily for me, my little brother was the other sucker in love with her in that room and did me a solid without even knowing.

"What did you wish for?" he asked.

I was watching her like a hawk, so there was just no chance at all of me missing the split second her eyes drifted to mine.

"Troy, honey." Mom pulled him back to give Clementine some space. "You know she can't tell you or it won't come true."

My phone buzzed. It was a text message.

Amy: My parents are out of town.

Lucas: A party?

Amy answered in a second.

Amy: No. Just the two of us. Chase is out.

I looked around thinking how easy it could be with Amy. No drama, no secrets.

Hannah was eyeing Tyler like he was the only thing in the world, and he was nothing but a train wreck. Their whole damn family was. Clementine included.

I felt sorry for Spencer. Her heart would be broken in no time if she continued this illusion. Just like Clementine broke mine.

Lucas: No, thanks.

Amy: Are you sure? No strings attached.

Lucas: Positive.

Even though I declined Amy's company, I still needed to get away.

"Well, we cut the cake, so I'm going out now."

"It's school night, you know the rules," my father warned me.

"Yeah. I'll be back before midnight."

I broke the rule. I came back at two in the morning.

The lights in our guest room were still on. I stopped by the door. Some pathetic part of my brain thought she was waiting up for me.

My father appeared next to me in the hallway. He looked pissed.

"Where were you?"

"At the beach."

"And why didn't you pick up your phone?"

"I left it in the car."

That was another rule I broke. I had to always be reachable whenever I was out at night.

"I'm not going to ask if you know what time it is."

He wasn't whispering but he was talking quietly enough not to wake up the others. He noticed I was staring at the light slipping under Clem's door.

"Don't even think about it. She's off limits."

"I know," I murmured. He sighed.

"You're grounded. Two weeks. No. Scratch that. I'll let your mother decide in the morning."

"Oh, come on," I protested. "She'll lock me up until graduation."

"You should have thought about that before you decided not to answer my calls. Go to sleep."

***

My mother decided I would be grounded for two months. A month for each rule I broke. I was allowed to go to school and play football. That was it.

It was my third Friday night at home. I was enjoying immensely the fact that I was grounded, and I could spend my time around Clementine without having to admit it was by choice.

We won the finals. I felt good about it, but it wasn't what I was expecting. Spending a few hours with Tyler on Clementine's birthday made me think about what I wanted to do now that high school was almost over. I always thought of him as some sort of a hero, but he was just a regular guy with lots for emotional problems and possibly a drinking problem. I didn't want to end up like him. Was I going in that direction? The answer to that question escaped me.

I couldn't find an answer to another important question. Why wasn't Clementine speaking to me?

She got her favorite cake. I didn't smash Dylan's head, even though he showed up in my house when I specifically told her not to invite him. It felt like she was thousands of miles away, even though she was sitting in front of me every night at the dinner table. It was both a nice, familiar routine between us, and, at the same time, I was about to explode with anticipation every time she turned her head in my direction.

"Where are you going tomorrow?" my mother asked Clem while I was cleaning up after dinner. They were making a cake.

So, my people-hating nemesis was doing something worth talking about this weekend, and I was planning on counting the cracks on every ceiling in the house. Oh, and apparently, I was doing community service, helping Mom in the backyard.

"Just hanging out," Clem answered.

My mother pointed to a tower of dishes on the counter and got back to their conversation.

"I know I'm not your mother, but you're living under our roof, and I'm responsible for you, so I have to at least know where he's taking you."

Fucking Dylan.

But I could handle it, right? They would bring Hannah with them. There was no way Clementine was going on a real date with that douche. Not after what happened between us on her birthday.

"We are going to a museum."

I suppressed a smile. She was the only senior in Southern California I knew who would agree to spend her Saturday in a fucking museum.

I loved that about her.

"Is Hannah coming with you?"

Yes.

"No."

My left eye twitched. It wasn't exactly an ideal situation. But I've been through that before. Her going out on first dates. Me preventing her going out on a second one. The only difference was it was Williams. No biggie. It would be a challenge staying home doing nothing, knowing she was strolling around with him, but it wasn't impossible, right?

"Which museum?" mom asked.

Clem hesitated, then answered, "The International Banana Museum."

What was that again? I fished for my phone and typed the words that sounded like something made up for a weird porn script.

Nope. Not a porn movie. A real place.

I took some of the clean plates to put them back into the kitchen cabinets, and I started laughing quietly. With every second I felt my body submitting to the laughter. When it came out of my mouth It. Was. Loud.

I laughed so hard I had to put down everything I was holding and lean on the counter. My shoulders were bouncing up and down. A few seconds later, I managed to at least stop the hysterical laughter and control it to a semi-normal smile. It felt like it was about to slash my face into two, but at least I wasn't howling now. Isolation did weird things to normal people.

I turned around to face them. They were both looking at me like I was the stupid one.

"I'm sorry. Don't mind me," I snorted while suppressing another loud laugh. "Please continue."

I turned my back again on them. It was hilarious. I couldn't wait for her to get back from that date, just so I could see her face.

"Where was that exactly?" my mom continued her interrogation.

"It's in Mecca."

I burst out laughing. From all the fun places he could take her and really be a good date, that idiot picked that.

"I'm sorry. I can't...," I couldn't even finish my sentence. "I'm sorry, Mom, I can't".

I left the kitchen laughing so hard that my father and Troy, who were checking what homework he had for the weekend, both looked at me and smiled, anticipating a good joke.

"What?" Troy asked impatiently with a huge grin on his face.

That only made me laugh even more.

"Banana...banana...," I tried to answer, but I couldn't.

"What?" Troy was jumping up and down. Dad looked behind me, and I turned. Mom and Clem were standing there. Mom was smiling.

Clem was looking at me, biting her lower lip, not wanting to show she was laughing with me.

CHAPTER FIFTEEN

Clementine

I got back on Saturday night and the whole Cole family was in the living room. Lucas smiled at me.

"How was the date?" he asked with a smug face I wanted to punch.

"Amazing. I've never had that much fun. *Ever*."

That wasn't true. Two years ago, Matt Pierson took me out for a walk and ice creams, and he made me laugh so much and so hard my face hurt and I almost peed my pants. Twice. Of course I wasn't going to say that to Lucas, so I lied and tried to rub my pretending-to-be-perfect date in his handsome face. It was petty of me, and I knew he probably didn't care, since he laughed like a maniac yesterday when I said where I was going, but I wanted to ruffle his feathers a bit.

"Best date ever."

Not that we had a bad time. It was fun. Sort of. Okay, it was dumb but in a fun way. It was perfect to hang out with friends, which was the whole point.

The truth was I came up with that weird museum idea, because I was scared Dylan was planning to take me out on a real date without actually calling it that. It was true he asked both me and Hannah to go out with him, but when she said she was busy, and he didn't cancel it, I started feeling uncomfortable.

I strolled over to the kitchen. Lucas followed.

I realized I couldn't ignore him anymore. At least when he was not ignoring me. The minute he started talking to me, I forgot I wasn't speaking to him.

"Were there any apes out there? Beside your boyfriend, I mean."

I took a deep breath. I wasn't having the Dylan conversation again. I left the word *boyfriend* slide this time. After all, I had more important things to worry about. Like the offer my mentor made me the other day.

"It's a museum, not a zoo." I started digging in the fridge. I wasn't hungry, but I needed to do something, so I didn't have to look at him. "You should visit one someday. Just to have an idea what it's all about. You could actually learn something other than knocking people off on the football field."

"Thank you," he smirked. "The correct term is tackle, by the way. And sometimes I too get *knocked off*. I'm not the Greek god you might think I am. I know I have the looks, so I get your confusion."

I cocked my head. "A Greek god? Seriously? Try Narcissus. I've never met another person so self-absorbed and in love with himself. You know what happened to him, right? In fact, it was the goddess *Nemesis* who punished him for his vanity. Isn't it funny that you call me exactly that?"

"So I'm not a god, but you're a goddess, and not just any goddess, but the one of revenge and retribution?" I was surprised he knew who Nemesis was, and he got that from my expression. "Yeah, Clem, I play football, but I can also read, you know." He wasn't offended. He looked amused by our conversation, pleased he managed to astonish me.

Comparing him to Narcissus reminded me of the reason I was there in the first place. What Elizabeth hoped for.

"You can mock me all you want, Lucas, but you can't deny the similarities. Narcissus was beautiful." I pointed at him. "Many fell in love with him, but he treated them with nothing but disdain. Ring a bell?"

I tried to sound casual when I called him beautiful, but Lucas being Lucas couldn't let it go without a comment.

"Ouch. Poor Williams. Calling another man beautiful after your first date? Harsh, Clem. Was he that bad?"

"You're..." I started, irritated.

"Unbelievable?" He interrupted me and took the jar of pickles. "You keep saying that." He opened it and passed it to me with a charming smile. "You're welcome."

"Deluded also fits."

This back and forth between us has become natural to the point I couldn't even remember the feeling of anxiety I used to have about passing him by in the school's hallway.

He watched me silently while I ate the sandwich. I was impressed with myself for not trembling under his scrutinizing look. I used to feel uneasy around him, but not anymore. I had the feeling he was noticing the change too.

"You're not saying anything about the girls." I paused and waited for him to answer. He didn't, so I pressed. "You hate them."

"I don't hate girls. I love them." He flashed me a suggestive smile. Jealousy crawled into my stomach. What was I supposed to say to that? "Why do you want to talk about the girls?" he looked intrigued.

"I don't."

"Liar." He leaned forward and looked straight into my eyes, like he could see the answer to all his questions there. "What are you hiding, Nemesis, goddess of revenge and retribution?"

"You're changing the subject." I shook my head. "You're the one that's hiding something."

"I'm not. You know everything. You just don't want to think about it because you'll have to deal with it." He took a lock of my hair and played with it. "And you prefer to cover your problems and mistakes with piles of lies and secrets."

His voice was soft and alluring, not at all judgmental. I licked my lips and my eyes drifted to his mouth. All I could think about was our kiss on my birthday. I thought about it a lot. I didn't mean to, but my mind just kept going back to that moment. He read my mind and chuckled, releasing my hair from his hand.

"You'll have to dump your boyfriend if you want me to kiss you again, nemesis." His tone changed. He was teasing me again.

The rest of the Cole family entered the kitchen with a loud laughter. Lucas immediately leaned back. I saw his father giving him a warning look. Great. Garret suspected there was something between us.

"Clem, how was the date?" Elizabeth asked enthusiastically. "Was it fun?"

"Yeah. It was... different."

"It's stupid," Troy added, and we all looked at him. He looked smug, just like Lucas did so often. "I Googled it. He should have taken you to the Railroad Museum. That's awesome!"

"That's in Sacramento, sweetie. It's too far away." Elizabeth ran her fingers through Troy's hair.

I glanced at Lucas. He was enjoying every second of this. Even his ten-year-old brother thought my date was boring.

"They had great banana desserts there," I started. "You'll love it. The ice cream was amazing."

"You can eat bananas here too. And you don't even like ice cream. You eat chocolate." I knew Troy had a little crush on me, but I didn't expect him to get mad that I went out on a date. It made me smile.

"Buddy," Lucas intervened with a serious face. "I think Dylan wanted her to eat one very special banana."

Elizabeth gasped. My mouth fell open.

"Lucas," Garret warned.

"What? It's my duty to explain to my little brother about the birds and the bees, right?"

"What are you talking about?" Troy looked between his father and brother. "I don't get it." He knew they were talking about something he shouldn't be hearing, and he wanted to be in on Lucas's joke.

"People make jokes about bananas," Lucas started. "...because they look like..."

"Out! Now!" Elizabeth pointed at the door. Lucas grinned.

"Sorry, bro, Mom wants you to stay ignorant," He got up and took a banana from the fruit basket Elizabeth always left fully stocked on the kitchen counter.

"All this banana talk made me hungry. Are you hungry, Clem? I could share my banana with you," he pointed at me with the banana, his eyes daring me to answer his sexual innuendo.

"Out!" Elizabeth threw a tablecloth at him, and he lifted his hands in surrender.

"Troy, don't listen to Mom, OK? You can share your banana with any girl you want to."

"Lucas, I swear to God..." He smacked a kiss to his mother's temple and got out of the kitchen, humming something.

I lingered downstairs for about half an hour. I thought about the conversation Lucas and I had before he started acting like a twelve-year-old. It felt meaningful in some way. Like it changed something between us.

I went up to my room, and I threw myself on the bed. Something was pressing to my back from under the covers. I pulled them down. A banana and a note.

"If it's not enough for you, I have another one at your disposal."

The asshole went into my room. How dare he? I took the banana and waltzed over to his room. I burst inside without a knock. He was in his bed reading a book. I tossed the banana at him. He tilted his head and dodged it, not tearing his eyes from the pages.

"You read weird shit, nemesis."

I looked at him confused. He closed the book and showed me the cover.

"Stay. Out. Of. My. Room," I spat, infuriated. "Don't touch my things. Don't get near my bed again, you got it?"

"I'm sorry, your room? Last time I checked, this was still my house. So your room is actually my room. And as I come to think about it, you're sleeping in my bed. I could decide to pay you a visit some night."

The image of Lucas sneaking in my bed made my skin hot.

He was still casually lying and not at all surprised I was here. No doubt he expected me to do exactly that. Show up kicking and screaming. He held up the book for me to take it back. I reached out for it, the book fell on the floor with a thud, and he grabbed my wrist. In a second I was on top of him on his bed. I straddled him without even thinking about it.

"It's a nice change." His voice was low. "You pressing me against a surface and not the other way around. No need to throw things at me though. Next time you want some attention, just ask politely, like a lady."

I should have bit his head off for this comment, but I wanted other things at that moment. I leaned forward, and our breaths mixed.

"Why can't we stay away from each other anymore?" I asked.

"Hormones," he answered. But I could see it's not even close to what he really thought. "Did you kiss him today?" he asked, and I shook my head. "Why?"

"It's not like that. We're friends."

"So? We were friends and I was in love with you."

It was like a punch in the stomach. It wasn't a secret, but he said it aloud for the first time.

"Do you realize you're doing the same thing you did back then?" he played with my hair. "You ignore the one chasing you, and you go after the one who doesn't care about you. The roles are switched this time around. Not yours, of course. You're still in the middle."

That hurt more than I wanted to admit. Lucas didn't care about me. Truth was, I didn't care about Dylan back then, and I didn't care about him now. But I was already in a vulnerable position, and I wasn't keen on making it even more embarrassing than it was, so I remained silent.

Lucas rolled me off of him and we were now lying next to each other. He unbuttoned my jeans and slid his hand in. He used a finger to press the fabric of my underwear to my wet entrance. A smirk formed on his lips and he started rubbing me through my panties.

A quiet voice inside my head warned me we were in a house full of people. Not just any people, but his parents. And I wasn't just the neighbor. I was living here. If someone found out, it could be a huge problem, a deal breaker. My father would hold Elizabeth and Garret accountable. He would probably take me to Seattle, and it would be even more difficult for me to stick it to my family than it already was.

"What are you thinking about?" Lucas was watching my face attentively. "You're frowning," he kissed the spot between my eyebrows. "I would ask if you want me to stop, but since you're wet, breathless, and moaning, I would take a guess and say something else is bothering you."

Moaning? Was I moaning?

"Umm... I was thinking that someone could come in."

"Kinky!" he joked. "If that's your thing, I could deliver. Just not my parents and my brother." He paused for a second and then his eyes lit up. "I have an idea. I changed my mind about Williams. He's more than welcome to come and watch me eat you out anytime he wants."

I had no time to answer. His fingers moved my underwear to the side. He was spreading my wetness all over me, only a tip of one of his fingers slightly entering me every now and again. I started to twist so that I could get more friction where I wanted.

"Someone's impatient." He sucked on my neck for a second, teasing me. "Tell me about the guys in Seattle."

"What do you want to know?"

"How many?" he asked at the same time he slid a finger inside me.

"One," I hissed. "We only did it once."

"Did you enjoy it?" His voice was husky.

"Why are you asking?"

"Unhealthy curiosity. If you want to keep it a secret, I could tell you about my first time. Or any other time you want for that matter. But I think that would be a buzzkill."

"Does it even matter?" I moaned. "If I liked it?"

The answer was obvious. It didn't. We were not a couple. We weren't dating. We didn't even like each other. Except the last one wasn't true anymore.

"No. It doesn't matter," his voice was serious and low. "Other guys stole your first kiss and your first time. But I'll erase every memory you have that's not with me."

He removed his hand from my jeans and climbed on top of me. He leaned down and kissed me. It was a slow, deep kiss that melted my bones. Years of unexpressed feelings were pouring in that one kiss. It consumed me. I tried to remember why I was in his room in the first place.

The banana. He messed with my things.

I couldn't care less. I rubbed myself against him shamelessly. Lucas broke our kiss and exhaled. He looked frustrated. He kissed my nose and half smiled.

"Full disclosure?" he asked. "I need to tell you something before we go any further."

"Is it small?" I tried to keep the light tone. I had the feeling nothing good was coming out of his mouth. "No, wait. You're a virgin."

His lips barely moved when he tried to laugh. I pushed his chest, and we both sat on the bed facing each other with my legs wrapped around his waist.

"Oh, God," I gasped. "Are you? Is that the reason Chase got you a hooker for your birthday?"

Lucas scowled. "Hannah told you about that?"

"Hannah told me a lot of stuff about your parties," I teased.

"You know I'm not a virgin then," he looked at me with caution. "How would I make all these girls talk about the sex we had if I wasn't fu...?" he stopped talking. "Sorry, I didn't mean to say that. I just want to come clean about something. Just don't freak out, okay?"

"Come clean about what?"

"Remember how we talked about the fact no one was stupid enough to fuck you *here*?"

"We didn't actually talk, you just said so, but yes," I made a brief pause, then added. "Just spill it, Lucas."

"What would you say if I told you I was the reason for that?" his eyes were scanning my face. "I may have told some people you're off limits."

I moved back away from him. It took me a few seconds to digest the information, but finally I got up from the bed and distanced myself from him.

"What do you mean?" I asked. I thought I understood but I needed to hear it again.

"I made sure no one touched you the way I wasn't able to," he admitted directly. In his defense I could say he looked as if he knew he did something wrong, but I couldn't get pass the fact he fucked everyone in school while preventing me on purpose from doing the same.

"So, you basically fucked girls on weekends, and on Monday you drove away anyone interested in me?" A memory flooded my brain. "Is this the reason Matt Pearson stood me up on our second date and hasn't said a word to me ever since?"

He shrugged.

"They don't tell me how they do it, but I guess," Lucas said without blinking.

"You sabotaged my love life and you're not going to at least pretend you're sorry?"

"You did things years ago, and I'm still waiting for an apology. But that's not the reason I'm not going to apologize. I'm not sorry, and I don't want to lie. But maybe you want me to. Should I have fucked you and kept it a secret?" Lucas stood up too, but he didn't approach me. "If you stop being such a martyr all the time and think about why I did it..."

I cut him off and got in his face. My mouth was inches away from his when I whispered.

"I know why you did it. You did it to get back at me. To punish me."

Lucas shook his head.

"That's what I tried to convince myself, but now I know it's not true." He reached over to touch my hair, but I pushed him away. I was so angry, I could scream.

"You controlled a whole part of my life. You had no right," I spat.

"Oh, come on," he rolled his eyes. "What would Matt Pearson even do with you? You need someone to demolish those fucking walls you built up around yourself. He's not going to do that for you."

"Because you decided, not because he couldn't."

"Because he doesn't care. If he wanted you, he would have told me to fuck off and still gone out with you."

"You got some nerve. Is that what calms your conscience? You scared off every guy that showed any interest in me."

"Apparently not every guy. I missed one in Seattle," he smiled.

"Is this a joke to you?"

"No. But I won't say I regret doing it just because you think you need to hear it. You need something else."

"You know shit about my needs." I turned my back to him. What I needed was to leave his room immediately.

He put a hand on the door right before I opened it. "Don't run away. Stay. Talk. No more secrets." Then he removed his hand from the door and waited for my reaction.

The possibility of coming clean and sharing everything with Lucas Cole was something my body rejected violently. I got dizzy and felt sick to my stomach. My inside world was too ugly for him to handle. I opened the door and left him without a second look.

***

Three weeks later, I flew to Seattle to spend Christmas with my family. Everyone was coming, except Mom who was still in the rehab center.

I tried numerous ways to convince my father I should just stay with the Coles. I used my fear of flying, which was a lie, my overwhelming schedule, also a lie, and the need to feel somewhat home after everything that went down, which was the biggest lie of all. The answer was always the same.

"You're coming even if I have to ask Elizabeth Cole to drag you to the airport by the hair."

It was a bit of a shock for me. My father usually caved when I wanted something. So I got off the plane with that awful feeling in my stomach. Something had changed. I had no idea what and it made me jumpy.

Dad waited for me at the airport.

"Where's Adina?" I asked when we got in the car. I wasn't exactly interested in his girlfriend's whereabouts, but I preferred to talk about her than let him ask questions about me.

"With her parents. I told her I wanted to spend Christmas alone with my children."

"Good call, since she's younger than some of us..."

My father frowned but said nothing.

The rest of the drive we spent in an awkward chit chat about the weather, Madison and Tyler's travel to Seattle and, of course, Mom. She would soon be released from rehab.

"I talked with the contractor the other day. He thinks they could pull it off around the time your mother gets back. Of course the house would be empty, but you'll have one bathroom ready to use and a bed. You won't be able to use the kitchen though."

I wasn't sure how I felt about going back to live in that house. But I knew for sure I didn't want to live with Sylvia anymore. I wondered what Dad thought about that. I had three days to find out.

"Worst case scenario," he continued, "you'll have to spend a few more nights with the Coles than we originally planned. A week tops. I know you want to leave their house as soon as possible."

Don't be so sure about that.

We got to his place, and Tyler came out with a huge smile on his face.

"Hey there, little monster," he hugged me and whispered. "A friendly heads-up. The big monster is on her period or something, so watch it."

"Great," I murmured.

I hadn't seen Madison in a whole year. We hadn't talked on the phone. We sent some texts for our birthdays, and she said something once in our group chat with Tyler that I thought was directed to me, but I wasn't sure, so I just didn't answer.

"How's your friend?" my brother asked.

My head snapped towards him. He laughed.

"Relax, I'm not asking about Cole. Although judging by your reaction, maybe I should."

He stood there waiting for an answer. I glanced at dad who was unloading my suitcase while talking on the phone, probably with Adina...My first instinct was to change the subject or lie. To tell him to mind his own business. But the truth was I felt the need to talk about it.

"He did something."

"Another girl?"

"More like a hundred," I snorted. "But it's not like that. We weren't together then. We are not together now either."

"It seemed to me you were headed in that direction on your birthday party," Tyler frowned.

"Well, you were wrong. But anyway. Promise me you won't make fun of me."

Tyler burst out laughing, "No way I'm promising that. I need something to entertain myself for the next couple of days, and your story may be the only thing I got."

I rolled my eyes.

"Forget it. I'm not telling you anything."

"Come on. Spill it. I'll behave."

"Apparently he scared off everyone that ever wanted to date me. He just told guys to stay away from me."

I exhaled loudly feeling relieved. I haven't told that to anyone. Not even Hannah. I was too embarrassed. Too angry. Too confused.

"Wait a second," I stopped and looked at his face. "You were asking about Hannah, weren't you?"

Ty looked at me like my question was making him uncomfortable. Then he tried to get out of it the same way I did when something felt unpleasant to me. He lied. I saw it on his face.

"I tried to make small talk," he shrugged it off. "Your story is way more interesting. So? He scared off other guys?"

"Yeah. Can you imagine?"

Tyler thought about it and nodded more to himself than to me. "Sure. Why not? He's the most popular guy in school and the captain of the football team."

"Excuse me?" I was outraged.

"And those guys listened to him, so they were obviously pussies. I don't see why you're mad at him."

"Seriously?"

"Yes. Seriously."

Dad caught up with us.

"What are you talking about?" he asked but didn't wait for an answer. "I have to make a call. An hour tops. Maybe two. Ty, order food in. Clem, I'll leave the suitcase in your room. Madison will show it to you. You two are sharing one. See you later, kiddos."

"Ugh." I preferred to sleep on the couch. No, on the floor. I would even sleep in a tent in the backyard or go back to California on foot, just not share a room with her. Tyler read my mind.

"Just suck it up like everyone else."

That reminded me I was not the only one that wasn't enjoying this family gathering. I wasn't sure if even dad enjoyed it. I had the feeling he did it because he felt obligated.

I nodded and took a deep breath.

"I will."

***

Madison showed me our shared room. We exchanged not more than five sentences in total and she went to the bathroom to take a bath. Tyler and I ordered Italian for dinner and lay on the huge couch in dad's living room for the next hour.

When the food came, my mouth watered. It smelled so good, and I was starving.

"I say we eat some pizza while the ice queen tries to unfreeze her heart in the bathtub," Ty flashed me a smile.

"I heard that," Madison's voice flew from the staircase. "Is dad still on the phone?"

"That," Tyler nodded. "Or he hides from us in his office."

I stuffed my mouth with pizza. I preferred to remain silent in Madison's presence. Our relationship had been pretty much nonexistent for the past few years. Ever since she graduated actually. She was my constant in our home. When she left, I felt betrayed and deserted by the person who provided me with stability and emotional support.

I couldn't believe how much she resembled Mom. Not only on the outside with her gorgeous blond hair, green sparkling eyes, and her fashion model cheekbones, but on the inside too. She was so reserved. Cold. So concerned with her appearance and performance. So judgmental.

I felt her scrutinizing gaze on my face. I was munching, and I stared at the pizza with such intensity, one could decide I was trying to move it to my mouth with the power of thought.

"How's school?" she asked.

I nodded and lifted a thumb up. When I swallowed, I added.

"Good," then took a large bite from my pizza slice.

"And college applications?"

I snickered and shot her a look, then answered with my mouth full.

"Are you asking or Mom?"

That gave her pause. She just blinked at me. Dad entered the room, ushered us to set the table and eat like a family.

The dinner was silent if we didn't count some sports talk from dad and Tyler. By the desert Madison couldn't hold it anymore.

"Can we talk about the living arrangements for Mom and Clem?"

"Yes, of course. We can discuss everything you feel we need to," Dad supplied reluctantly.

"Why do you care?" I intervened. "You live in New York, and a lot of the time, you're not even in the States."

"So?" Madison frowned at me. "I'm allowed to have an opinion. I think you should live separately. Mom needs a calm environment, or she'll start drinking again."

My head snapped up from my plate. I stared at her beautiful face.

"Are you saying I'm the reason she had been drinking?"

"Of course not," Madison said and sounded sincere. "But you're pushing each other's buttons. And let's be frank here. You told no one she was drinking."

"Maddie," Dad warned.

"Okay, fine. All I'm saying is she's eighteen now, and she can be on her own."

Okay. That sounded better and in my favor. And it also saved me the effort to start this conversation with my father on my own. A gratitude towards Madison started to spread in my chest. Then she spoke again.

"Maybe you could rent Clem an apartment somewhere. I think Mom should stay in the house."

"I don't think now is the best time to decide anything, Madison." Dad's voice suggested he wasn't enjoying this exchange. "Actually, I wanted to talk with Clem in private."

He pointed with his thumb behind his back to his home office. I stood up and followed him. The room wasn't as spacious as all the others, but it was cozy. We sat down, and he took a pencil from his desk. He played with it while he talked.

"I think this conversation is long overdue. There is something that came up during your mother's therapy. I always thought we could just skip that and never talk about it. That it would just disappear with the years, but it didn't. Your mother's therapist thinks we both have to tell you our side of the story. I guess your mother will do it when she comes back next month."

"Okay. What story is that?"

He scratched the back of his head and avoided looking at me.

"Remember how your mother sometimes jokes around about you being an unplanned baby?"

"I know she wasn't joking if that's what you're trying to explain," I said a little bit too rudely.

"No, that's not it," he tapped his leg with the pencil. "Your mother thinks your bad relationship is partly my fault. She was so tired and overwhelmed when we found out she was pregnant with you. She wanted to..." he paused trying to find the right words.

"To terminate the pregnancy," I offered.

"I pushed her not to. I don't regret it," he quickly assured me. "I love you, and I can't imagine not having you, but if we look from your mother's perspective back then..."

"It was wrong of you to pressure her." My voice was almost a whisper.

Dad threw his pencil back on his desk and took my hands in his.

"That's why I've been so soft with you over the years. I felt guilty that your mother was so cold and demanding. I think she punished me through you. I wanted to give you enough love for the two of us, since she wasn't able to do it. But she loves you. I'm sure she does."

"Yeah, right," I snorted. Dad grabbed my head between his palms and made me look at him. His eyes were full of tears.

"She loves you. We all love you. But I think your mother's right. I did widen the gap between you two. You saw me as the good parent, and you demonized her more than she deserved. Which made her even more harsh. It was a vicious circle. It's not your fault. You were just a kid. We should have known better."

I felt my tears falling down my face.

"Dad, you're wrong. She regrets she had me."

"No. She regrets she screwed it all up," he wiped my tears away with his thumbs. "Ask her why she named you Clementine. Let's call her now."

I shook my head violently.

"No. I don't want to."

"Clem. You both need this."

"No," I removed his hands from my face, stood up, and walked over to the door. "I don't want to talk to her." I was already in the hallway, going back to the living room. "I don't want to see her. The mere thought of her coming back is making my skin crawl."

I saw the condemning look on Madison's face. She didn't like my outburst. Too bad for her because I wasn't going to hide it.

"You were old enough to remember," I told her. "She didn't want me, did she?"

My sister swallowed hard. She hesitated, but then she replied.

"She spent the whole nine months repeating that."

"Madison!" Dad yelled. "What are you doing?"

"Stop protecting her from the truth," Madison raised her voice. "You don't give her a chance to accept it and deal with it," she attacked him.

"Why did she call me Clementine?" I asked her and she shrugged.

"I have no idea."

"I can tell you that," Dad started, but I cut him off.

"No. I don't want you to lie. I want someone who will tell me the truth."

"Your mother will."

"I'm not calling her, Dad. Is that the reason you wanted me to come so much? To bully me into calling that bi..."

"Stop it right now!" Dad yelled. "She's trying. She's suffering because she understands now that she did horrible things to you."

"To me?" I snorted, outraged. "You think she did it only to me? What about the two of them?" I pointed at my siblings. "Open your eyes, Dad."

I turned my back on him and went upstairs to my room. No one came after me. Not even Tyler.

I took a long shower, then dried my hair. Why did my sister get the pretty name and I got the grandma name? There was only one answer to that. Because my mother wanted to show me in yet another way she hated me. I was already used to it, I still didn't like it, but I was used to it. But I wasn't ready to let my mother off the hook.

I opened up my suitcase to find the pajamas I packed. I left Tyler's tee back at the Coles. I didn't want to look weak for wearing it to bed.

On top of the clothes there was a small box. I immediately recognized the wrapping paper. It was from Elizabeth. Her Christmas presents had been ready and under the tree for about a week now. She must have put mine in here when I wasn't looking.

I was gone for a day, and I already missed Elizabeth. I missed them all. I couldn't bring myself to think about the fact that I was leaving them soon.

I sat on the bed and wondered if I should wait until tomorrow morning to open the present. But I was feeling down, and Elizabeth was exactly the kind of person to give the best presents.

I tore open the wrapping paper, and I found a jewelry box. I opened it and with one look I knew I was wrong. Elizabeth didn't give the best presents. Her son did.

CHAPTER SIXTEEN

Lucas

Four years ago

A loud knock on my door followed by my father's annoyed voice added to my agitated state.

"Lucas, hurry up!" he yelled from the hallway.

My throat was clenched. I didn't answer. I couldn't answer. I knew they were waiting for me to go to the New Year's party we were invited to, but I just stood in my room like a statue.

I was planning on kissing a girl tonight.

I had already kissed a girl. Twice.

Kiss number one happened when we were five. I was reluctantly participating in a pretend wedding ceremony with my best friend.

"You can now kiss the bride," Hannah Spencer squealed, and out of nowhere Clementine leaned in and kissed me on the mouth. It was only for a second. She saw my confused expression and shrugged it off.

"It's what people do in the movies."

Kiss number two? The same girl. Even a more awkward situation. We were twelve. She was bawling her eyes out after her mother had messed up her birthday cake. I mean how hard was it? She had three kids and three types of cake to remember.

I was sitting with Clem on the floor in her room. It wasn't the first time I was witnessing her crying over something her mother did or said. I always did something goofy to make her laugh. This time around, however, I sensed she didn't need a laugh.

She was angry. It was a look I wasn't used to. She was still crying, but there was something dark about her that day. Her jaws and fists were clenched. Her eyes squinted while she looked down at our feet.

I felt the need to tame her.

Our shoulders touched, but she didn't show she knew I was there next to her.

I thought about things I could do to calm her down. I reached out to hug her over her shoulders, but I backtracked before I even touched her. I wasn't used to being so close to girls. She was my best friend, but hugging? I mean, it was weird. How long would I do it? Did I need to say something first?

I decided a quick kiss on the cheek would be enough to make her feel better.

The moment I leaned in with eyes tightly shut, I sensed her moving. Our noses bumped, but it still happened. This time *I* kissed her on the lips.

We both pretended it had never happened. Never spoke of it. I tried not to even think about it until this fall.

Clementine's parents divorced in the summer, and her father moved to Seattle. She went for a visit. When she came back, she was changed. There was make up on her face. Her clothes were different. Tighter. Shorter. Her hair was shiny. She looked older. And I started to think of her more as a girl and less as a friend.

Suddenly, I had no idea how to even talk to her. How to be around her. But I knew one thing. I wanted to kiss her again. This time for real.

My father knocked again, and this time he opened the door. My clothes gave him pause.

"What the F are you wearing?"

I was asking myself the same question for half an hour now.

"Mom will freak if she hears you."

"I didn't say it. I just said F," he winked at me.

I thought about asking my father about his first real kiss, but I stopped myself. Instead, I answered his question about the clothes.

"I decided to try something new."

I usually wore jeans and a tee. Never any of those shirts Mom bought for me. They just hung in my closet, untouched, until she replaced them with new ones when I changed sizes. Dad made a serious face and nodded. Then narrowed his eyes at me, and a hint of a smile twisted his lips.

"What's her name?"

I unbuttoned my shirt a little. It was suffocating me. Or was it the fear? I couldn't tell. I saw my face in the mirror. It looked grayish. Dad sat on my bed, making himself comfortable.

"Is it Clem?" he pressed. "Your mother has been waiting for this development ever since you punched that kid for pushing her when you were ten."

"He pulled her hair," I clarified.

He was referring to the day Dylan Williams was trying to catch her in our backyard.

"Whatever," Dad waved me off. I felt my palms sweating, and I rubbed them in my jeans. "Are you planning on telling her?"

No, dad, I plan on kissing her at midnight, but I'm not going to tell you that.

"I'm thinking about it," I said. "Don't tell Mom, okay? She'll make a big deal out of it, and I'm already nervous."

"Why? You've known Clem your whole life. You are friends."

"She's changed," I shook my head. "It's not the way it used to be between us."

"Yeah, feelings are messy and complicated sometimes." My father stood up and patted my back. "I have to go check on Troy and your mom. He messed up his clothes trying to bake cookies for Katie while your mom was getting dressed. I may have had to watch him, but ended up watching a game." Dad wiggled his brows. "Don't go into the kitchen."

I laughed. Troy was still letting mom dress him up like she wanted, and tonight was the annual New Year's Eve party Chase's parents were throwing. The whole street was going. That meant Troy was dressed at least as sharp as Dad.

"He thought he could bake cookies while Mom was getting dressed?" I mocked my little brother.

"I get the feeling he's going to be a hopeless romantic like your mother. And he's also six. You, on the other hand..." he took a look at me from head to toe. "Keep the shirt, it won't hurt. But don't put so much pressure on it. Everything is going to be fine."

Turned out even my father was wrong every now and again, because that night was a complete disaster.

CHAPTER SEVENTEEN

Lucas

The present

The music was so loud I couldn't hear anything from the conversation Chase was having with the girl on his lap on the other side of the couch. I presumed it was a dirty talk by the way she was pressing herself to him.

It was New Year's Eve. Chase's parents were throwing a party, as they did every year. My parents and Troy were there. The last time I went to that party was four years ago.

Not that I didn't visit their house. I did. Just not on New Year's.

My mother had begged Clementine to go with them ever since she got back from Seattle a few days ago. She refused. I got it. It wasn't her style to waltz in Amy's house when the two of them weren't talking at all and pretend nothing ever happened. And I also hoped that house brought her bad memories.

Even though I was still grounded, my mother agreed to let me come. I was going to ask Clem to come with me. Not as a date. She wasn't ready for that. But as a peace offering. I knew Hannah would be there. I thought it could work.

Clem, however, made that impossible. Every time I went into the room, she found a reason to leave five seconds later. I even tried to go to her bedroom. I knocked and waited for her to invite me in. I heard her walking to the door. Her shadow appeared under it. She hesitated for a moment, then locked it.

I considered staying home with her. No. I wanted to. I needed to. It had been physically difficult for me to distance myself from her ever since she got back from Seattle. I was so used to her presence around me that her being away for three days made me wish for her closeness even more.

But I knew her. Pressuring Clementine into anything would only make her resist it even more. She needed to feel free to make her own choice.

I felt a punch in my shoulder. I cocked my head and looked at Chase. His eyes were already glassy from the alcohol.

"What the fuck, man?" he asked.

I knew what he meant. I was pouting again. I shook my head signaling him I wasn't going to *share* my feelings. Not that I was ashamed of them. I just wanted to share them with my hazel-haired nemesis first. Then shout them out loud for everyone else to hear.

A hand snuck on me from behind. It went down from my neck to my chest. I knew who it was before I even looked at her. I tilted my head back, and Amy's breasts were basically in my face. If I stuck my tongue out, I could lick them.

"Hey, I brought you something," she purred and showed me a bottle of vodka.

"No, thanks. I'm not drinking."

She rounded the couch and stood in front of me. She wore a short skirt that barely covered her ass. Her tits were almost popping out of her top. She wasn't wearing a bra, so I had a perfect view of her nipples. She was looking at me with determination that irritated me. "Why? You're always wasted on New Year's."

"I decided to try to get through it sober this year."

Something caught her eye on the other side of the room, and Amy came closer. Almost climbing on top of me.

"You might reconsider."

I knew what I was about to see the moment I noticed the smirk on her face. I sort of always knew this fascination Amy had with me wasn't just about me. It had to do with Clementine. She wanted to fuck me because she thought it would hurt her.

I turned my head and I saw my beautiful nemesis. She was with Hannah. And unfortunately, just like I thought, Dylan. He was slightly behind them looking around the room. Clem's eyes were pinned on me and Amy. Her face showed no emotion; I gave her that.

It looked like she was waiting for me to touch Amy just to have a reason to tell herself she was doing the right thing by pushing me away. I wasn't going to give her that satisfaction.

"Amy, get off my face, would you?"

I didn't even look at her when I said that. I was still looking at Clementine. I got up and went straight to them. I saw the horror on her face when I stopped right in front of her. I turned my gaze to Hannah.

"Spencer! Nice seeing you here."

"Cole," she smiled and nodded. "Let's go get some drinks." She pulled Dylan's shirt and pointed to the kitchen. Smart girl.

I couldn't help but smile when Clem realized Hannah was Team Lucas. Her face became red. I wished it was from embarrassment and her feelings towards me, but I knew her. It was that irrational anger always lingering inside her body, waiting to explode.

"You're welcome," I teased.

"For what?" her voice was sharp, but she couldn't tear her eyes away from me.

"For the necklace," I drifted my gaze down. Her collar neck dress made it impossible to see if she was wearing it. My eyes lingered down her body, and she started stepping from foot to foot. She turned her gaze to the kitchen. I didn't. I was looking only at her.

"Did you like it?" I asked.

"Lucas, can we just pretend nothing ever happened? Forget about everything?"

"No."

She cocked her head sideways.

"No?"

"No," I shrugged. "You said it yourself. We can't stay away from each other anymore." I took a step closer to her. Her pupils dilated. I loved how her body reacted to mine.

"You said it was hormones."

I nodded. Of course I said that it was hormones. But my gift suggested something else. She knew it and she wanted that to disappear.

"In that case we could just focus on someone else?" she suggested.

"Like a threesome? You Hartleys seem to love them," I joked. She rolled her eyes with a hint of a smile on her lips.

"Like maybe you should pay some attention to Amy instead of me. She seems... interested."

"And who would you pay attention to?" I was enjoying this immensely. "No. Wait. It doesn't matter. I'll explain to you why." I leaned even closer. Our bodies touched. She was panting. "I fucked enough girls to know this, so listen carefully. It won't work. You can fuck every guy in here and you would still want me."

I knew I was being a jackass, and it would piss her off, but I was losing patience. I needed her to figure out this shit between us before I died of old age.

"I might test that theory," she said, her eyes throwing daggers at me.

"Sure, be my guest," I moved away and stood behind her. I traced her spine with my finger. I leveled my mouth to her ear and whispered. "You know the one rule though. Williams is not on the menu."

Obviously there were no rules. She could fuck him, and I couldn't do shit about it. I was just pushing her buttons. I had the feeling she would go straight to him after this, and it could go two different ways. She could fuck him or decide not to. Either way, it wouldn't magically redirect her feelings for me to him.

"We'll see about that," she spat and left me laughing.

***

Two hours later I was still alcohol-free and beginning to regret the way I played my cards. Clem was drunk. She was a fun drunk. A little dorky. She snort-laughed, bumped into people, and explained out loud every time she had to go pee.

When I deliberately pissed her off earlier, I hadn't thought about the fact that she would get drunk. It put her in a vulnerable position with that dickhead she wanted to bang just to prove a point.

So, I spent the last two hours watching over her. I didn't want her to do something stupid and regret it tomorrow morning. But, unfortunately, my role for the night included me watching her throwing herself at Williams every time her eyes met mine.

I knew the alcohol was the reason for her behavior. She never touched him like that when she was sober. She was leaning her body into his. His hand was glued to her waist.

I knew she had every right to be angry with me about intervening in her love life for years. I really did. It was shitty of me, but I just couldn't bring myself to feel bad about it.

It was almost midnight, and Hannah was shooting me concerned looks. After the third time my eyes met hers, I decided to go over there.

"Hey, roomy," I said, and Clementine looked at me with annoyance. "Am I going to have to carry you home tonight?"

"Nemesis," she supplied, and I grinned. It was the first time she called me that. "Maybe I will crash somewhere else tonight."

In your dreams, baby.

I leaned over to Hannah. The music muffled my words, and she was the only one hearing me.

"Do you want to bitch slap her now or you're going to wait until she's unconscious and this asshole fucks her in the bathroom?"

"What kind of a friend do you think I am?" She looked at me offended. "I stopped drinking the moment I realized she wanted to get hammered. I've been holding my pee for forty minutes now because I don't want to leave her alone."

"Jeez," I huffed. "That's why you were eyeing me for? Because you want to go to the bathroom? Go, Spencer. I'll stay."

Hannah leaned over the counter and tried to look Clem in the eyes. It was a difficult task, considering the latter couldn't hold her head up without moving it. I sent Williams a warning look. He ignored me.

"Clem, I'm going to the bathroom. I'll be right back, okay? Don't move."

Hannah smacked my shoulder and looked at me with a serious face. I rolled my eyes.

"Don't worry, I'm not leaving her."

My closeness sobered Clementine up a little. She stopped leaning in on Dylan, and he removed his hand from her body. He looked around. Then he pressed his mouth to her ear and said something that made her frown. She shot me a look. I couldn't take it anymore. I put my hand over Dylan's shoulder and asked politely.

"Will you give us a minute?"

I squeezed his shoulder harder than I had to. I wanted to send him a message. He was giving us that minute one way or the other. He moved a few feet away, and I took his place next to her, hiding her body with mine so that he couldn't see her. I put a finger under her chin and lifted her head up trying to catch her gaze.

"What did he say to you?" I didn't think she would tell me, but she surprised me.

"He asked me to go upstairs with him."

"Will you?"

"I might."

"Don't."

"You still think you can make this decision for me, don't you?" A dark chuckle escaped her lips.

"No. I'm asking you not to go. The decision is all yours. But you're pretty drunk, so I'm not letting you go upstairs tonight. You can fuck him tomorrow when you're sober."

"Why did you give me *that* necklace?" Her eyes demanded an explanation.

"On Christmas people usually give each other presents. I'm still waiting for a present from you, by the way. It was pretty rude you didn't get me anything."

"You asshole," she tried to round me, but I stood in her way.

"Don't even think about it. I promised Hannah I wouldn't leave you alone. You're stuck with me."

"Fine. You can watch."

I tilted my head back and laughed.

"I'm starting to think you really like the idea of being watched. I wonder why you closed your curtains on me for so long." I rubbed her cheek with my thumb. "I would have watched you every night, you know. You're so beautiful."

"Stop it," she hissed, pushed me away, and strolled towards Dylan. She took his hand and dragged him to the dance floor. She was bumping into people, but she didn't care.

I knew she wouldn't be doing this if she was sober. But she was angry, confused, and, unfortunately, wasted. And I was the reason for all three. My punishment consisted of me watching her rub herself on Dylan while they danced.

It wasn't my first choice of entertainment, but I decided to give her the chance to get back at me. I could see how confused she was, and I knew she needed to feel in control, and unfortunately her idea of being in control included hurting someone, oftentimes herself.

The image of their bodies pressing together almost caused me a burst of every blood vessel I had in my brain. I could feel the rage taking over my body. It was humming in my veins and bones.

Hannah showed up looking around frantically.

"Where is she? I told you to stay with her!"

"That's what I'm doing," I pointed ahead. Hannah's jaw fell open.

"I didn't think she would really do it," she whispered, and I laughed.

"If you think she's doing this tonight, you're crazy. One wrong move from either of them and I'm stopping this shitshow."

Clem threw her hands around Dylan's neck.

Don't kill her. She's drunk and you're in love with her sorry ass.

I wanted to go there and yank her from his arms, but I refrained from it. I approached them slowly; Hannah was at my heels. I didn't want to pretend I wasn't going to physically remove him from her if I had to. So I slammed my hand on his shoulder, looked Clem in the eye, and explained in a very calm manner how things were going down.

"Hannah and I are taking you home. Now. You're going to take a shower and go to bed, and I hope tomorrow you'll wake up with the worst hangover ever," I looked at Dylan next. "Fuck off. You have five seconds before I punch you in the fucking face."

He laughed.

"Dude, get the hint. She doesn't want you."

I took his shirt in my fist and dragged him closer to me.

"Fuck off. Last warning. She's drunk." I stared at him waiting for a reaction. He looked at Clem and probably decided by the way she was wobbling, that it wouldn't be a good look for him to fuck an intoxicated girl. He stepped back and left.

Hannah and I dragged Clem back home. I went straight to my room. I couldn't hear anything from Clem's room, but about half an hour later I heard Hannah leave.

I was in the darkness. In total silence. That was the first time Clem and I were alone at night. It would probably be the last too.

I heard someone's footsteps in the hallway. I knew it was her. Not only because my parents and Troy would make a lot more noise if they were coming home, but because I started to feel her presence around. Even when I couldn't see her.

She opened the door of my room without a knock, stepped inside, and closed it behind her. She leaned on it. Probably giving time to her eyes to get used to the darkness.

"Talk about double standards, nemesis," I mocked her. "If I go into your room without asking, you'd cut my head off."

Silence.

I was so sick of her only thinking and never actually talking. I craved her words more than everything else. I sat up in my bed and faced her, waiting for her to react, do something. Anything. She didn't move a muscle.

"I'm not going to make it easy for you this time around," I warned her. She nodded and pushed herself from the door, took a few steps in, and stood right in front of me.

"I'm sorry," her voice cracked.

"You'll have to elaborate. You've got quite the record." It was a shitty thing to say, but I said it anyway. She was chewing her lower lip, deciding something. Then she turned her back on me, but still remained an arm's length from me.

"Could you unzip my dress, please?" Clementine picked up her hair to reveal the zipper that started high on her neck.

"Are you that hammered?" I raised my voice and stood up gently pushing her forward to give me some space to get away from her. "Are you that determined to fuck someone tonight?"

Clementine sighed.

"Just do it. Please."

Being a sucker for her, I did what she asked me to. I started to unzip her dress slowly. I could only hear the sound from the zipper and her shallow breaths. I wasn't even in the middle of her back when she stopped me.

"That's enough."

She turned to face me, pressing her dress over her chest with one hand and trying to take the top of it off. I saw something sparkling on her naked skin. She managed to reveal everything from her neck down to her still-covered breasts. She was wearing the necklace.

"I wear it every day. Obviously not all the time. You would have seen that. But every night when I go into my room and I know I won't be seeing you until the morning, I put it on."

"Why?"

"Why do I put it on?" She seemed confused.

"Why are you hiding the fact that you are wearing it?" I touched the daffodil pendant. I didn't mean to buy her a present at all. In fact, I had decided I wasn't going to. But then I saw that necklace when I took Troy to the mall to pick up presents for Mom and Dad, and I remembered how she called me Narcissus.

"Because I love it. I don't want to ever take it off, and I can't handle that.".

I wanted to tell her what that pendant meant to me. What *she* meant to me. But I didn't want to scare her off. I didn't trust her that she wouldn't run away again. I took her face in my palms.

"Hide it then," I whispered.

Clementine dropped her forehead to mine, then pressed her lips to my mouth for a second only.

"Thank you for the necklace."

"You're welcome."

I reached and helped her put on her dress again in total silence. Then I took her hand and dragged her downstairs into the living room. I could see the fear on her face. Fear that I was going to make some grand gesture or say something that would be so big that we could never ignore it.

I was no idiot. I wasn't doing anything remotely close to that. I just turned the TV on and sat on the couch. She sat next to me. Ten minutes passed and she summoned the courage to talk to me again. She was her usual sassy self.

"Are you going to ask me about Dylan?"

"No," I smirked. "I don't want to talk about him."

"Since when?" I heard the doubt in her voice.

"Since you just told me everything I need to hear for the moment."

I shot her a look, just to see her reaction. Her face reddened. She changed the subject immediately.

"Maybe I should go to bed. I'm not used to drinking alcohol."

I reached for her hand and squeezed it.

"Stay for a while."

My parents got home at some point. Troy was walking like a zombie. I was pretty sure he was half-sleeping. Dad shook his head when he saw us on the couch. He was worried about the consequences, but got upstairs with Troy. Mom's feet were glued to the floor. She was looking at us. Her chin trembled. She came closer, planted a kiss on my head, took a blanket and tossed it over Clementine, who was sleeping with her head on my shoulder, then followed Dad and Troy. I turned the TV off and closed my eyes.

CHAPTER EIGHTEEN

Clementine

The morning after the New Year's Eve party I woke up with the worst headache in my life.

Did Lucas wish me the worst hangover last night?

I opened my heavy eyes and looked around. I was in the living room. Memories about last night started to flood my brain, and I felt mortified.

I got drunk and almost made out with Dylan.

I deliberately pissed off Lucas.

I got home, snuck into Lucas's room, and made him undress me.

And the worst of all, I told him I had feelings.

Well, maybe not with those words, but the message was pretty clear. I had to do some damage control, but I couldn't bring myself to sit up.

It felt like every move could make me puke. And the taste in my mouth was already bad enough.

Eggs and bacon were stinking up the room. I heard voices coming from the kitchen.

"I think it's because of Sylvia," Elizabeth told someone. "Richard called after she boarded the plane back from Seattle. Apparently, they got into a huge fight."

"About what?" I heard Lucas's low voice ask. Warmth filled my belly.

"I don't know. But it must be something important if she got so drunk last night. You should give her some space."

"I'm giving her plenty of space."

"You slept on the couch together last night." There was an accusation in her voice. It made me cringe. "Don't you think it's inappropriate? She's our guest. Her father trusted us to take care of her. I'm not sure he would appreciate you two cuddling in the middle of the night in the living room. And Troy saw you. He's only ten, Lucas."

"Are you mad we were cuddling or that you saw it?"

This conversation was getting too personal for my ears. I wasn't ready to hear Elizabeth say I'm not good enough for her perfect son.

"I love Clem. I don't mind you two being together. And I don't want you to hide. But having said that, I really do think you're not thinking this through. Both of you. She needs stability. What if her father decides he's not okay with her living under one roof with her boyfriend and moves her again?"

Boyfriend? He's not my boyfriend.

I snorted. In my mind at least. I didn't make any sounds or movements, because I was scared of them finding out I was eavesdropping.

"First of all," I heard Lucas's voice, "I don't need to think this through. I know how I feel and I know how she feels. Second of all, her father left her here, knowing she would be living with boys," he paused. "And third, don't call her my girlfriend," he said with an icy tone. I felt like someone squeezed my heart to death. "You'll scare her away. I need her calm and relaxed to seal the deal."

Seal the deal? Did he mean sex? Did he just tell his mother that?

"I hope you're not suggesting sex," Elizabeth murmured, and Lucas chuckled.

"Thanks for the vote of confidence, Mom."

They changed the subject after that. I slid my legs down to the floor and got up as slowly as humanly possible, not only because I didn't want them to know I was awake, but also because I was scared everything my stomach contained in that moment would make a sudden appearance and color the carpet. I went upstairs to take a shower and brush my teeth before I died from poisoning from my own breath. Moving around actually helped a little with the nausea. And I was hungry.

Half an hour later, I entered the kitchen. Troy was there. He jumped from the barstool and came to hug me.

"Happy New Year! You were sleeping last night when we came back, and I couldn't say it."

Lucas snorted.

"You were sleeping and walking, bro. But I will give it to you. You stayed awake longer than this party animal over here." He pointed at me, looking...happy? He was smiling at me calmly. His eyes were warm and I loved the way they scanned my neck. The pendant was under my shirt, but the chain was visible. Now that I have told him I loved it, I could wear it as much as I wanted.

"Troy, go find your father, please."

Troy made an unhappy face. He knew Elizabeth was kicking him out because she wanted us to talk alone but left the kitchen anyway.

"How are you feeling?" Elizabeth asked with an accusatory tone. She was looking at me with her *don't-bullshit-me* expression.

"Not so good," I confessed.

"You are aware I have to tell your father about this."

"Yes," I looked down at my feet. I couldn't bear the fact that she was disappointed in me. "I'm sorry, Elizabeth. I hate that I'm putting you in this position after everything you did for me."

This was the first time I acknowledged her help, if you don't count the kiss I gave her on my birthday. She smiled.

"Well, I don't want to nag about the alcohol, it's obviously illegal, but...you should be more careful. Think of the consequences. What if something happened to you last night? I'm sure you weren't the only one drunk at that party." She shot Lucas a look.

"I was only drinking water the whole time." He lifted his hands up in front of his chest.

"Anyway," she continued. "That should always be on your mind. You're going to college soon, and there will be a lot of parties. Don't put yourself in that vulnerable position."

I nodded but guilt spread inside me like it infected my blood. No one knew about my college application situation.

I changed the subject.

"Dad said that the house will probably be ready by the time Sylvia gets out of rehab."

"Probably," Elizabeth nodded. "The contractor showed me the place last week. It's turning out great. I have a spare key if you want to check it out."

"No, thanks," I shook my head. "I'll wait."

"Okay, I'll go tell Troy he can come back now." Elizabeth passed me by and squeezed my hand for a moment.

"I'm hungry," I turned to Lucas. "Does greasy food really help with hangovers?"

"Only if you eat it before you start drinking," Lucas said.

"What should I eat then?"

He reached behind him to take something. When I saw it, I burst out laughing.

"A banana is always a good choice."

We all spent the day home. I helped Elizabeth with the cooking, which I found out I really enjoyed. Lucas, Troy, and I watched a movie together. Lucas was sitting on the ground, his back pressed against the couch. Troy and I were sitting on it. I had one leg under my butt and the other down on the floor. At some point, I felt Lucas's big warm hand sliding on the back of my leg from my ankle up to the knee. His fingers caressed my skin, and it prickled. I saw him snicker.

In the evening, Troy and I played board games. Lucas commented on our skills or the lack thereof, and made us laugh like crazy. He didn't play with us, but he didn't leave us either.

By the end of the day, I was so tired I actually dragged my feet from the bathroom to my door. I opened it lazily, and I saw Lucas in my bed. Under the covers.

"What are you doing?" I whisper shouted while I closed the door as fast as I could.

"Relax," he chuckled and removed the blanket. "I'm fully clothed."

He was wearing gray sweatpants, but he was naked from the waist up. I glanced at his bare chest, and my pulse quickened.

"Do you know what fully clothed means? If your father catches you here, we will have a problem."

"All important parts are covered," he smirked. "And what would that problem be? You're going home in two weeks. He's not going to rat us out now."

I was still standing by the door, as if I was waiting for someone to come in and catch us, and I wanted to be as far away as possible from the bed. Lucas cocked his head sideways. I bet he was trying to guess what I was thinking.

"To answer your question, I'm sleeping here tonight. As I intend on doing every night from now on."

I tried with everything I had in me not to smile at him, but I failed.

"I don't remember inviting you to my bed."

"I don't see you removing me from it either."

I went to the bed and stood in front of him. I wanted him to stay. More than anything.

"It's not about sex," he started. "I just...Last night was...You fell asleep on my shoulder and I..."

Lucas Cole was trying to say a coherent sentence and he was failing. That was a first. Since he had already helped me multiple times with clearing my own thoughts and formulating them for me, I decided it was a good time to return the favor.

"I liked sleeping with you too."

He smiled and tapped the other side of the bed. I turned the light off, lay next to him, and closed my eyes. I took a deep breath. Everything felt so right.

"Does it feel normal to you too?" I asked.

"Yes," he answered, and I wasn't at all surprised he knew what I was thinking. He always knew. "I'm kinda pissed about it though."

I shot him a surprised look. He laughed.

"I could have slept in your bed for three months, and now I only have two weeks."

It was sweet and, at the same time, a rude thing to say. He put an expiration date on us. Not that I could blame him for it. I worked pretty hard to fuck everything up between us.

"What will you do if I give you a tee with my number?" he asked suddenly.

The first time he asked me that, we were barely talking to each other. We were in a different place now. But I decided to give him the same answer anyway.

"I'll burn it," I whispered and smiled. He chuckled.

"Liar."

We turned to face each other and just laid there. He reached and played with the neckline of Tyler's tee.

"Can I take this off?" he asked. His eyes were burning mine. I swallowed hard and nodded. He shifted, and my body followed him. We sat up, and a second later I was shirtless.

I thought that he would get all over me, but he just looked at me for a moment, then lay back down on the bed, dragged me into his arms, and pressed my back to his chest.

"Go to sleep."

***

The college talk in the Cole residence had become more and more frequent even before Christmas. In the beginning of my stay no one asked me about my plans. I was a totally different person now, and Elizabeth talked to me like I was one of her kids. I liked it. No. Loved it. But I hated that I had to lie to her face now. And it was getting harder for me to do it. So every time she tried to ask me about it, I found excuses to leave the room and pretended I had to call Hannah or Dad that very second.

I saw how they all looked at me. The suspicion. The fact that I was lying to them was tearing me up inside. They knew something was up. I just hoped I could hold on to that secret a little bit longer. I was scared that Elizabeth would tell my parents if she found out the truth.

And I wasn't even remotely ready to think about Lucas's reaction to my yet another secret.

It was the first day of school after New Year's, and my palms were sweating. I knew I would see Dylan there. I had no idea what he was thinking. I acted like an idiot at that party. I led him on. Used him. He had probably figured that out by now.

I was chewing my lower lip, staring at my reflection in the kitchen window, when Lucas came behind me. He pressed his body to mine and reached out to my mouth. His thumb released my lip from my teeth. He kissed my hair.

"Everything is going to be fine. Forget about it."

"How do you know?" I turned around to face him. "What if he's mad?"

Lucas shook his head.

"What would he even say? That he tried to take advantage of you while you were drunk? Believe me. Even if his ego is hurt, he won't say a thing."

"But people saw me there. With him. Someone must have seen me leaving with you."

"Clem, chill. I'm the golden boy, remember? People love me," he hesitated for a moment, then continued. "Leave your car here. I'll drive you today."

"Yeah, I don't think so," I rounded him and tried to escape him. He took my wrist, and I stopped.

"Why not? What are you so scared of? If anything, if people know you're with me, they will avoid pissing you off because they will know it would piss me off."

"What do you mean *with me*?" I asked, the panic taking hold of my body.

"You know exactly what I mean."

Lucas got into my face and leaned in for a kiss. Alarm rang in my head and I pushed him back.

"Your mother is here."

"So? I don't want to hide."

"Maybe you should include me in that decision?" I squinted.

"Like you include me in yours?" he pressed.

"I...we have to go."

I left him standing there alone without finishing the conversation. I knew it would backfire later, but the anxiety had me by the throat and I needed to get away from him just to be able to breathe.

I managed to avoid Dylan in school for two whole hours. Then I bumped into him. He wasn't smiling as he usually did. He looked at me with an expression I couldn't read.

"I'm so sorry," I said, and he shook his head immediately.

"I'm the one who has to apologize. I did it again, didn't I?" I knew what he meant. I saw the similarities of it, but I was a willing participant. Both times actually. "I let things go too far."

"They didn't."

"No thanks to me. I felt like it was my last chance to get somewhere with you. I saw how you and Cole were looking at each other the whole night. I knew if I don't make a move, I may not have another shot."

I felt the urge to deny the connection I had with Lucas. To lie again. But I didn't.

"I'm sorry, Dylan. I was so confused. And he was pissing me off. I used you. And now we can't be friends..."

"Of course we can. Now I'm sure that we can never be anything more than that."

"Really? You're not mad at me? We could still be friends?"

"Sure." He shrugged like it was nothing. It gave me pause. Shouldn't he be at least a little angry? I gave him the impression I was into him just to make Lucas jealous.

"If you need some time away from me, I would totally understand."

"Oh, Clem," he put an arm over my shoulders and hugged me with a smile on his face. "I don't need to spend time hating you. My ego isn't that fragile."

I didn't miss the hint.

He came with me to my locker. A few minutes later he left to go to class but not before he hugged me again.

The emotional roller coaster I was riding was making me distracted. I was late for class. I rushed down the empty hallway. A door flung open and a hand I was very familiar with these days dragged me inside a small dark room. It was full of cleaning supplies.

Lucas closed the door behind me, then plastered my back to it. I couldn't see his face clearly but I saw his clenched jaw, and it was enough for me to guess his mood.

"What are you doing?" I asked, trying to hide my sudden arousal from being in that dark, narrow, *locked* space with him.

He was looking at me without moving. Without saying a word.

"Why do you have a key for this place?"

He placed his hands on the door, caging me. There was at least a step of empty space between us.

"I got the key from the previous captain of the football team, and he got it from your brother."

His voice was lower than usual. He was in a bad mood. Was it because I refused to come with him to school today?

"And why are we here?" I asked nonchalantly, even though my mouth was dry. I felt something was about to happen. Something I was going to enjoy.

"I decided you're deaf since you don't understand a word I'm saying," I felt his hot breath on my face. "So I'll try something else. And I locked the door to calm your nerves. I don't care if people see us. But I know you hate the thought of that."

"What? No...," I tried to explain, but he pushed my notebooks from my hands and they fell on the floor. I was in shock. He was never so abrupt with me. So rough. I squeezed my thighs with anticipation.

His eyes were deadly, and he scanned my cleavage. I was wearing a strapless dress. No bra. With one movement he pushed the top down. I looked down at my naked breasts to check the view. They looked good from where I was standing.

One second passed. Then five. Ten. He wasn't making a move. I felt heat radiating from his body to mine and vice versa.

"Um, excuse me?" I half-smiled.

He lifted his gaze to meet mine and licked his lips. He looked at me like he couldn't decide if he wanted to yell at me or devour me.

"Are you out of your mind?" I obviously was, since I liked what we were doing. Last night when we slept together, he didn't touch me, even though I thought he would. I wanted him to. "I have to go to class."

He rubbed one of my nipples with his thumb, and I moaned. I moved my hips forward, I needed to feel him pressed against me. I was met with more empty space between us.

"You are excused from that class," he slowly slid his hand from my breast down to my stomach, pushing the top of my dress even lower, below my belly button. Wetness was pooling up between my legs. I remained silent, enjoying his touch.

He used his both hands to move the bottom of my dress up. It was now gathered around my waist.

He was testing me. He thought I would stop him, no doubt. When I didn't, he cocked an eyebrow.

"No questions? No arguments?" he asked, and I shook my head. He narrowed his eyes. "Good."

He took a step closer. Our bodies almost touched. He lowered his head to my breasts, and I stopped breathing, waiting for his tongue on me. But then he changed his mind. He lifted his head back up and looked at me.

I felt his fingers tracing my ribs from both sides, and I trembled. He was moving so slowly I wanted to scream.

"Touch me," I said, looking him straight in the eye.

"Where?" His voice was husky.

"Everywhere."

His thumbs rubbed the sides of my breasts in circles.

"You'll have to be more specific than that," I heard the smile in his voice. "Or you could just be patient and wait to see what happens. You decide."

"You want to torture me," I said out of breath with desire.

"Torture you. Teach you a lesson. Whatever you want to call it."

I squeezed my eyes shut.

"Suck my nipples."

I hadn't even finished the last word, and his mouth was on one of my breasts. I yelped. He put a hand on my mouth to keep me quiet and released my flesh from his lips with a popping sound.

"As much as I would like for someone to catch us and get this over with, I don't particularly enjoy the thought of anyone hearing those sexy noises you're making."

His tongue flicked my other nipple, his hand still on my mouth. I licked it and he groaned. He pushed his thumb between my lips, and I sucked on it.

He lost control.

He pressed his knee between my legs and kissed me hard. I buried my hands in his hair. It felt like every cell in my body pulsated. I pressed my clit against his leg. My underwear was soaked. I was probably going to stain his jeans.

"Need some help with that?" he pushed his hand between my pussy and his leg, moved my underwear to the side and began spreading my juices all over. He pushed two fingers inside me, and I pressed my head against the door, arching my back.

Every time his fingers pushed in and pulled out, I could hear my wetness.

"This sound is driving me crazy," he murmured.

He kneeled down, removed my panties while I balanced holding on to his shoulders. I thought he would stand up and enter me, but he didn't.

His tongue touched my clit, and I instinctively spread my legs wider. I couldn't stop moving. He pressed a hand over my stomach to pin me to the door. His mouth felt so hot on my skin down there.

"Has anyone kissed you here before?" he groaned, and it felt like the sound entered my body and echoed in every cell.

"No," I whispered.

His tongue penetrated me, and I dug my fingers in his head again. The pleasure was almost too much. The thrill of being in public pushed me closer to the edge. His fingers and tongue were everywhere. Touching, sucking, rubbing my sensitive spot.

I came with a loud moan.

I was still shaking when he removed his mouth from me and stood up, his fingers still inside me. He started moving them faster and harder. His palm pressed my clit with every stroke, and I felt another orgasm washing over me.

He dropped his forehead to mine. I could see the desire in his eyes. He kissed me. His lips were swollen from eating me out, his fingers still inside me. I reached down to his jeans but he caught my wrist.

"Not now," he removed a lock of damp hair from my neck. I was sweaty. Panting. Satisfied but wanting more.

"If I see his hands around you one more time, I will break them on the spot. I get you two have some strange friendship. I don't like it, but I can't tell you who to be friends with. But he's not touching you anymore." I blinked his way, still trying to recover from what we just did. "Explain to him that you're mine," he continued, "or I will do it my way. This is my last warning, Clementine. No more Dylan Williams shit. I've had enough of that. Stop testing me."

"I'm not testing you." My voice was low and filled with desire, even though he made me come twice. "I felt guilty, and I wanted to apologize. He knows I want you."

I saw the relief on his face second before a smirk appeared on his lips.

"That's the first time you say that. If I knew an orgasm was all you needed to confess it, I would have made you come on the first night you spend in my house."

I lifted an eyebrow in question, knowing he would once again read my mind.

"Yeah," he shrugged. "I wanted you even then. I think there never was a day I didn't want you to be mine."

CHAPTER NINETEEN

Lucas

"Where the hell are we going?" she whispered while I was sneaking us out in the middle of the night.

"You'll see," I smiled and pushed her out the front door. I closed it slowly and then grabbed her by the waist and planted a kiss on the tip of her nose. She giggled.

Fuck. I love that laughter.

I spent the entire day with a raging erection and images of her naked body flashing before my eyes. What we did in that room in school was completely improvised. I saw her and Dylan and they were hugging *again* and I snapped.

I had that key for two years now. I had used it with other girls a few times. I didn't plan on taking Clem there. But I saw her with him, and the need to mark her mine arose. I was done with playing games and moving backwards.

Hearing her saying she wanted me made my rage evaporate in seconds.

The control that girl's words and actions had over me was unfathomable.

I pushed her in front of me, my hand on her lower back, navigating her. Touching her, even with her clothes on, made me lose my mind. I was still amazed by my restraint in that room. The only thing that helped me control myself and not flip her over and fuck her from behind was the fact I was trying to make a point.

I waited for her to find out where we were going. I was ready for resistance.

"Oh, no. No way," she smacked my hand away and tried to go back to my house.

My house? Our house? What was the correct term? I had no idea anymore.

I caught her after only two steps. She used her body weight and tried to drag me back. I didn't budge.

"I know you hate it," I ran my thumb over her cheek. "Just trust me, okay."

"I don't want to go in there. Not yet," she protested. "Did your mother make you do this? Is this because I refused to see it when she asked?"

I shook my head, not tearing my gaze away from hers.

"This has nothing to do with my mother. The house is just... a means to an end." I took a step away from her, holding her hand. She was walking backwards to my house, and I used some force to pull her to me. "Trust me, Clem."

"I trust you," she huffed. "I just hate the fact that the house is..."

"Almost ready?"

She nodded. Fuck. I was back to being an eight-year-old that couldn't stand her being sad for a second.

"I'll be right here. Like always." Then the old instincts kicked in and I felt the need to make her laugh. "Mom will continue to watch your every move like a hawk. And I'm pretty sure Troy will try to kill me in my sleep when he finds out about us. He's crushing on you so hard; I feel sorry for the little guy. Although I'm pretty sure anyone who sees us together would think the same about me."

She gave me a fake, one-sided smile. Maybe I couldn't make her laugh and forget about moving out, because I dreaded that moment just like she did. Maybe even more.

I tried to pull her towards her house, and she followed. My heart began to beat faster. Every time she followed my lead or trusted me with something, like earlier that day, when she trusted I wouldn't let us get caught in that room, I felt like she was giving me a little bit more of her. And I collected those crumbs of her affection with the hope I would one day get her everything. Every little piece.

We were at her front door and was fishing for the keys in my pocket, when she blurted out.

"Your mother invited me to live in your house because she wanted you to forgive me." I stood still for a moment. Then I turned to face her. "She wants you to fall in love and she thought you needed to forgive me to be able to do that."

I cleared my throat.

"I know. I figured that out a while ago," I said. "She was on the verge of crying every time something good happened between us, and she never meddled when he fought. She just watched as if she was waiting for something."

"But you look surprised?" she asked, confused.

"I'm surprised you told me."

My answer made her uncomfortable, so I bumped my shoulder into hers and unlocked the door. I walked in first and lit a flashlight.

"The power is out."

I glanced at her. She was looking at the walls and the floors. They were ready.

"Do you want to look around or...?"

I knew she didn't care about the house, but I wanted to give her a moment if she needed one.

"Or?" she asked.

"Or get with the program?" I grinned at her.

"Get with the program, please," her voice was a whisper.

I took her upstairs to her room. She walked in, and I stayed in the hallway. The room was completely empty if you didn't count the bed. I saw it delivered a few days ago. So all I needed to do was bring sheets and a blanket.

"Now I get why we're here," she tried to hide her amusement.

"Do you?"

"That's pretty self-explanatory," she pointed at her bed.

"I decided I had a better chance here than three steps away from my parent's bedroom."

She looked at me, head to toe.

"You decided right."

"Can I come in?" I was still standing in the hallway. "I know you hate people going into your room without asking."

She laughed and pointed at the made bed again.

"I think you have once again broken that rule."

"At least I didn't take anything this time." I walked in slowly.

"Only because there is nothing to take."

"True." I was only a step away from her. "I want to take everything you have to give."

Silence fell between. She broke it first.

"Why are you looking at me like that?"

"Like what?"

"Like you're about to hunt me."

"Actually I was hoping you would put me out of misery and take the last step between us for a change."

I still needed the reassurance she was choosing me. She erased the space between us without any hesitation and looked up at me.

"Are you sure you want to do this?" she asked. My laughter jumped off the walls and echoed in the empty room. It echoed inside me.

"I think I'm supposed to ask you that, nemesis."

"I love that nickname."

She pressed her forehead to my chest in total despair. I ran my fingers through her hair, buried my nose in it, and inhaled deeply. I was addicted to that pink grapefruit shampoo she was using.

"I know," I pulled her hair back to see her face, and I kissed her. It was slow and deep. She wrapped her hands around my neck and pulled me closer. Something had changed. I could feel it. She lost control when she was with me and that put all kinds of ideas in my head.

Ideas about the future we were going to have to face soon.

"I never wanted him," she said out of breath when I broke our kiss to lick on her neck. I smiled, but I didn't stop to suck and nibble on her skin.

I slid my hands down and lifted her up. She wrapped her legs around me, just like she did on her birthday when I pressed her against the wall. I placed her on the bed and took her shoes off, then unbuttoned her jeans. She lifted herself up on her elbows staring at the ceiling.

"Lucas Cole, you are the most arrogant person I have ever met."

I took her jeans off, and I lifted her shirt a little to kiss her flat stomach. I chuckled with my mouth pressed to her skin.

"You seem to enjoy that." I grabbed her wrists and pulled. She fell on her back again, her face right under the huge fluorescent daffodil sticker. "I wanted you to look at that every time some douchebag you brought from college gets on top of you on this bed."

That was a lie. If I had it my way, the only one to climb on top of her in any bed would be me.

"Oh?" she cooked her head sideways, not tearing her gaze away from the sticker. "Why so subtle? You should have put your face up there," she teased, trying to keep the mood light.

"I don't want you to get obsessed with me," I lied. That fucking daffodil around her neck and the one on her ceiling were me marking my territory.

"Bullshit," she saw right through me and I didn't mind all that much. I had no problem with her knowing my true feelings.

I managed to undress her completely while we had that conversation. That was the first time I ever saw her without a single item of clothing. She looked like she came out of a dream.

"You're so hot. You have a porn-star-worthy body," I told her instead. I was fond of my balls and wasn't ready to hand them over to her, giving our history of her smashing my organs, namely my heart. "Minus the breast implants."

She looked down to scan her body.

"Should I get breast implants?" She narrowed her eyes.

I shook my head and cupped them. She sighed.

"They're perfect. You're perfect."

I was torn apart between speeding things up and fucking her immediately and taking my time to touch and lick on every inch of skin, slowly driving her insane with need and desire.

"Thank you," she flashed me a wicked grin. "Now let's see if your reputation is deserved, shall we?"

Driving her insane it is.

I kissed and rubbed her everywhere except between her legs. At some point she was twisting under me so much that she managed to rub her clit on my abdomen. She moaned so loud I almost came in my pants.

I stood up and took my clothes off.

"I can't believe you did all of this," she said, staring at the ceiling. "We could have just done it at your place."

"Do you like it?"

"Yes."

I lay on top of her with my mouth right above her belly button.

"Good. That was all I wanted," I sucked on her skin around it, lowering myself down to her clit. I was still avoiding it and her entrance, but I licked her everywhere else.

She figured out what I was doing and tried to chase my mouth. I laughed with my head squeezed between her thighs. I put a finger on her clit. A violent shiver went through her entire body. I slid it down to her entrance and pushed inside.

"Soaked," I hissed and sucked on her clit hard. She yelped. I pushed a second finger inside her. A minute later she was panting and twisting. She was close.

"Oh, God," she cried out, and her muscles clenched around my fingers. I somehow felt that clench on my dick.

She was steadying her breath, and I reached under the pillow and pulled out a condom. She watched me put it on in silence.

"Are we doing this?" I asked, leaning over her, watching her face for any sign of regret or hesitation. There wasn't any.

She nodded frantically and wrapped her legs around my waist, pulling me closer to her.

I angled myself and entered her in one go. We both groaned.

"I know you don't want to hear it, but I'll say it anyway," I was moving slowly because I didn't want to come in five seconds and I also wanted to see every emotion she would show me. "I love you, Clem. I know you're scared of that, but I just can't hide it anymore. I *don't want* to hide it."

She closed her eyes. A frown appeared between her brows. I kissed it and then invaded her mouth. I reached down between us and pressed her clit with my thumb. She arched her back with pleasure. My movements became faster and harder.

I felt my orgasm building up. She was also close. Her hands were squeezing my shoulders, leaving dents in my flesh.

"Come for me, baby," I groaned. Moments later she did, and I followed.

We spent the next couple of hours in her new bed in almost total silence. Only our moans were filling the air around us and the dirty things I whispered in her ear.

When we got dressed to head back to my house, she grabbed my wrist and stopped me as I was passing through the door. I looked at her face and worry changed the satisfaction I was feeling three seconds ago. She looked tormented.

"Are you okay?" I pulled her into my arms. For a moment I thought she wouldn't let me hug her, but she did.

"I'm not a good person, Lucas," she started crying. "You were right all along. I lie, I keep secrets. And that's not even the worst thing I've done."

"I'm not your mother, Clem," I stroked her hair. "I don't need you to be flawless. I just need you."

We went back home and didn't speak another word that night. I slept in her bed again. She broke into tears a couple of times, and I kissed her face dry every time, squeezing her into a tight hug.

CHAPTER TWENTY

Clementine

The morning after Lucas and I had sex for the first time, I woke up feeling like shit. He was already gone. He always left and snuck back into his room before everyone else woke up.

I didn't regret that we had sex. On the contrary. I thought it was the natural end point of things. *End* being the important word here. For the few days we spent together after New Year's I found out that my heart swelled a little every time I saw him beaming at me. Because of me. I felt untroubled around him.

But I also knew it would end. He was bound to this town in so many ways, and I was going to leave it for good.

I sat up in my bed, and I touched my pendant. The fact that he loved me didn't surprise me. I knew it the moment I found his present in my luggage in Seattle. I saw how he scanned my neck for the chain every time we saw each other for the first time in the morning. The relief and pleasure smoothing his face when he realized I wore it again.

I wished I could tell him that I loved him. But I had no right. I was about to blow everything up once again. I knew it was for the best. We weren't right for each other. He was way too... too everything to be with me. Too popular. Too desired. Too good.

I was vindictive, full of hate and unresolved issues. I was a total mess. I didn't deserve him. But more importantly, he didn't deserve to be with someone like me. I saw it now. He was meant to be with someone like Amy or Hannah. Someone normal.

Would he be able to have a girlfriend now? Fall in love? Make plans for the future with someone.

The thought of him with another girl turned my stomach upside down. But that was what I was here for. I just didn't know if I helped or did more damage. I didn't think the path Elizabeth envisioned in the beginning of my stay included us having sex and professing our feelings to one another.

I got ready for school and went downstairs. Garret was joking around with Lucas, who shot me a quick look full of worry. It was like he gulped a part of my anxiety along with my tears last night. Troy was talking to Elizabeth. She was oddly quiet. She looked distant. Something was wrong. And being the person with the secrets around here, I just knew it had everything to do with me.

Maybe she knew we were sneaking around to spend the night together.

I knew I had to face her. She did so much for me. The least I could do for her was to be honest.

I lingered around long enough for everybody else to leave. I noticed Elizabeth had asked Garret to take Troy to school and that she wasn't ushering me to go. She didn't care that I was about to be late. Lucas noticed it too. I saw the questioning looks he was shooting at me, but he didn't say a word in front of his mother. I knew he did it because of me. He wanted to give me the space I needed.

The moment the front door closed behind Lucas's back, we both turned to each other.

"Are you and Lucas together, Clem?" she asked, her voice cold like I never heard it before. "Or are you just having fun?"

Was that it? She didn't approve of us being together? I knew she was worried we lived under the same roof, but I never thought she didn't like the idea of me being with her son.

"We're together," I admitted. I had no desire to lie to her. Not her. She was the one that helped me. "I think we are. We hadn't specified it."

"Does he know you're going to London?"

The air inside my lungs left my body. I closed my eyes.

She already knew the answer to that. She knew her son well enough to know that he wouldn't be so calm and happy if he was aware I was leaving not to college but to another continent. But I owed *her* every hope that blossomed into my heart the past few months, so I answered anyway.

"No."

Elizabeth started pacing back and forth in the kitchen.

"I got suspicious about your applications, and I asked Duncan if you mentioned something to him. Can you imagine my surprise when he told me about your arrangement?" she sighed. "Does your father know?" I shook my head. "God, Clem!" Elizabeth raised her voice.

"I'm sorry. It's not because of you or Duncan, I swear. It was my plan all along. I mean, not going to London, but skipping college."

"Why? Why do you want to do that?"

"I...I wanted to defy my mother. Show her that I'm making my own decisions. I started to put away some cash. I wanted to graduate and leave. That's what I did with the money from the jewelry. I had a shoe box filled with cash. It burnt in the fire."

I paused to give her a chance to say something. I hoped she would say she understood. But she just looked at me in total silence.

"After the fire, I thought I lost my chance to leave this town and get away from my parents. Then you invited me here and introduced me to Duncan and...At the beginning he didn't like anything I did, but then I made something different, and he liked it. He started mentoring me. Like really giving me advice and at some point, he said I had potential and that if I wanted to, I could go to London. It's a paid internship, Elizabeth. It's probably paid because of you. I would have to live under a bridge with the rent there, but it's London, right?"

I tried to lighten the mood. It didn't work.

"And where does Lucas fit in all of this?"

"He doesn't," I shook my head. It hurt like shit to say it out loud. "I'll tell him. I just need some time. He'll understand." Or at least I hoped he would.

"He's in love with you."

"I know."

"Are you in love with him?"

The questions squeezed my throat, but I managed to answer.

"Yes."

"Then why do it?" Elizabeth raised both her hands in the air in desperation with my bullshit. "Why do you want to break it off and move to the other side of the world?"

"It's not because of him. It's me. I'm not...like you. You love each other, you support each other. I'm nothing like that. Lucas deserves someone better."

"Love helps to round the edges," she said with a plea in her voice.

"No. I need to get away from my mother, Elizabeth. I'm sorry. I can't breathe around her. I can't. She suffocates me. She makes me feel like I have no soul. My feelings towards her subsided while she was away, but now that she's coming back...It consumes me all over again. I'm so close to getting away. Please, don't tell my father."

"Oh, Clem..."

"Please. I will tell them. Just not now. Please, keep my secret a little longer?"

"I can't hide it from my son. You're about to break his heart. Again." There was no judgment in her voice. Just sadness.

"I will tell him next week. When I move back home. I promise."

I missed school that day, and Lucas became suspicious of me and his mother. He had every right, of course. But I wasn't ready to drop the bomb yet. I needed to have space between us, and the two inches that separated us lately didn't do the trick for me.

"I was just tired, and I asked your mother to stay home. That's it."

I had been repeating that for three days. I hated that I was lying to him *again*, but compared to everything I kept from him, this lie wasn't even in the top five.

I also tried to keep our relationship mostly physical and avoided serious conversations at all costs.

"You're lying," he roared while he was entering me. I was lying on the bed in my room. He was on top of me. Everyone was home. We were being reckless.

I couldn't care less. I needed to feel as much of him as possible while I still had the chance. I shook my head.

"I'm not lying."

"Why the distance then?" he asked and a miserable chuckle escaped my lips between my moans.

"What distance? You are literally inside my body."

"What's eating you then?" he frowned.

"Hopefully you are."

He pulled out of me and flipped me on my stomach. He entered me again in one stroke.

"Oh, God," I hissed.

"I'm listening."

Again with his favorite joke.

"Don't stop," I moaned into the pillow.

He pounded into me until we both came. Then we just lay in bed not touching each other, watching the ceiling.

"That's the ugliest chandelier I have ever seen," I said repeating my thoughts from the first night I spent in this room. "I can't believe your mom bought that."

"She didn't," Lucas said with a distant voice. "It's a gift from my dad's sister. She hates it, but she can't say no to people if you haven't noticed."

"I have," I said thinking about my last request to her. I could see it on her face. It was torturing her. The thought that I was doing something that would hurt her son and that she was a part of the lie. But she agreed anyway.

"Stay here," he said. His eyes were digging holes into the side of my face. I played stupid and refrained from looking back at him.

"What do you mean?"

"Stay here until graduation. Your house is not ready. You have a bathroom and a bed. That's it. It looks like a mental institution."

I squeezed my fists and my fingernails hurt my palms. But I remained silent. I didn't move.

"I feel like you're running away from me, and I have no idea why."

"I'm tired," I looked at him with a smile. "Maybe you should sleep in your room tonight."

The pain on Lucas's face made my soul ache. He tore his eyes away from mine, shook his head, and stood up. He left my room without a word.

I couldn't sleep. Everything I did and everything I was about to do haunted me. It was too much to hold in. But I couldn't burden Elizabeth with my self-loathing. She had already done enough for me and crying on her shoulder about breaking her son's heart was a bit too much to ask.

I took my phone from my nightstand to text Hannah.

Me: I did something horrible.

Her answers started coming a few seconds later.

Hannah: Please don't tell me you slept with Dylan...

Hannah: I'm rooting for Lucas now.

Hannah: He was amazing at the party last week. Dylan not so much.

I wondered where to start. I had to just pour it out of me. Everything. So I did. I told her why Elizabeth wanted me here in the first place and what happened with Lucas since I moved in in his house. I told her about the shoe box. About Duncan's proposal. About me accepting it. About Elizabeth knowing about it and hiding it from Lucas. I dumped it all at once, not giving her time to answer any of it. Then I just stared at the dozens of texts and wrote the last one.

Me: Are you mad?

Hannah: No... I'm just processing. Give me a minute.

I gave her a few. When my phone finally buzzed, the texts I got broke my heart.

Lucas: I get you have things to work out.

**Lucas: I don't want to, but I'll give you space if that's what
you need.**

Lucas: Whenever you are ready.

He wanted to wait for me.

I didn't answer.

The next days were excruciating. I just stared at the wall that was in
front of me. Hannah was supportive, but when she tried to convince
me for a second time not to go to England, I just asked her to drop
the subject. She did, but it was obvious she thought I was making a
mistake.

Lucas was quiet but always present. I could see the torture in his
eyes. On my last night in his house, we were all eating dinner together
and the mood was so depressing that even Troy didn't speak. Lucas's
fork rattled on his plate and we all lifted our gazes.

"I can't do this," he stood up, came behind me, and kissed my hair.

My eyes watered the moment his lips touched me, but when Troy
came and hugged me seconds after Lucas turned his back on me and
went upstairs, I broke into tears.

I spent the night sobbing.

The next day Elizabeth, Garret, and Troy helped me move my stuff
into my house. Elizabeth was looking around and her eyes spotted the
narcissus sticker on my ceiling.

"Did you ask for that?" her finger was pointing at it. "It's not really
your style."

"Yeah," I smiled grimly. "It's a joke. Lucas did it. I once called him
Narcissus. You know. The myth."

Elizabeth's brows shot up.

"And the necklace you're wearing?" she asked, already knowing
the answer to that. I felt the burning in my eyes again. Apparently, I
couldn't stop crying.

"Yes," I muttered through tears. "He gave it to me."

Elizabeth came and hugged me while I wept. At some point, I felt she waved off Garrett and Troy. I heard them leaving the house.

"Are you sure you want to do this, Clem? You are clearly suffering. It can't be right if it makes you so miserable."

"I have to. I have to," I was saying frantically shaking my head. "I'm just going to miss you all so much."

She looked at me for a few seconds, she was hesitating.

"I talked to Lucas last night. He knows that there is something wrong and that it is big enough to mess you up like this, but he still has hope, Clem. If you are sure you're leaving, tell him. Give him closure. It doesn't have to be ugly. I even think he'll understand."

I nodded.

"I will. I will. I just need to pull myself together."

I wondered where Lucas was. He wasn't home when I left. And three hours after his family left my house, his room was still empty. I could see it now. My curtains were open.

The doorbell rang, and I jumped up from my bed, running downstairs, thinking it was him.

I swung the door open, out of breath.

My mother was looking at me from the other side of the door, dressed in a pencil skirt and a shirt. Her hair was up, her make-up perfect.

I was wearing jeans and a tee. I had zero make-up on, and my hair was a mess. We were so different. Two strangers. She had no idea who I was. She only knew who she wanted me to be. And I had no interest in finding out who she was.

"What are you doing here?" I asked.

"I came to see the house."

Of course. Not me. The fucking house.

Her gaze was moving over my body.

"You put on some weight."

"And I see you haven't changed one bit." I plastered a fake smile on my face. It was true. I had put on a few pounds, but I looked healthy. When she left for rehab, I was really skinny. "Please, come in. Take a look around."

I moved away from the door and waved her in.

She didn't apologize, didn't mention the fire. She didn't ask how I was doing or anything about the Coles or the fact that the least she could do was to thank them for taking me in. She just looked around and whatever thoughts she had, she kept to herself.

Rehab might have helped her with her drinking problem, but sure as hell hadn't changed anything between us.

"You know, Clementine, you're the only one that never came to visit me in the rehab center. Even your father came twice."

Did he now? He went to visit his ex-wife twice, but he didn't come to see me even for my birthday. What was that all about?

"Good for you. Listen, Sylvia," I exhaled. "I know that Dad rented you an apartment. Why don't you go there and call the others?"

I pointed at the front door. She moved towards it.

"Everyone is coming next weekend," she said when she stepped outside.

"Everyone?" I asked, but I couldn't care less.

"Your father, Ty, and Maddie," she chimed. "Your father plans on flying out here at least once a month now. He wants to be more present."

"What difference does it make? I'm graduating soon. I won't be here anyway."

"Well, about that. We talked, and we decided you should stay in California. Your father has some connections, and he could help if you're not accepted."

My throat bobbed, and I felt a scream building up inside it.

"No," I said shakily. "No, I'm not staying here. You can't decide that for me."

"It's not negotiable, Clementine. We don't trust you enough to let you live too far away. You're unstable. Your dad told me about your outburst on Christmas."

"I don't care if you trust me or not. I'm not staying here."

I felt the urge to shout the truth out. To tell her where I was going and that she had no power over me. But it was too soon. And I had to tell Lucas first. I couldn't risk him hearing it from somewhere else. I owned him at least that.

"Well, since your father and I are financially supporting you..."

"You mean Dad is."

"...it's not really your decision."

I snorted.

"I don't believe that he agreed to this."

"If you had played along and participated in my healing process, maybe we could have let you decide. But your behavior proved you're just an angry child. And your father and I agree you need to stay close. He's traveling a lot for work and sending you to Seattle is not an option."

"And Dad knows about this?" she had to be lying.

"Of course he does. He wanted us to tell you next week, but since you mentioned moving away, I decided that the moment is as good as any."

I wanted to wipe the smirk off her face.

"Why do you want to keep me here, since you never even wanted me? What kind of sadist are you?"

Her voice was sad when she answered.

"The same as you, honey. That's what we have in common. You may look nothing like me on the outside, but on the inside..."

She turned her back on me and walked away.

***

My mother's words were stuck in my head for two days.

The same as you, honey.

At first I was pissed at her. I told myself she was wrong. That I wasn't like her.

But then I started thinking about all the times the two of us hurt one another. She was mean to me, and I fought back. Not only that. I was actively thinking of ways to torture her. Humiliate her. Just like she did it to me.

I even went as far as hiding her alcohol abuse from everyone, taking pleasure in the fact she was suffering.

I couldn't stand myself anymore.

The worst part of it all was I realized I did to Lucas what she did to me. And he didn't deserve it. He was always there for me, from the day we met. He never hurt me. And I? I had no mercy. I crushed him, and I was still doing it. By not telling him the truth. By not explaining we were over. I knew he was still waiting for me and did nothing about it.

The realization I possessed every bad quality my mom did hit harder that anything. Hannah and Dylan were trying to cheer me up at school, but it was pointless. I wasn't even listening to them.

"Do you want to go to the beach?" Dylan asked after school. Hannah had to stay. She had practice.

"I don't feel like driving for two hours just to spend one on the beach," I refused.

"I could drive. You will look out the window and think about that thing."

"What thing?" I frowned.

"I have no idea. The thing that has you so worked up."

I thought about my options. Going home to spend the rest of the day so close to Lucas? Or going to the beach and maybe sketching a little.

"Okay, but no talking. I'm not in the mood."

"Sure. No talking." His smile was kind, but there was curiosity in his eyes. I hoped he would keep his promise and not try to question me.

He drove us to the beach in total silence. I felt emotionally exhausted. The moment my bare feet touched the sand, all I wanted to do was just lie down. So I did.

I felt Dylan sitting next to me for a long time. My eyes were shut. I had no idea what time it was. I was just breathing and listening to the waves.

"Your hair is full of sand," he said at some point. I didn't answer. I didn't even try to come up with something to say to that. "You're a fascinating creature," he continued and sounded baffled.

"No talking," I reminded him. "Don't forget we're with my car. I could just leave you here."

"You wouldn't do that. Seems like you keep your needs for inflicting pain exclusively for Lucas Cole."

I shot up straight and heard the sound of sand falling off of me.

"Why would you say that?"

"I've been here for five months now, and he spent most of the time in your personal purgatory. I thought you were together after New Year's but lately he's been even more..." He tried to find the right word.

"Miserable?" I supplied.

"Wrecked."

Wrecked. I wrecked him. And he didn't even know the whole story yet.

"I'm about to make it worse, you know."

I felt the need to talk about it. Dylan cocked his head sideways exploring my face. I told him about Duncan and London. About me knowing Lucas and I were over from the very beginning but leaving him clueless.

"That's insane," he was focusing his gaze on the ocean. I couldn't bear to look at it. It had the same color as Lucas's eyes. So I looked at Dylan's face. He was concentrating. Like he was trying to solve a puzzle. Then he turned to face me. His smile sent goosebumps all over my body. "Thank you for sharing."

CHAPTER TWENTY-ONE

Lucas

I tried my best to give Clem the space I promised her. Most of the time it felt like a knife was cutting my body, but I knew cornering her was going to do more damage. And I was not going to accept damage. I wanted a different outcome. I wanted her.

Her hanging out with Dylan instead of me was painful, but I knew it wasn't about him. It was about avoiding me. So, I kept my jealousy under control.

My mother was trying to talk with me, but I ignored her. I needed to talk *to* Clementine, not about her.

One day I was particularly impatient, and I texted Hannah. I preferred to humiliate myself in front of her than not keep my promise to Clem. I wanted her to feel my word was something she could count on. Not something that depended on my mood.

Hannah: Her mother is giving her a hard time.

Hannah: And they're having a family dinner or something like that on the weekend, so...

The dots, indicating Hannah was typing more, wiggled on my screen, then stopped. It was a long pause, but she started writing again.

Hannah: There is one more thing, but you need to hear it from her.

Hannah: Maybe you could, I don't know...

Hannah: CALL HER???

Lucas: I can't. I promised her I'll wait until she's ready.

Hannah: You two are idiots.

That day I went home and asked my mother if she knew something about the Hartleys family dinner. I knew one gathering could push Clem over the edge. Whatever that edge she was standing at was.

"Lucas, Clem has issues that are beyond your relationship."

"I know," I hissed.

"Give her space."

"That's what I've been doing!" I shouted out of frustration. She covered my hand with hers.

"I know you're hurting, but she's confused and I'm not sure she'll be able to give you what you need."

"You don't get it," I shook my head. "We were good. And then I told her I loved her, and she just...It was like she couldn't handle that. Like it was the worst thing on earth."

"Relationships are hard. You are young, and maybe she's just not ready for that. You have to respect her choice. She has to do what's best for her. And you have to do the same."

I stood up and left the conversation. I couldn't stand listening any more of the breakup hints my mother was dropping. Clementine didn't close her curtains anymore, but she obviously spent most of her time in another room because I only caught her in hers twice. It was in the middle of the night. She pretended she didn't see me, turned off the lights, and went to bed.

I wasn't sleeping much. Days blended into each other.

"You look like shit," Chase murmured on Friday morning.

"I feel like shit too," I was beyond hiding my feelings now.

Two days ago, Chase sent me a picture. Clem and Dylan sitting on the beach. I didn't blink that night. I knew the lack of sleep was making me irrational. I was barely holding on to the promise I gave Clementine. I was about to let go and just go confront her. I was planning on waiting for her by her car after classes. She had to talk to me eventually and for me eventually was today.

I was sulking and playing in my head an imaginary conversation between us. I just couldn't figure out what got her so upset that she couldn't just be a normal human being and tell me she loved me too. Because I knew she did. I felt it when we were together even though she never said it. And she was still wearing my necklace. Every day.

Chase was sweet-talking a girl that I could swear I was seeing for the first time when Amy appeared next to us. We were standing in the hallway. Chase and I had a class together. I just needed to wait for the asshole to finish making his move.

"Did you hear?" Amy sang in my ear. "Guess who has a thing with some old dude in England?"

Chase and I ignored her. Spreading gossip was never our thing. But the girl whose name I didn't know was interested, and she leaned forward waiting to hear everything.

"Clementine Hartley."

My heart stopped beating for a second with the mentioning of her name.

"Bullshit," I cut her off. "Stop spreading rumors."

"Oh, it's not a rumor. It's true. I heard it from a trustworthy source."

I rolled my eyes. I had enough of this stupid war Amy was leading against Clementine.

"He's a designer," I started explaining, not even sure why. Probably to save Clem from the embarrassment of that stupid gossip. "He helps her with her jewelry-making thing. My mom introduced them. Check your sources next time you decide to talk shit."

Amy grinned and cocked her head.

"So you do know then?"

"I told you. It's not true. There is nothing to know."

"Then why is she going to England after graduation?"

My head went blank. My brain probably stopped working to compensate for my heart which was hammering louder and louder with every second I spent replaying the sentence.

She's going to England. She's going to England.

Fuck. That's it. She's going to England.

"She says it's for an internship, but come on," Amy continued her theory about the affair. "Why would a fifty-year-old guy ask an eighteen-year-old girl to move across the world for an internship? She's not that good. I bet there are thousands of girls in London that are even better. She's sleeping with him."

"But how?" The other girl asked. "If he's in England and she's here?"

"He's famous and he's loaded. He probably visits."

I knew that part wasn't true. Clementine wasn't having an affair with him. But leaving for an internship part? That was something she would do to run away from her family and to run away from me. That was something that could make her distance herself from me.

I left the others and started roaming the hallways. I had to find her immediately.

"Is it true?" I smashed my palm on her locker. Her eyes were big and sad, and I had to fight my need to make her feel better and actually grow a pair and demand answers for a change.

"Is what true?" she asked breathlessly.

"London?" That's all I could say without raising my voice. But it was enough. I saw it on her face. It was true.

I stumbled backwards.

"I can't believe you did that" I shook my head. "Were you planning on telling me or you were just going to string me along until graduation and leave without a word?"

Tears started streaming down her face. She didn't answer. What a surprise, huh?

I was aware everyone around us was looking. I didn't care.

"Answer me, damn it!" I shouted. I felt someone's hands on my shoulders pulling me back. Then I heard Chase's voice.

"Leave it, man."

I shook off his hands and took a step towards Clementine.

"You really are a coward, Clem. You're so scared of letting go of your secrets that it ruins everything and everyone around you. You will never find what you're looking for in London. What you're looking for has been living next door your whole life. But I don't have it in me to make you see that."

I left her crying in the hallway and stormed out without a second look.

CHAPTER TWENTY-TWO

Clementine

Four years ago

I was looking at my outfit in the mirror. Dad's assistant said it looked amazing on me when we bought it in the summer while I was visiting him in Seattle. She was extra nice, super young, and had a guilty look on her face every time I tried to look her in the eye, so my guess was she was screwing my dad.

She was dedicated to the task of making me feel good and have fun using my father's credit card. She took me to a hairdresser. Then we did our nails. If I knew from the beginning that she just wanted to please me, I would have asked to dye my hair pink. But, unfortunately, I figured things out much later. When we were shopping.

I didn't need nor did I want new clothes, but I saw an opportunity to piss off my mom by wearing something she wouldn't approve of. I knew exactly what she liked. She wanted to dress me up like a doll. Like she did with Madison when she was still here, although as far as I knew my sister, she was still dressing and acting like my mother trained her.

I used the nameless, at least to me, personal assistant to get me what I knew my mother never would.

It was New Year's Eve and we had to go to the twins' house. Chase and Amy's parents threw a party every year. That night, I had two tasks to accomplish with my appearance.

First, I had to rebel against my mother in a public way so that she felt not just challenged but also embarrassed. A few years back, I found out she loathed being humiliated in front of other people. After the divorce, she started to care even more about other people's opinions. I didn't know that was possible, but apparently it was.

My second goal for the evening was to make Lucas Cole kiss me. For real this time.

So I picked a pair of ripped denim shorts and loose baby pink t-shirt that revealed the better part of my belly, thinking that outfit would help me with both my tasks. Everyone attending that party would be dressed as if they were going to a wedding, so no doubt my outfit would embarrass Mom in front of her fellow snobs.

And I really hoped it would appeal to the neighbor who made my mind go blank every time he tried to talk to me.

I put on some makeup. It made me look older and my mom hated it, but I wanted Lucas to see me in another light. Not just as the girl he knew his whole life who embarrassed herself in front of him in every possible way a child could. I wanted to make him forget I ever showed him my snot when we were sick or that I accidently wet my bed when we had a sleepover at the mortifying age of seven.

I went downstairs. My mom looked at me with narrowed eyes.

"Go change your clothes, Clementine."

"But Dad's girlfriend said I looked great in these," I pretended I didn't understand what her problem was. Also, I wasn't sure that PA was his girlfriend, but I wanted to irritate my mother. I blamed her for the divorce. I didn't care that my dad was the one cheating. I would cheat too if I was married to someone like mom. She was the coldest person on earth.

"You look like a slut. But I guess your dad's girlfriend is one too, so no wonder she told you that."

"Oh, thank you, Sylvia. That was the look I was aiming for."

Her face twisted, and her eye twitched.

"What did you just call me?"

It just slipped out of my mouth, but seeing the look on her face was priceless. I was going to use that again.

"Isn't that your name, *Sylvia*?"

She asked me that question every time I reminded her not to call me Clementine.

"You ungrateful little..." she exhaled and closed her eyes. "I don't have time for this. This is my first social visit without your father. I'm not going to let you ruin it."

Like I was the one ruining anything.

We went to the party on foot, it was just a few houses away from us. I had invited Hannah to come with us. Amy's parents didn't mind us kids inviting friends over, because it meant we were entertained and less prone to wreck their home.

My mother left me and Hannah alone the moment we entered the house.

"I can't believe your mother let you come dressed like that," Hannah laughed.

"She has more pressing issues than that, but she didn't miss the opportunity to tell me I looked like a slut."

"What issues?"

"Impressing the neighbors? Pretending she's fine? I don't really care." I paused. "Do you see him?"

"No. I don't see his parents either, so maybe he's not here yet." Hannah looked me head to toe. "I wish I was as brave as you and just go to the party the seniors are having and kiss your brother."

"Ugh, gross." I pretended I was gagging. "He's turning eighteen in a few hours and you're fourteen."

"I know," Hannah sighed.

"Clem!" I turned around and I saw Elizabeth Cole waving at me. I hadn't visited their house since my father's affair became public knowledge. At first, I was embarrassed and then, when I got back from Seattle in the summer, Lucas was looking at me differently, and I kept my distance from his entire family.

Elizabeth came and hugged me. Then she whispered in my ear.

"You won't believe what Lucas is wearing."

I peeked behind her and there he was. Standing with his father and little brother. Looking at him made my pulse beat in my ears.

"He looks...good."

"You should tell him that when he comes over," Elizabeth kissed me on the cheek. "How are you? Is everything okay at home?"

It was no secret my mother and I didn't get along.

"Yeah. It's fine. Ty is still here to lighten the mood. The real treat will begin when he graduates in a few months."

"I'm sure it will be fine. You can always come talk to me if you need anything."

"Sure," I said, but I wasn't planning on doing that. I didn't like talking about our family drama. Elizabeth said a few words to my best friend and headed back to her family.

Lucas looked me straight in the eye. He said something to his father and walked over to us.

"Do you want me to leave you alone?" Hannah whispered when he was only a few steps away.

"Don't move," I roared. Seeing him now made me scared to death.

"Hey," Lucas stood in front of us.

"Hey," I answered breathlessly.

"Where are the others?"

"I don't know," I said without even glancing around us to try to figure it out. "We just got here."

"Let's go find them," Lucas waved his hand towards the back door. Every year we just hung around in the backyard. This time we were the oldest of the group of the children here. We would probably have a separate party next year and we would never again hide in the darkness of this yard.

"You look pretty," Lucas leaned into me while we were walking by the adults.

"Thanks." I felt my breath hiss. He smirked. He knew he was making me uncomfortable. I should have been mad or embarrassed, but I felt good. Excited. *He cared.*

We found the others sitting on blankets on the ground. I thought Lucas would go sit with his best friend Chase, who was kissing a girl at that moment, but no. He settled next to me.

It is happening. It is happening.

A shiver passed through me, and he asked if I was cold.

"No," I said with eyes glued to the ground.

I felt his hand sneaking into mine, and he gave it a little squeeze. Then he laced his fingers with mine.

He nodded to a boy sitting across from us that I hadn't paid attention to up until now.

"Hey, Dylan," I greeted him. "I didn't know you were here."

"Surprise," he smiled at me.

Hannah hugged him and sat next to him. They talked, but every once in a while, I caught Dylan staring at my hand. It was still in Lucas's. It made me feel uncomfortable. Was he judging us for holding hands in public? My fingers twitched. Lucas felt it and turned his gaze to me. He smiled and ran his thumb on the inside of my palm. It squeezed my heart.

At some point I had to use the bathroom. Lucas was joking around with Chase and wasn't paying any attention to me, so I decided it was a good time. I tried to pull my hand away, but he tightened his grip and turned to face me.

"Are you okay?" he asked.

"Yes," my thumb caressed his. "I'll be right back."

I didn't want to tell him I was going to the bathroom. Why would I want to tell that to a boy I intended to kiss?

There was a bathroom on the ground floor with a line in front of it, so I decided to sneak upstairs. I wasn't allowed to. Amy's parents didn't like it when we did that, but my need to pee was too overwhelming for me to stand in the line. And I wanted to get back to Lucas as fast as possible. I liked how he squeezed my hand when I tried to pull away.

Someone knocked on the door when I was in the bathroom. I wasn't the only one not wanting to wait to pee.

A minute later I got out, and I saw Dylan. His back was plastered to the opposite wall.

"Hey, I thought you left," I smiled at him.

Earlier he got inside the house and never came back.

He was taller than I remembered. He looked at me with a huge grin on his face.

"And I thought there was a rule that said we shouldn't come up here," he teased. "Do you like breaking the rules?"

"Do you?" I asked with a snort.

"Yes."

I felt a knot forming in my stomach. There was something weird about him being here. Did he follow me here?

"I had to use the bathroom and the one downstairs was occupied. What are you doing here?" I asked again.

"Same. But now I'm eavesdropping. A couple is making out behind that door over there. But I don't think they are a real couple."

I looked down the hallway and tried to listen carefully. A few seconds later a loud moan and some male groaning filled the silence. I was mortified. I was standing in a hallway alone with a boy listening to people moan.

It wasn't like I never talked about sex. There were occasional jokes that boys shared with us. But it was different now. He wasn't telling a joke, and we were alone. I heard the noises the couple was making, and I felt my skin reddening with shame. I was so shocked I didn't know what to do.

"Do you want to see them?" Dylan asked. "You would be able to tell me if they are a couple or not."

"No, thanks," I tried to figure out a way to leave. "Does it matter anyway? If they are a couple?" He shrugged.

"Aren't you interested just a little bit if they are having an affair? You probably know them."

I thought about my father's affair. I had enough of that for years to come, so I definitely wasn't interested in who the people behind that door were.

Also the noises were becoming way too inappropriate for us to listen.

"I don't really care about gossip, so I'm going back outside," I murmured.

"To your boyfriend?" Dylan asked with a curious tone.

Before I had the chance to think of an answer to that, the woman behind the door spoke.

"And you're going to kiss your wife with that mouth?"

My jaw slacked. My pulse quickened. I froze.

Sylvia Hartley, ladies and gentlemen!

A moment later, I began to tremble, and I clenched my fists preventing my hands from shaking.

"Do you know who the man is?" I asked through my teeth. Dylan looked at me and understood in a second.

"No, but I bet you know who the woman is."

I tried to take control over my body and nodded.

"My mother."

That hypocrite! She was sleeping with a married man after all the time she spent insulting dad about his affair. She still called his PA the *homewrecker*. And she was doing it at a party while all our neighbors were here and obviously this man's wife. She was so concerned about what other people thought about her when they were looking at me and my behavior, but apparently, she could do whatever the hell she wanted.

"Maybe you should go," Dylan said, and I shot him a look. "Listening to your mother's moans? Twisted!" he smiled and looked interested in my reaction.

He was right. It was twisted. Part of me wanted to cut my ears off. Another part of me wanted to kick the door down and expose that witch!

"What are you thinking about?" Dylan asked, and he looked strangely excited.

"That I want to humiliate my mother."

His eyes widened, and he grinned.

"You want them to get caught."

I wasn't going in that direction, but when he mentioned it, it made perfect sense.

"Yes," I hissed. Then I imagined the consequences if I did that. "But I can't do it. She'll make my life miserable if I embarrass her like that."

"I can do it for you. Go to the bathroom; I'll come in a second."

I did what he told me. Standing in that bathroom though I wondered if I could trust him. He wasn't a perfect stranger, but he was still a stranger. An acquaintance. But rage clouded my judgment. I didn't stop him. I didn't even know what he was about to do, but I didn't care.

All I could think about was how this was going to affect my mother. It would destroy her.

Everyone would know she screwed a married man while his wife drank wine downstairs. The bathroom door opened, and Dylan walked in. He flashed me a wicked smile waving his phone in his hand.

"I thought about taking a picture, but they were so into it, I managed to film a whole video."

I pressed the play button on his screen. My mother was sitting on top of a washing machine. Her legs were spread wide and between them there was a man. He was all over her.

I recognized his shirt. It was baby pink. Earlier that evening when we came, he greeted us and made a joke about us wearing the same color. The video ended. I pressed my sweaty palm to my forehead.

"You have to delete this. You can't tell a soul."

Dylan frowned at me.

"Why?"

"Just do it."

"Not before you tell me why. You wanted to expose them a minute ago. Who is he?"

"Chase and Amy's father.'"

I couldn't do this to my friends. Expose their cheating father. They had a good family. Their parents always seemed happy.

This is Sylvia's fault.

"Dylan, please, delete it. I can't do this to them. What if their parents got divorced? They would be devastated."

Dylan hesitated.

"But you wanted to humiliate your mother, remember?"

"Yes, and that was before I found out she was making out with my friends' father. Please, delete it. And don't tell anyone. Ever."

He munched on his lip thinking. I could probably take his phone from his hand and delete it myself if I was fast enough.

"Okay," he finally said. "I'll delete it and I will never tell anyone. If that's what you want."

"Thank you," I sighed and closed my eyes in relief.

"But I want you to kiss me."

My eyes flung open. I looked at his face. He wasn't joking.

"Are you kidding me?" I asked anyway.

"No. Not at all."

I thought about Lucas. I wanted him to be my first kiss. Not this semi-stranger.

"It's just one kiss, no big deal," Dylan started. "It's not like we're seeing each other a lot anyway. No one will know."

"Why kiss then?" I asked. "What's the point?"

There had to be one, right? He shrugged.

"I like you. You're pretty. And I filmed them because you asked me to, remember?" That wasn't exactly true. I didn't know he was going to film them. He saw my hesitation and came closer. "No one will know," he repeated.

I thought about Amy and Chase again. I remembered the hurt and humiliation I felt when everyone in town found out my father was fucking another woman. And now I would be even more humiliated, considering my own mother was the other woman. The woman that could break my friends' family apart.

They would never speak to me again.

"Just one kiss and the video will disappear," Dylan's quiet voice filled my ears.

My feet sort of walked on their own closer to him. I felt emotionally disconnected from it, and I just wanted to get it over with. I couldn't risk bargaining with him when someone could hear us. And that video had to be deleted.

"I want to see you delete it."

"Kiss me and you can delete it yourself."

"Just one kiss," I whispered, offering my lips.

"Promise."

He leaned in. He placed his hand on my back and pulled me closer. His lips touched mine. It felt wrong. I tried to think about something else. About someone else. About Lucas. But the moment his face appeared in my head, I felt like someone kicked me in the stomach. I gasped. Dylan took that as an invitation to invade my mouth with his tongue. The moment it touched mine, I jerked back. He laughed, and I was so appalled by what we just did, I forgot about my mother, the video, everything. I rounded him with the intention of running back down, when I saw a figure standing in the hallway looking at us through the opened door.

"I...," I started to explain myself.

Lucas turned his back on me and left.

I slacked down to the floor. I asked Dylan to leave and stayed in that bathroom long enough for my mother and Amy's father to stop their make out session, or whatever they called it. I heard them go downstairs one by one. One of them tried to use the bathroom, but I had locked the door.

When I finally managed to calm myself down enough to get out of there, I tried to call Lucas. He didn't answer. I went downstairs and told my mother I was going home. It was almost midnight and she just shrugged, letting me go by myself like she didn't care. She probably didn't.

I ran back home crying. I got upstairs to my room and looked through the windows. Lucas's room was dark. It seemed empty. Maybe he was still at the party. I lost count on the times I tried to call him. Send him dozens of texts. Nothing.

I endured a sleepless night. I was going to talk to him first thing in the morning. I had to explain. My phone rang around seven o'clock. It was Amy. My heart flipped inside my chest. She knew. I didn't know how, but I was sure she knew.

I answered the call. She asked to go outside. I did. She was waiting for me.

"I can't believe you did this to me," she snarled.

"Amy, I'm so sorry," I tried to touch her, but she swatted my hand away. "What happened? Did Dylan send out the video? Who else knows?"

"No one. I just grilled Dylan for an hour before he finally came clean and told me what happened."

"Did he delete the video?" The thought of my mother's recorded moans was becoming unbearable.

"Yes. You did your part of the deal after all."

"You know about the kiss?"

"Lucas told Chase. I guess what they say about the apple and the tree is true after all."

I shook my head violently. But the thought sank even if it made me want to disappear. I was like my mother. She kissed someone and hurt his family. I kissed someone and hurt Lucas.

"I'm sorry." My tears were falling down my face. "I didn't know it was your father. I tried to make it right."

"Please explain to me how you kissing Dylan could possibly make it right?" Amy roared, stepping closer to me. "Your whore of a mother was making out with him while we were all there. If Dylan talks, it will be the end of our family." She spat every word in my face. "Make sure your mother stays away from my father."

"How?"

"I don't care. If our family breaks apart because of you two, I will make your life a living hell. Don't tell anyone what happened."

"I have to tell Lucas. I have to tell him. To explain why I kissed Dylan."

Amy released a dark chuckle.

"Lucas will never look at you again. Believe me. Chase told me every word Lucas said. It's over between you two."

"I can't lose him. He's my best friend."

Amy cocked her head sideways looking at me like I didn't get the whole picture.

"You just kissed a random guy when it was perfectly clear to everyone that something was happening between you and Lucas. Do you think you will change his mind about you by explaining to him what your mother did? You're dead to him."

"Did he say that?" I whispered.

"Yes. He said he never wants to see your face again."

CHAPTER TWENTY-THREE

Clementine

The present

I went to Amy's place later that Friday evening. I really hoped I wasn't going to bump into Lucas there. That was the last thing any one of us needed after that scene in school earlier that day. I knew Dylan and Amy were behind it. And since I was done with Dylan forever after that betrayal, I had to confront Amy. The following day was our family dinner and I wanted to get this over with before I had to deal with my parents and their plans for me.

She opened the door. The moment she saw me a smug smile formed on her face.

"Finally," she murmured.

"Can I come in?" I asked. I didn't want to make a spectacle for the neighbors if this got out of hand.

She stepped away for me to enter. As soon as she closed the door, I turned to face her.

"How long have you and Dylan been together?"

"Since New Year's. He found out you were never going to give him a chance."

Good. At least there was some part of our friendship these past few months that wasn't a lie.

"And you found out Lucas wasn't going to give you a chance," I added. Amy didn't comment on that.

"We're not together. But we have a common goal."

"Ruin my life?"

"The nerve," she scoffed. "You did that on your own. No one made you lie all the fucking time."

It hurt to admit, but she was right about that.

"We just revealed some of your secrets. It's not like you could actually move to England without anyone noticing."

"Interesting how you think I should reveal my secrets, but you keep yours," I stepped closer to her. "Your father was responsible for that night four years ago. He shouldn't have cheated. You took advantage of the fact that I was feeling guilty about my mother's involvement. It wasn't my fault he was in that room with her."

"Why did you kiss Dylan then?"

"To spare you and Chase the heartache."

"Oh, the martyr. Please, if you want to spare me something, let it be your acting."

"Why did you forgive Dylan for shooting the video, but you couldn't forgive me, even though I tried to make it go away? We were friends."

"Yes, we were. But I had always hated you. Just a little. At first, I felt bad about it. I knew I was jealous and that it was wrong of me. But people always chose you over me. Hannah chose you. Lucas chose you. And you weren't even trying. You were a total mess. But everyone adored Clem."

"That's not true," I tried to cut her off, but she didn't let me.

"And even after everything that happened that night, they continued choosing you. Hannah stopped talking to me and took your side. And Lucas? He should have been with someone like me. But he never got over you. He couldn't even stomach the fact that you would actually have a boyfriend, and that it wasn't going to be him."

"Did he even say all those things about me? That I was dead to him? That we were over?" I questioned everything.

"Not that night he didn't," Amy smiled. "But time passed, and you never apologized. Never sought him out again. And he started saying those things. I think he said them trying to convince himself they were true."

I shook my head.

"Bitch."

"I think he finally truly hates you now. I mean, it's the second time you smashed his heart. And this time you hammered it to death."

***

"Do you think Dylan told her about London on purpose?" Hannah asked. We were laying on my bed staring at the daffodil on the ceiling. I had to peel that thing off.

I sat up and looked at her. I thought about it a lot mainly because it took my mind off Lucas and the fact he would definitely hate me for the rest of his life this time around. I occupied my brain with Dylan to distract myself from that depressing thought.

"I think he did. I thought it was weird he wasn't angry at me after New Year's. And what do you know? He was already in a secret alliance with Amy."

"He's done playing games. I will tell the whole football team to make his life a living hell."

"You founded an anti-bullying club. I think this goes against its values," I murmured. "Leave it. The damage is done."

Hannah shot up.

"No way! You and Lucas could have had a chance if it wasn't for those assholes."

"No," I shook my head and started crying. "That's not on him. I was keeping the secret. Dylan and Amy just smelled the blood and went for it. But I was the one that made us bleed in the first place."

Hannah squeezed my hand and started talking.

"Maybe you could still fix it. You hurt him, but he loves you. You can go over there," she pointed to his house through my window. "You can explain and..."

"No, I can't."

"Clem," she looked at me with a serious face. "You're making the same mistake. Go to him and explain."

"No," I frowned. "He deserves better. And I can't even look Elizabeth in the eye."

"So you're not even going to tell him about Amy and Dylan?"

"What's the point? I did this. Not Dylan."

"See," Hannah yelled. "You're doing the right thing now. You're taking responsibility for your actions. Isn't that what Lucas wanted all along? He will forgive you."

"I don't want him to forgive me. I will leave after graduation. It would be easier for everyone if he hates me."

"So you aren't even going to consider staying?" Hannah was disappointed. I understood that. I would miss her too.

"I don't want to stay. I want to leave. You will go somewhere, hopefully far away from Boston," I shot her a look. "Lucas will go somewhere too. Everything will be fine."

We stood there silent for a moment.

"Are you worried about tomorrow?" she asked, referring to my family dinner.

"Worried? No. But I still have no desire to participate."

"Everything will be fine," she repeated my words. She believed in that statement just as much as I believed in it. Not at all.

"Can you spend the night?" I asked.

"Sure. I'll call Mom," she reached between us and grabbed my phone thinking it was hers. "Oops, that's yours," she said but stared at my screen. "Umm, Clem? You have a lot of missed calls from Elizabeth Cole. Texts too."

My heart sank. I knew she deserved the right to yell at me, but I was scared to death that she finally started to hate me.

"Let me see the texts. I can't call her back now."

I took my phone and read while Hannah explained to her mother she would sleep at my place tonight.

Elizabeth: Clem, pick up.

Ten minutes later.

Elizabeth: I'm not mad. I just want to talk.

Elizabeth: I know it's hard, but you have to talk to him. It's not about his closure only. You need it too.

An hour later.

Elizabeth: I'm not going to stop. Pick up.

I had five missed calls from her. Not even one from Lucas. I had to say something to her or she could show up at my door anytime.

Me: Soon. I promise. Just not tonight.

Her text came immediately.

Elizabeth: Soon better be in the next couple of days, Clem, I mean it.

Hannah leaned in to look at our conversation.

"You two really are close. Why don't you call her now?"

"I can't. I need some time. And this stupid dinner thing tomorrow? I have a bad feeling about it."

"You'll have to tell them about London. Now that everyone in school knows. What if your parents find out the same way Lucas did? It would be insane."

"Fuck," I rubbed my temple. "It wasn't supposed to be like this. I need more time."

"You're out of time."

***

I had a hard time letting Hannah go the next day. Lucas was right. I was a coward.

My father was the first one to arrive. He was team Sylvia now as far as I could see. He called me to tell me that he was going straight to my mother's apartment. Madison came to the house two hours later. She walked around the empty space, making small talk about the color of the paint in the kitchen and the nuances of the new beige bathroom tiles.

When Tyler finally arrived, the first thing he announced when he set foot inside the house was the time his plane for Boston was leaving tomorrow morning. Then he hugged us and dragged me upstairs to his completely empty room. Madison stayed behind talking on the phone.

"Love it," he said looking around. "Suits Mom perfectly. It's so clinically clean and neat. I bet she caused the fire to burn my posters." I laughed. When he was in high school his walls were covered in posters of naked women. "I thought she would take them off the minute she saw my back after graduation, but she didn't," he said and looked at me. "Did she tell you why?"

"We weren't exactly talking. Why did you have them anyway? I always wondered. You had so many girlfriends, and I know you were having sex."

"It made you, Mom, and Madison uncomfortable, and you stayed out of my room."

I burst out laughing.

"You look tired," he smiled at me.

"Yeah, Hannah spent the night, and we didn't sleep that much."

I watched for his reaction when I mentioned her. I still remembered how he asked me about her on Christmas. Tyler looked at his shoes.

Interesting.

I stayed silent to give him time to continue.

"I got the impression she was mad at me on your birthday. Did I offend her?"

"Um, I think you pretty much offended everyone at the table when you called us kids."

"Is that it?" Tyler sounded shocked. "I called her a kid and she looked at me as if I had skinned her cat."

"Hannah's a dog person."

"Who cares?" he mumbled.

You, apparently.

"I don't think it's that simple," I started. "She's my best friend, and you did some shitty things when we were little. You once overheard us talking about her first real date. You were a senior. Remember?"

"No. I don't," he spat way too fast. I suppressed a smile.

"You spend two hours telling us stories about how you and your friends talked about the girls you went out with. She stood her date up because she was scared of the things he would say about her later."

"Big whoop," Tyler rolled his eyes. "She missed a date with a pimply freshman."

"He was a sophomore," I narrowed my eyes. He was tapping with his foot and that was the longest conversation we ever had about a girl. "And he asked her out again next year when you were already gone. They ended up dating for a few months."

"Turns out I did no harm, did I?" he was pouting.

"Where are you?" Madison's voice came from the hallway and interrupted our conversation.

"In my room," Tyler yelled and seemed relieved she showed up to save him from our exchange.

Madison's face appeared at the door, her eyes shut.

"Is it safe to look? Did he bring new posters?"

I didn't answer for a moment. Then my brain signalized me that the question was obviously for me.

"No," I cleared my throat. "It's fine. You can look."

Madison opened her eyes and smiled.

"I love how empty those walls are," Madison joked.

"Oh, don't tempt me, monster Maddie. In half an hour I could turn this place into a sixteen-year-old virgin's room again."

"Sixteen?" Madison and I asked at the same time.

"I was a wallflower," Tyler batted his long eyelashes our way.

I felt strangely calm and pleased. I almost forgot the thing I was going to have to suffer through tonight.

"Does anyone know what's so important to discuss?" Tyler asked.

"Sylvia," the three of us dragged and laughed.

"Has anyone had a normal conversation with her?" I asked.

"Today or like ever?" Tyler deadpanned.

"I sort of did," Madison said. "She saw pictures of an event I helped organize in a magazine. She spent ten minutes explaining to me why I am bad at my job. Does it count?" She was looking at me like her eyes were extracting information from my brain without me noticing.

"Stop that," I frowned at her. Her pink lips parted as if she was about to say something, but she changed her mind.

"OK, enough with the small talk." She clapped her hands together. "Get your asses downstairs. We're going to that dinner and you're both starting to talk to Mom. I'm done entertaining her with my life while you two ignore her."

Madison turned her back at us and left the room. The sound of her heels irritated me. It reminded me of Mom.

"She's right," Tyler surprised me.

"About what?"

"We tend to leave her to deal with Mom and Dad while I distance myself and you play the victim part. It's not exactly fair."

***

Sylvia and Richard Hartley looked at me with suspicion. For a moment I thought they knew about London, but I dismissed that theory fast. If they knew I hadn't submitted one single college application, they wouldn't just look funny at me. It would be just like Hannah said. Insane.

We were all sitting around the table in Mom's new apartment. She made the effort to cook for us, something she stopped doing altogether when Tyler moved out. She said it wasn't worth the hassle for only two people. It seemed easier to me to cook for two, instead of five.

My stomach was empty. Everyone was munching something, but I couldn't eat. I hadn't had a proper meal for days. I was poking the food on my plate thinking about what Tyler said about Madison. Did she really take more shit from Mom and Dad while the two of us played roles that helped us skip a thing or two?

The more I thought about it, the more I realized that yes, she did that. For years. Probably from the moment we were born. I just couldn't remember that far back. But I remembered all the hairdos, how she picked me up from school when I was little. She was playing the role of a mother to me. And I used her to fulfill my parents' dreams of a perfect daughter while I had the luxury to be the rebel. I had that luxury because of Madison.

Dad cleared his throat.

"Well, kiddos. You're probably wondering why we're all here," he sighed. "I'm glad we're. That fire could have really changed our family forever. Your mother and I want to make some changes. To start a healing process of some sort. We want our family to be a safe environment for you to share everything that concerns you."

"If there is anything," Sylvia looked at us one by one, "Anything any of you wants to share with us, we're here."

I snorted deliberately. I wanted her to know I wasn't buying it. Dad laughed nervously.

"Well, Sylvia, maybe they need more time. It's not like a light switch."

"Do you want to start, Clementine?" She ignored Dad.

I got used to my name while I was living with the Coles. But from my mother's mouth, it irritated me all over again.

"No, but we know you're going to try to make me."

"No one is making you do anything, sweetie," Dad supplied.

"Bullshit. Mom told me about *your* decision. You want me to stay in California."

Dad looked at Sylvia with an accusatory look.

"We're open to suggestions..."

"That's not what we agreed on," Mom cut him off. "You're doing it again. Giving her what she wants. Trying to be the good guy while I end up being the bitch."

"I don't think that forcing her would do her any good..."

They started fighting while the rest of us listened. I looked at Madison. Her eyes were pinned on me.

"She's not ready to live on her own," Mom said with a tone that suggested she wasn't taking any objections. "In fact, I think I should move back in. She's just a child. An angry child. Do I have to explain to you how this is a bad combination? Do you want her to run away with someone covered in tattoos, driving a motorcycle?"

"That's more likely if I live with you." I grinned at her.

Madison laughed grimly. Everyone turned their gazes to her.

"Clem is not the innocent child you make her out to be," she said, looking straight into my eyes. "Just admit it, Clem," she was challenging me. "You kept your mouth shut on purpose." No one was talking, not even me. "You saw the possibility of playing the victim and you took it. Like you always do." She leaned forward and looked me straight in the eyes. "I give you one chance to say it yourself."

"Say what?" I yelled at her.

"That you hid Mom's alcoholism on purpose. It wasn't because you were a child or didn't know what to do. You took pleasure in her misery. Just be an adult and say it. If it wasn't for the fire, you would have never told anyone."

I thought I would feel ashamed if it ever came to the point to confess that, but I felt strangely unaffected.

"Yes! I would have done exactly that," I hissed. "What about you? You talk with her on the phone every fucking day. I bet you sensed there was something."

"Of course I did. But I thought she was just unhappy. How could I know she was drinking herself to sleep every night?"

"Jeez, I don't know," I pretended I was thinking. "You could have asked. Have you ever considered picking up the phone and calling *me* instead of her? Asking *me* what was going on? None of you asked," I looked at Dad and Ty, then I turned my focus back to Madison. "But especially you. You never ever called me."

That wasn't the only thing I accused her of. I hated that she started over somewhere else and forgot about me. I knew I had no right, given everything she did for me when I was little, but I felt like she deserted me the moment her foot was out the door.

"Because I couldn't stand your whining! Talk like the adult you pretend to be, and maybe we could have a bond. You chose to play that game. Clementine against everyone else. I didn't force that on us. You did it."

I couldn't sit anymore. I shot up and so did Dad. He was still silent, but his face twisted with worry.

"I did that because you left me! You took care of me more than anyone in this room and you just left me. You became the perfect daughter. The pretty one. The smart one. The one that was presentable. The one that exceeded all the expectations. You were the *wanted* one. The one with the beautiful name. I was the one that should have never been born."

Madison rolled her eyes.

"This again?" she asked.

"About that name," Sylvia tried to speak. I cut her off.

"I don't want to hear it."

"You should. There is a whole story."

She sounded calm. Like we were not in the middle of a fight.

"I don't care about your stupid stories! I wanted a mother that loved me. And you made quite the effort to point out you were not that mother."

"Clementine, calm down," she ignored my statement. "You have it all wrong. It's true I didn't want a third child..."

"Oh my God." I shook my head in disbelief. "You won't stop, will you? Even when I tell you I don't want to hear it."

"You need to hear it. To understand."

"I don't want to understand you. I want to get away from you. Madison is right. I wanted to hurt you. You were hurting yourself with your drinking problem, and I decided it was good enough for me. I knew, the *whole* time I knew, I could just call dad and say the word, and he would help you. I just didn't want to."

I paused for a second. An idea was already forming inside my head. The anger made me drop the last bomb.

"I didn't apply. Not to a single college." My mom's face went blank. I knew it. "I did it to piss you off. To make you feel ashamed in front of all your friends and neighbors. You know, the people who really matter to you. And not only that, but my *hobby* got me an internship. In England. I'm moving, and I'm never ever coming back."

"What?" Dad's voice boomed. I straightened my back and looked at him.

"I'm leaving."

"You can't do that."

"Really? After everything I said, you think it's as simple as that? That I'll give in just because you said so?"

"You're not leaving, Clementine." Dad sounded determined. "I have some connections. We will get you into a college and you'll stop with this nonsense now."

That was the last straw. I took my phone, shot a quick text, and ran out of the apartment. Thirty seconds later, Tyler caught up with me.

"Do you want to talk?"

"No."

"Okay."

I laughed grimly. He frowned.

"What are you laughing about? You said you don't want to talk, and I agreed with you."

"Because it suits your interest. Why would you burden yourself with problems when you can just go with the flow? *Clementine wants to leave. She doesn't want to talk. Okay then. No worries,*" I did a poor imitation of his voice.

"You really are confused. I think some time away would do you good."

"Confused?" I raised my voice again.

"Yes," he said calmly. "You scream you don't want anyone telling you what to do. Then you scream at people who respect that wish and accuse them of not caring. I think you are confused."

"I'll clear my head then."

"At Hannah's?" he asked. I hesitated.

"Yeah. Is that a problem?"

"No. I just don't want you to be alone in that depressing house. We just want to know where you're going."

I unlocked my car.

"It's *we* now? I can't believe you, Ty. Seriously."

"Do you need a ride?"

"You don't have a car."

"I could drive yours and then walk to my hotel," he suggested.

"No. But thank you for the offer," I hugged and squeezed him. "I love you," I said. I couldn't remember the last time I said it to anyone.

"Love you, little monster. Call me when you calm down?" he asked.

I nodded, and I got inside the car. I looked in the back view mirror, and I saw them all. They had followed me. The look on Madison's face was curious. Dad was crushed, and Sylvia just stared at me. This time there was no judgment in her eyes, no annoyance. She contemplated the end of our relationship. And she accepted it.

CHAPTER TWENTY-FOUR

Lucas

About ten hours after Clementine left the Hartley's family dinner, Hannah Spencer called me to inform me that she had boarded a plane in the middle of the night and left for London. Hannah also told me everything Dylan Williams and Amy did from the first time he kissed Clem up until the day I screamed at her about London.

A day later, on Monday morning, I saw the two of them strolling in the school hallway. Perfectly calm. Perfectly happy. I knew that Clem hadn't confronted Dylan at all. The thought of him getting away unscarred from it all made my blood boil. Our eyes locked and he smirked.

I just pounced on him. It was way overdue. The moment I hit him I realized I wasn't going to stop until I saw his face covered in blood. It took three people to get me off of him.

I had no idea who my parents charmed and how exactly, but I got suspended for only two weeks. When I came back, Hannah became my misery buddy. She was as mad as me. Clem lied to her brother that she was going to spend that night after their family dinner at her place. Instead, she met my mother at the airport without even texting her BFF she was leaving.

"I'm so pissed at her. This is classic Clem," she murmured the first time we talked after my suspension. We were sitting on the bleachers. I was staring at the grass on the field; she was flipping pamphlets for prom.

"Cruel and selfish?" I supplied, not expecting an answer, but it was Hannah Spencer. Of course I was getting an answer. That girl talked more than my mother.

"What?" She looked at me like I was crazy. "No. She's not cruel. I meant her sneaking out like that. It was so impulsive. What was your mother thinking, by the way?"

"She thinks she did her a favor," I ran my hand through my hair in a nervous manner. "This was the worst thing she could do. Clementine needs a whole different thing."

"I know!" Hannah squealed.

We had a lot of talks like that one, Hannah and I. The person I didn't want to talk to at all was my mother.

"Are you going to start talking to me soon?" she asked while I helped clean the kitchen after breakfast one morning.

"Don't hold your breath."

"Come on, Lucas," she sighed. "It's March already. It's been more than a month. It's a little excessive, don't you think?"

"Excessive?" I played the word in my mind a few times. "No, I don't think so. I was perfectly fine before you invited her here. All of this could have been avoided if you just didn't get involved. But you can't do that, can you? You always have to meddle in other people's business."

"Whose business is that? Clementine's or yours?"

"Both."

I tried to remain calm and not engage in the conversation, but I was on edge, and she was becoming pushy lately. At the beginning, she gave me space to deal with everything. But with every day that passed, she was forcing me to talk. I left a glass on the kitchen counter with a thud. Mom immediately turned to face me. She was ready for an outburst. I planned to be totally in control.

"Okay. You want to know what I think. Here it is. *You* introduced her to that old creep who lured her in London. *You* knew about it, and you didn't tell me. And finally *you* bought her a ticket and boarded her on a fucking plane without even considering I might have a problem with that."

"No." Mom looked at me like she had to tame me. "I knew you would have a problem with that. But it wasn't about you. She needs this."

"Bullshit."

I noticed she didn't comment on my language. She didn't even make a face.

"You love her, right? Then you should be happy that she's happy."

"What if she's not?" I asked more aggressively than I intended. When the fuck did she even get into this jewelry making shit? "Why are you so sure she's happy?" Mom opened her mouth, then closed it with a guilty look on her face. I chuckled.

"You two are talking, aren't you?"

"Yes."

That chicken. She talked to my mother but didn't answer any of my calls or texts.

"Fine. Tell me where she is; I'll go find her. If she can talk to you, she can talk to me."

"No! Lucas, grow up," Mom came closer to me and put a hand on my shoulder. "I'm not letting you harass her. She's not ready to talk to you. You can't force her."

Her nagging tone was getting on my nerves. This exchange could turn into a fight any minute now.

"Well, I'm not ready to talk to you, and you are forcing me." I took my car keys and went to school.

These days I was so hostile that even Chase had a difficult time making me do anything. I was spending a lot of time with Hannah. At first, we talked only about Clementine, but I started to like her. She wasn't as annoying as I thought.

"Do you think she'll come back?" Hannah asked me while we were eating chocolate waffles the same day I told my mother I wanted to go to England and find Clementine.

The question pierced me like a knife. I wasn't ready to think about any other possibility. I didn't answer though.

"Tyler thinks she'll come back, but I'm not so sure anymore," she added while stuffing a large piece of waffle in her mouth. I looked at her and pretended to be shocked. She laughed.

"I know you know. Clem told me you figured me out on her birthday. He asked me for my number before he went back to Boston, just in case she contacted me."

"So you're talking?"

"Texting," Hannah tapped her mouth with a napkin.

"Sexting?" I raised a brow.

"No!" she roared and glanced at me. "But a girl can dream."

"I can't see you with him. You're too put together. He's all over the place."

"People change. Clem did when you were together. If you two had more time, I think she would do everything in a different way."

"Or you're finding excuses for your best friend."

She leaned across the table and almost whispered.

"Can I tell you something embarrassing?"

"Do I have to reciprocate after?" She rolled her eyes. I laughed. "Go ahead."

"I'm jealous. Tyler told me Clem was only talking to your mother and Madison. I get your mother. But Madison? She can talk with her, but not with me?"

"Believe me, I'm having the same sentiment regarding my mother. In your case, I think she'll come around. You're her best friend."

I knew Clem would reach out to Hannah. And me? I had no idea what she thought about us anymore. I came back home later that day feeling restless. I tried to entertain myself, but every room in the fucking house reminded me of her.

I stormed out. I didn't know where I was going until I saw her.

Sylvia Hartley was just coming home and passing through her front door. She moved back in just two days after Clem left. I marched over there, and I rang the bell. She opened the door and cocked her head sideways, waiting for me to speak. I didn't.

"Can I help you?" she asked with a tone that implied she wanted to get rid of me.

"Can I come in?"

"Why?" She narrowed her eyes. Well, that's where Clementine got her suspiciousness. I leaned a shoulder on the door frame and exhaled loudly.

"I'm mad and I want to scream at someone. My mother's kind of used to it, so I decided I could scream at you for a change."

Sylvia smiled, moved away from the door, and waved me in.

"Come on in then."

I did. Memories of the night Clementine and I spent in this house flooded my brain. I wondered if the daffodil was still on her ceiling, or if she peeled it off the day I publicly dumped her in the school hallway.

"I'm not actually planning on screaming at you," I explained. "I just need a distraction."

Sylvia ignored my words and led me to their kitchen. She opened the fridge, looked inside, and closed it with a thud.

"I'll order some pizza."

Two minutes later, she hung up the phone and sat at the table across from me.

"So, is she talking to you?" Sylvia asked.

"No."

"Me neither."

"How is she?" I asked. Sylvia raised a brow as if I was stupid. "I know she's talking to Madison. I presume she tells you everything. She's your favorite child."

Sylvia looked at her perfect nails and pouted.

"Well, I like Tyler too."

We looked at each other for about a minute. Then she smiled and added.

"I love all my children. I really messed things up with Clementine, but that doesn't change the fact that I love her. We just got used to hurting each other, and no one was ready to let go of that. It was the only thing we knew."

"I don't think she sees things in the same light as you do."

"Well, like I said, I messed up," she paused. "She's fine, according to Madison."

"Good."

"You know, we never really talked after I came back from rehab. Thank you for getting us out of the house that night. You saved our lives."

"I did it for her. Not you."

"Mm...I'm not so sure about that," she scanned my face. "You are Elizabeth Cole's son. That woman is famous for her never-ending need to help others. I get the feeling you take after her."

"Great," I murmured. "I hope I'm not prone to jeopardizing my relationships with my loved ones just to help total strangers."

Sylvia smiled, looking like she was enjoying our conversation way more than she expected.

"I talked with your mother a couple of times since Clem left. She wanted to help my daughter when she invited her to stay with you, but Elizabeth mostly hoped it would benefit you."

"Yes, I know. She wanted me to forgive Clementine for kissing someone else when we were fourteen. Turns out, it wasn't exactly my problem after all." My tone was sharp.

"What do you mean?" Sylvia looked intrigued. I took a deep breath.

"I was obsessed with your daughter. I never really hated her. I kept telling myself I did because I had to attach a feeling as a reason for my obsession. Love was not an option. So, I repeated to myself that I hated her until I forgot there was another feeling lurking inside me. So what my mother really did was expose me to an unhealthy amount of Clementine Hartley on a daily basis until I couldn't fool myself anymore."

"Was that a bad thing?" her tone implying it really wasn't.

"Considering she's an ocean away from me and not returning my calls?"

"Have you thought that maybe she would return and have a clear idea of what she wants? Do you want her to be here trying to figure herself out while making mistake after mistake, all of which you would be an audience to? Or do you want her to come back some day and give you closure without hesitation?"

"I don't want closure. I want her," I said through my clenched teeth. Sylvia paused for a moment.

"Don't judge your mother, okay? She helped a girl you obviously love. Is that a good or a bad thing?"

What happened to that woman? Before I could find an answer to that question, she continued.

"That's what I asked myself. Elizabeth helped my child. Should I hate her for it or should I be grateful? Don't get me wrong." She lifted a hand and slid it over her hair. "I didn't come up with that on my own. I wanted to strangle your mother at the beginning. My therapist pointed me in that direction."

"So you're not mad at my mother?" I asked, perplexed.

"No, she did the right thing for Clementine. I'm thankful for it."

I spent a couple of hours in Sylvia Hartley's empty home. The house looked huge for a single person. I felt sorry for her. Later that evening, when Sylvia was seeing me off at the door, I looked at their staircase.

"Can I go up to her room for a second?" I asked.

"I guess," Sylvia dragged. "You're not doing anything perverted, are you?" She looked disgusted from the possibilities that went through her head. I laughed.

"Just a quick look. I'm not turning into a stalker, I swear."

She nodded, and I went to Clementine's room. I immediately looked at the ceiling. The daffodil was still there. I was glad she hadn't peeled it off in a nervous breakdown.

I went back home. Everyone was in the living room. No one talked to me, since I hadn't really been talking to them for more than a month. I threw myself on the couch next to mom. She looked at me with caution.

"Was she wearing the necklace when she left?"

I felt three pairs of eyes staring at me. Mom rubbed her cheek.

"Sorry, honey. She was crying. I was worried. I didn't pay any attention to that."

"Okay," I said calmly. "I understand."

I gave her hand a gentle squeeze. I felt good for the first time since Clementine first started pulling away from me.

"Thank you for helping her. I'm sorry I was a dick. You did the right thing. She needed you."

I saw on her face she had a million questions to ask me, and I lifted one finger in the air.

"Only one, please."

"How do you feel about her decision to leave?" she cocked her head waiting for my answer. I thought about it for a second.

"I want her to be happy."

CHAPTER TWENTY-FIVE

Clementine

I got back to my tiny room in the house I shared with eight other people to find my sister Madison with two empty wine glasses in her hands.

"Oh, good, you're home," she smiled.

She landed in London three days ago and although we were in a better place now, and I really enjoyed seeing a familiar face, I really needed her to go back to her hotel room. Apparently she wanted us to drink wine.

I was in a bad mood. Duncan turned out to be an even bigger asshole in person. I didn't know that was possible. I had been here for two months now, and I hadn't seen him smile. Not even once. Most of the people who worked with him rarely dared to even look him in the eye. What the hell did Elizabeth see in this guy?

I asked her that on the phone on the way home today. She laughed.

"Well, I was young, and he was older, talented, famous. I was attracted to his dark vibe."

I loved to talk with her on the phone. I asked about everything and everyone except Lucas. I couldn't bear hearing news about him. Although I was dying of curiosity. Where was he going after graduation?

"Honestly," Madison was looking at me with a face that suggested I had something gross somewhere on me. I glanced down. My clothes were fine. "You're starting to look as grumpy as you describe that boss of yours. I think London doesn't agree with you. You should come back home with us."

Us meant Madison and Sylvia. Maddie was here with a client. I had no clue what Mom was looking for here, but I wasn't going to ask.

Madison and her renowned boss were traveling with their newest client. The daughter of a third-generation politician was marrying the son of one of the richest financial investors in London. The bride could pretty much buy every bridal dress in Europe, which obviously made her indecisive and irritated Madison.

"Are you even going home? I thought you were going to Paris in a few days?"

"Not if that spoiled brat buys a dress. I have two days to make her buy something. I want to go home."

"Poor Maddie." I made a pouty face. "Forced to sleep in five-star hotels in every capital in Europe, while the bride-to-be picks up the check for everything." I looked at her as if she was personally responsible for my misery, and I continued with annoyance. "You don't even have to go out. They bring the dresses to you. You could go to Paris, Madison, and instead of trashing every dress you see here, you want to press her into buying one, just so you can go back home?"

Madison passed me a glass of red wine. I raised a brow.

"It's allowed here and I'm the safest person to get drunk around, I promise."

I believed her. I couldn't imagine Madison getting drunk. She would have to set aside her manners and risk compromising herself. And we all knew she had to be perfect all the time.

I took the glass from her hands and left it on my nightstand. I haven't touched alcohol since the New Year's Eve party, and that night was still haunting me, so no wine for me, thank you very much.

"Where did you even find those glasses?"

"I bought them on my way here. I don't want to drink from a cardboard cup."

"Well, feel free to leave at any time."

Madison watched me for a couple of minutes while I was nervously cleaning up a bit, then started talking.

"You should come to the hotel. We'll have a girls' night."

"When did we ever have a girls' night?" I snorted.

"Tomorrow," she cheered. "We will drink some champagne. Oh, no wait. I forgot Mom was an alcoholic. No drinking... Nails? Maybe some facial..."

"Are you out of your mind?" I hissed.

"She wants to talk to you," Maddie shrugged as if it was no big deal.

"Do you want to get kicked out of the hotel? Imagine me and Mom in a closed space for the first time since I ran away."

Madison thought about it for a moment.

"I don't see a problem. You are coming." She started collecting her phone and purse.

"No, I'm not," I tried to get her attention.

"Tomorrow," she said, already at my door. "After work. We'll be waiting," she shut the door behind her before I had a chance to say anything else.

The next evening, I was sitting on a chair in Madison's room, and I kept my mouth firmly shut. Her boss made her go to a boutique and scream at someone who apparently stood them up earlier today and didn't send the wedding dresses they were supposed to.

Mom was looking at me grimly from the other side of the room. I had the sudden urge to say something. Madison's job was a safe subject.

"When is she coming back exactly?" I asked.

"I don't know," Mom said with a soothing voice. Her eyes were still scanning my face. "She left a couple of hours ago, so probably soon."

"Would you please stop?" I asked with a sharp voice.

"Stop what?" she cocked her head.

"Looking at me like you're about to dissect me."

Sylvia chuckled.

"Is that how I look at you?" she asked. "That must be unpleasant."

I couldn't read her expression or her tone, so I had to ask.

"Are you making fun of me?"

She scowled.

"No. Not at all."

I saw it for a moment only; she covered it up so fast. But it was there. The awkwardness between us. It was a mutual feeling, and it made my throat unclench a little. I took a deep breath.

"How is the therapy going?"

It was a stupid question, but I honestly had no idea what to talk about with my mother. Madison should have been here as a buffer between us. She always had some chit chat ready on the tip of her tongue.

"You should ask my therapist about that," she joked. "Good. I think. It opened my eyes on some difficult topics."

I couldn't help it. I had to ask.

"Like what?"

"Marriage. Parenting," she sighed. "You."

I crossed my legs and tried to find a more comfortable position on that freaking chair. There was none. I stood up and started walking around the room.

"Why are you here? If you want to make me come back with you, you're wasting your time. It's not happening."

Sylvia shook her head.

"What then? A little vacation with Madison? Shopping? Sightseeing?"

"No. I came to see you. To talk to you. But I'm not pressuring you into coming back. Although I wouldn't mind if you decided to do it."

"How is Dad?" I asked, trying to postpone the inevitable part of the conversation.

"Worried. Proud," she smiled. "We didn't think you could manage being here alone."

"Of course you didn't. Is there anything you ever thought I could do?"

"Yes. As a matter of fact, there is."

"And what is that?" I asked with a snort.

"I thought you could forgive me."

My eyes started burning. I turned my back on her. I couldn't bear her seeing my tears. I waited for a second just to be sure my voice would sound normal and not like I was about to weep.

"Maybe that's the one thing I would never be able to do," I finally said.

"Maybe," she agreed. "Can I tell you the story? About your birth? About your name?"

I hesitated.

"It's fine if you're not ready. But I want to tell you someday."

I'd lie if I said that I wasn't interested. And she seemed calm and in control. She wasn't bitchy or snarky. So I turned to face her, and I nodded.

"I was so excited to get back to work. I wasn't sure what I was going to do, but I wanted to do something. Madison was six. Tyler was finally three. He was so unwary. Boys, you know. Maddie was jealous of the attention I had to pay to him, so she acted out. Your father was constantly working. I was so tired and so sick of it. The potty training, the baths, the tantrums. I just couldn't take it anymore. Going back to work was a huge thing for me. And just when I thought I was done with all that baby raising and I could finally go back to being a normal human, we found out I was pregnant with you."

Tears started filling up my eyes again, but I didn't look away this time.

"Your father was so happy. He told everyone. Your grandparents, his colleagues. And I felt like my life was over. Like I would never be able to have what I wanted. I hated you. I'm sorry. I know it sounds awful. But I did. And I hated your father for wanting you. It was like you were more important to him than I was. We spent nine months arguing, and I was in tears most of the time. Then I gave birth to you, and I felt so incredibly guilty. I couldn't believe I had spent the previous months hating something so small and innocent. So I decided to name you Clementine. I've told you what it means. A lot of times. Merciful. I wanted you to have mercy on me and forgive me for all the months I spent hating you."

I was sobbing by the window, not even trying to hide how upset I was.

"But it looked like you picked up on my feelings in those nine months. You were always crying. All day long. I couldn't pacify you, no matter what. And then your father would come back home in the evenings and you would calm yourself down in his arms. It was messed up, and it probably was related to my depression, but I had the feeling that all the hatred I felt for you during my pregnancy was piled up inside you. I could swear you were punishing me. With the years, it became a vicious circle. I felt you were provoking me with every step, with every word. And I had the twisted need to control you because of it. I was a horrible mother to you. I wasn't the best mother to Madison and Tyler, but I was a horrible one to you."

Sylvia stopped talking for a few minutes. Probably to give me some time to calm down, and when I stopped crying, she continued.

"That's the reason I named you Clementine. Not because I wanted to punish you or make you feel out of place. I named Tyler and Madison on a whim. I just liked those names. But I wanted yours to have a meaning. It's selfish, I know. Wanting you to forgive me instead of giving you what I owed you as a mother."

The door flung open, and Madison waltzed in.

"Hey, sorry I'm late. What did I miss?" She was smiling, but after one look at my no doubt red and swollen face, her smile dropped. "Are you okay?" she asked me and looked at Mom with narrowed eyes.

I paused to assess my current state of mind. Then I nodded.

"I want to splash my face and then...girls' night?"

Both Madison and Sylvia looked at me like I had a second head. I rolled my eyes.

"Nails or facials first?" I shouted on my way to the bathroom. "You decide."

***

Two months later

It was the middle of June and I had spent more than four months in London. I was nowhere near where I wanted to be. I wasn't enjoying the internship. The fascination I used to have with Duncan and his work was long gone. I wasn't exactly happy with my living arrangements either.

The excitement I felt when I first landed here had evaporated. I no longer felt I was doing the right thing, and I definitely felt like I wasn't where I was supposed to be. I missed Hannah so much. I had no idea if she would ever speak to me again, since I ignored every single one of her calls, texts, and emails. She stopped reaching out about three months ago. There was just no point in my calling her now. I had to make things right in person. You couldn't possibly apologize to your best friend for freezing her out for four months over the phone.

Or could you?

A thought was lingering inside my head all day long. It appeared after a short but irritating exchange with Duncan.

"I want you to come with me to a meeting. To take notes."

"Okay. Where is Ana?" his PA usually accompanied him to those meetings.

"Who?" he asked with a frown. He had changed six assistants for the four months I had spent here. He fired five of them. I was sure Ana's fate was no different.

"Your last PA," I specified. "You hired her two weeks ago."

"Ah, yeah. I fired her."

"Shocker," I whispered to myself because, let's face it, I was scared of him.

"Wear something nice. Ditch those ripped jeans for once. I'm thinking of a pencil skirt and a shirt."

"Sure. No problem." It was like living with my mother all over again, but he was my boss and it was his meeting, so...

"Oh, and would you please get rid of that necklace of yours? It's so tacky; it's an insult to our brand."

I pursed my lips together, swung on my heels, and left his office.

I never took off the necklace Lucas gave me. I wasn't going to do it for that stupid asshole. And my idea was born at that moment.

When I left work, I took my phone out of my pocket and scrolled down my screen to find Hannah's number, but I chickened out.

I dialed Elizabeth instead. She answered right before I hung up.

"Hey, what's up?" She sounded like she was trying to hide something. Probably the fact she was talking to me. I bet Lucas was around.

"I...I'm confused," I managed to utter.

"What's wrong? Is Duncan giving you a hard time again?"

She frequently offered to talk to her ex-boyfriend and to ask him to be nicer, and this time, like every other, I refused.

"It's fine. It's not about him. He just inspired an idea."

"What idea?"

"How is he?" I realized that the question was overdue. I had to ask that months ago. Elizabeth paused for a moment.

"He's better. I think he's still miserable but in a slightly more manageable way."

"What would you say if I told you I was miserable in an unmanageable way? That I hate London, Duncan, and I never *ever* want to make another piece of jewelry in my life?" I asked breathlessly.

"Hmm, what would I say?" Elizabeth thought about it. "I would ask if you wanted me to wait for you at the airport."

I heard laughter around Elizabeth. A familiar one.

"I'm sorry...Is that my mother?" I was sure it was her high-pitched laugh, but I couldn't possibly imagine her with Elizabeth.

"Mm…Yes. We're having a barbecue." Elizabeth sounded apologetic.

"On a Tuesday?"

"Garret took the day off. The kids are free." I could almost see her shrugging it off.

"And you invited my mother? When did you even get so close?" I couldn't picture the two of them as friends.

"I didn't invite her." Elizabeth sounded secretive. Then she sighed and added. "Lucas did. He visits her from time to time. He thinks she's lonely."

Lucas Cole and his fragile ego interacting with Sylvia Hartley and her scornful personality? I burst out laughing. I laughed so hard and so long my stomach hurt and my eyes watered.

"Just come home already." I heard Elizabeth smile on the other side.

"Will you buy me a plane ticket?" I teased.

"Oh? Another secret flight?" she replied. I thought about it for a moment.

"It would be a nice final touch. I left on the sly. Why not come back the same way? But I'll ask someone else to wait for me at the airport if that's okay with you."

"Sure. Go pack your bags. I'll call you later."

Three days later, I was looking around at the airport trying to spot my best friend's golden hair.

I had sent her a text to ask her to come get me when I land.

Clementine: I'm coming home, but it's a secret. We have to talk. Can you come get me from the airport?

Her answer was infuriating because I couldn't figure out if she was being sarcastic or she would really come.

Hannah: Sure.

I sent her the details of my flight, and she didn't say another word.

Lingering for ten minutes now, I began to wonder if I had to call Elizabeth. It was two in the morning. It wasn't a great time, but I didn't want to hang around here for hours.

"Did you miss me?" I heard the familiar but not so friendly voice of my best friend. I turned around, and Hannah was looking at me with a raised brow.

"Immensely," I answered.

She looked at my suitcase, turned around, and waved me to follow her.

"I'm not helping you with that."

Hannah drove in total silence for about ten minutes. She hadn't even turned on the radio. I finally lost my patience.

"Are you giving me the silent treatment?"

She cocked her head, her eyes not leaving the road.

"I thought you were the one doing that for the past four months."

I took a deep breath and shook my head.

"I'm sorry. It's unforgivable. I left in such a hurry, and I..."

"You tend to make bad decisions under pressure," she finished the sentence for me with her icy tone. I let it go without a comment. I didn't want to argue. Mainly because it was true.

"...needed some time to distance myself from everything," I continued. "When I finally summoned the courage to read my messages, I understood how much damage I had caused to everyone, and I just returned back to ignoring you all. It was easier."

Hannah released a sigh.

"Except Madison obviously."

"Okay, I deserve that. Yes, except Madison. It was easier for me to connect with her than with you. I knew I hurt you. By the time I was ready to talk, it was too late. You seemed over it, and I didn't have the intention of coming back then..."

"So you thought *Oh well, it was nice knowing you* and just forgot about me altogether?"

"Of course not. I could never forget you. You're my best friend. I can't imagine my life without you. I was a total douche."

Hannah pulled over and turned to face me.

"God, I want to scream at you so much!" She was trying to keep her tone casual; her whole body was tense.

"So scream," I simply said. And she did. She yelled at me for ten minutes, then hugged me and cried for another ten.

"Are you coming back for good?" she asked when she was finally turning into her normal self.

"If you're asking if I'm going back to London, no. I'm not. If you're asking if I'm going back home to live with my mother forever, then also no. I have to figure school out. I have to graduate. So obviously I will be here for a while. I have no other plans beyond that."

"What about Lucas?" Hannah asked, her voice warming up to me with every sentence. I shrugged in response. I didn't know what to say. "You're an asshole, Clem. But I forgive you." She paused. "He will too."

CHAPTER TWENTY-SIX

Clementine

I saw Lucas for the first time in four months on a Friday morning. He was going out for a run, and I was lurking around outside his house for hours.

He froze for a second. I saw the surprised look on his face. So Elizabeth really kept my return a secret.

For the past seventy-two hours, I had thought about that moment a million times. I imagined us screaming at each other, throwing accusations in the other one's face. Nothing like that happened in reality.

His gaze dropped down to my neck. I knew what he was looking for. It was there. Under my tee. The chain was visible though. He frowned.

"You look like shit," he mumbled.

"Thanks," I rolled my eyes.

"What are you doing here?"

Oh, wow. I wasn't expecting us to go to the important part so fast. I took a deep breath and started talking.

"I didn't really like it in London, and I..."

"I meant in front of my house?" he clarified, and my cheeks turned red. I could feel their warmth.

"Oh. I was waiting for you. Hannah told me you were running every morning so..."

I didn't finish my sentence. He took a few steps in my direction, probably waiting for me to talk. I felt my body itching to touch his. He was so handsome. His dark hair was a mess like always, and he looked at me with a scowl I wanted to erase with a kiss.

"Do you want to tell me something or you just came here to stare at me?" he asked, and I couldn't read his tone. Was he teasing me or was he irritated?

"I want to talk to you...I..." I looked around nervously. "I've been waiting for two hours. I really have to pee."

Way to go, Clementine. That's the first truth you decided to share?

"Go pee, Clementine," he nodded, pointing to his house. "I'll go for a run." He rounded me and added, "I'll come back in about an hour, and we will talk, okay?"

"Sure. Yes. I'll wait."

Two hours later, I was in Lucas's room, and we had barely said a word to each other. I was sitting on a chair next to his desk, and he was on his bed. His back was pressed against the headboard. His hair was still wet from the shower he took.

It was a long shower. He wanted to delay the conversation.

"Can I ask you something?" I was looking at my hands.

"I thought *you* were going to do the talking."

I shot him a look, and the scowl was still on his face. I swallowed hard.

"Yes. But I don't know how that conversation is going to turn out, and my curiosity is killing me."

He closed his eyes for a moment as if he was trying to compose himself and not yell at me.

"Shoot."

"Did you peel it off?"

We both knew what I was talking about.

"Is there another option?" he wondered, and I shrugged.

"My mother?"

"No. I did it. When I finally understood that this..." he pointed between him and me, "...is never happening."

That last sentence felt like a thousand knives piercing my skin.

"You could have just left it there." I realized I was sounding offended and I had absolutely no right to sound like that, but still...

"I knew you would eventually come back, and I couldn't stand the thought that it would still be there. Like a fucking *I Love You* banner. I didn't want to give you the wrong impression."

That was it. We were over. I had forgotten how bad it hurt when he rejected me.

"Yes," I said breathlessly. "Of course. I understand."

"I doubt you do." His voice sounded colder than in the beginning of our conversation. "You barely understand yourself."

There was a moment of silence.

"Why are you helping my mother?" I changed the subject, and he snorted.

"Are you just going to ask me questions? If I knew you were going to interrogate *me*, I wouldn't have agreed to this conversation."

"Why? What's wrong with asking questions?" I asked.

"Nothing. If you ask them at the right time. I think four months is a little bit too late."

"I'm sorry." I lifted my hands in the air with annoyance. "You have to admit it's weird." I tried to read his expression, but I couldn't. It looked like he deliberately was trying to hide himself from me.

"What's so weird about it? You left. I needed to vent. I couldn't talk to my mother, because I was pissed at her for helping you. So, I just ended up at your house one day."

I opened my mouth to ask him more questions about him and Sylvia, but he was obviously done answering because he cut me off.

"No more questions, Clem. It's your turn to talk."

"What do you want to know?" I asked, and I was feeling hopeful. I knew I wouldn't be able to fix everything with one conversation, but he was talking to me. It was a good beginning. He could have just kicked me out.

"Nothing really," he answered. "I just wanted to give you the opportunity to say what you have to say. You know? Closure and shit."

He had already come to terms with everything that happened between us. He was making that perfectly clear. He didn't even need to hear my part of the story.

"I wanted to apologize. To explain." My voice sounded distant in my ears, like I wasn't the one talking.

"Apology accepted. No need to explain yourself though. I know the whole story. Hannah told me. I know why you kissed Dylan at that party. I even understand why you left for London. The lying part was something I couldn't stomach for a while, but everything is forgiven and forgotten now."

"Is it though? Because you sound like you're angry with me."

His brows shot up.

"I guess I didn't think I would see you so soon, and I definitely didn't think that I was going to be the one to explain myself."

My hands started shaking. He saw it and came to my rescue. He always came to my rescue.

"Do you have plans?" he asked with a softer tone.

"Umm..." I rubbed my forehead. "I obviously have to graduate. I'll talk to Principal Smith on Monday. He will probably want me to repeat the whole year."

"Probably. The dick that he is. You should ask your mother to talk to him."

"I might," I hesitated. "And what are your plans? If I'm allowed to ask one more question."

"My mother didn't tell you?" he asked surprised.

"We didn't talk about you," I heard how bad that sounded, but it was already too late. His jaw clenched, and his eyes narrowed.

"So you never even asked about me? About how I was doing?"

I nodded, my heart was heavy with guilt.

"And did you ask about Troy?"

"Lucas, please..."

"It's a simple question, Clem."

"Yes, I did. I asked about Troy. I asked about your father. And I specifically asked your mother not to talk to me about you."

He shot up from the bed with a murderous look on his face.

"You used to tell me that I was the unbelievable one, but you're just off the charts." He shook his head. He opened the door and stood there waiting for me to leave. I stepped out in the hallway, and he continued. "Mom and Troy love you." His tone was emotionless. "You can come here anytime you want. I won't get in your way."

"Lucas," I pleaded.

"What?" he ran a hand through his hair. "What more could you want from me?"

I bit my lower lip. He didn't reach to release it with his thumb like he usually did. I had to say the right thing this time.

"Nothing. You gave me more than I deserved."

That was the last time we spoke before he left for Seattle.

***

Principal Smith agreed to give me the opportunity to graduate without attending classes. But I had to take tests and exams throughout the year. So I was definitely stuck in California. With my mom.

It was ironic. How much time I had spent preparing to leave, then, when I actually left and pissed everyone in my life off, I only managed to stay away for a few months before I ran back to my mother.

"Do you want to watch a movie tonight?" Sylvia cut off my thoughts. I was drinking a cup of coffee by the kitchen counter, preparing to go to work.

"Sure," I agreed.

Sylvia was pretty much her best self ever lately, and I thought I owed her to make at least the same amount of efforts she was making. She wasn't even commenting on my job, which was pretty impressive.

"Just no rom-coms," I clarified. I wasn't in the mood for watching some epic love story unfolding for two hours, considering I hadn't gotten over my own.

"Oh, okay. Something sad or scary then?"

"Scary, please."

I left for work, and I called Dad. We had that arrangement. I had to call him on my own twice a week. I usually did it early in the morning because I knew he would be in a hurry for work and wouldn't have time to ask a lot of questions.

He kept his promise and came to visit every month. He was still seeing Adina, which was a shocker to us all. I had a feeling my mom wasn't exactly happy about that, but at least she was acting civil enough for him to be able to visit without hiding he was having a relationship.

And now that Lucas was gone, I was a frequent visitor at his house. I played with Troy. I talked with Elizabeth, who was having a hard time accepting Lucas was never going to live with them again. I was having a hard time accepting that too. We baked a lot, and we ate a lot. I liked baking very much.

I had the early shift at the coffee shop that day. I had to be there at six, so that we would open on time at seven. It wasn't a big deal. I was just serving people coffee and sweets, but I learned more about baking, which had become a real passion after I started that job.

"Good morning, honey," I heard the friendly voice before I could spot its owner.

"Good morning, Mrs. Jones."

Mrs. Jones was both my boss and my co-worker. Another girl came for a couple of hours a day, but it was mostly us two.

"We're starting to take orders for pies for Thanksgiving today," she reminded me.

I dreaded Thanksgiving. I knew Lucas would come back home. Ever since our last conversation in his room, we hadn't exchanged a single word. Not in person, not in texts. I had no news from him whatsoever. I asked Elizabeth about him when he first moved to Seattle; she said he asked her not to talk with me about him.

It was painful, but I knew I deserved it. I just wished I had some teeny-tiny bit of information. Like if he was dating someone and had plans to bring her home in three weeks and rub it in my face.

Not that he would actually do it. That was something I would do. Something I had already done to him. And yet I knew he would never deliberately do it to me. But what if he was in love?

My shift was ending in the early afternoon, and I had this ritual where I sat on a table in the back of the coffee shop with a chocolate waffle and I texted Hannah.

Me: Are you still BFFs with Lucas? Could you do some spying for me and check if he has a girlfriend?

Sometimes, if she had time, she would call me. That day she didn't. I only got a text back.

Hannah: Why do you care?

Me: Oh, I don't know. Maybe to plan an escape to a foreign country for Thanksgiving weekend?

Hannah: I thought you already tried that (smiley face)

Me: Ha ha. Just ask him, okay?

Half an hour later and no word from Hannah, I decided to stop stuffing my face and go back home. I parked my car and checked my phone again. I had a text. Just not from Hannah.

Lucas: Are you trying to find out if I'm dating someone?

I will kill her.

I shot a text to Hannah first.

Me: WHAT DID YOU DO?

My heart was pounding. I tried breathing in and out to calm myself. It didn't work. I had to answer something. If I just ignored his text, it would be as if I confessed that it was exactly what I was trying to do.

Me: Hey.

Me: Yes. I was trying to find out if you're bringing someone home for Thanksgiving.

I was both shocked and impressed with my honesty.

Lucas: Why?

Me: It was stupid. I'm sorry. Forget about it.

Lucas: Clementine...

Lucas: Spill it.

Me: I spend a lot of time at your place, and I just wanted to know if I should stop doing that. Around Thanksgiving.

Seven minutes passed before he answered. I counted.

Lucas: I'm glad to find out my mother is keeping her promise.

He obviously meant the promise about not sharing any information about him with me. Did that answer mean he had a girlfriend and he was glad his mother was hiding it from me? Or that he was glad I was completely in the dark about what was going on in his life?

Me: Is that a yes?

Lucas: ?

Me: Yes, you have a girlfriend and you're bringing her home for Thanksgiving?

Lucas: Don't you think she would want to go home to her parents?

My heart sank. It shrank. I couldn't bring myself to answer that. He had a girlfriend. She wasn't coming with him, but he had one. Maybe she would come for Christmas.

I got out of my car and walked inside. I passed my mother, who asked something about the movie we were watching later. I waved her off.

"Just pick one."

"Are you okay?" she asked.

"Yes. I'm going to take a shower."

That evening we sat in the living room about to watch a movie I wasn't interested in one bit.

"Mom," I started, and her eyes widened. I hadn't called her that for quite some time. "Do you remember when I stopped talking to Lucas when we were fourteen?"

I wasn't really sure if she paid that much attention to me back then.

"Yes," she was looking at me curiously. "It's not exactly something you could forget. You were so close."

"I did something. To him. To you too. I asked a boy to help me. I wanted to humiliate you."

I told her the whole story. My mother sighed and leaned back on the couch.

"I'm not surprised."

"Of course you're not. You said it yourself. I'm just as sadistic and cruel as you are. Who else would do something so shitty?"

"Everyone does shitty things, Clem. I meant that you were angry and needed to get that anger out somehow."

"I was planning on exposing you while you kissed one of our neighbors. Aren't you mad at me?" I raised my voice.

"Not at the moment. Do you want me to get mad?" She asked, sounding confused.

"Yes."

"Why?"

"I don't know," I shot up on my feet and started walking back and forth. "I need..."

"To vent? To yell at someone?"

"Yes. But I don't have a person to yell at, because I'm the one doing everything wrong."

My mother narrowed her eyes. "Do you want me to get mad at you so we could scream at each other?"

"I guess." I stopped pacing. "No." I let out a breath. "I don't want to scream at you. Can we leave the movie for another time? I'm not feeling up to it. Besides, I'm covering the first shift again tomorrow and have to get up early."

"Another time," Sylvia nodded.

I went to my room, and I grabbed my phone.

Me: Dad, can Mom and I come to Seattle for Thanksgiving?

I received a reply almost immediately.

Dad: Of course, honey.

I saw the texts from Hannah from earlier, and I finally opened them.

Hannah: I asked if he's bringing someone home for Thanksgiving.

Hannah: He knew it was you asking.

Hannah: It's not my fault he knows you so well.

Hannah: I'll forward you his text

Hannah: Lucas: Mind your own business, Spencer, and tell your friend to ask ME next time she has a question about my personal life.

I threw my phone on the bed and then nervously picked it up immediately.

Me: Forget it. I'm sorry I asked you to do that.

Me: We're going to Seattle for Thanksgiving, so we're not going to see each other.

Hannah: Are you talking about us two or you two?

Me: Both.

CHAPTER TWENTY-SEVEN

Lucas

I thought Clementine Hartley had already done everything she could have to push me away and stomp all over my feelings for her, but she surprised me.

I got home for Thanksgiving with a blossoming hope for the two of us. She had, after all told the truth, about her inquiring if I had a girlfriend. I thought she was finally starting to open up. And then I got back home just to find out she chickened out once again and left for Seattle.

Another month passed, and she was still not talking to me. No surprises there.

I had to fly back home for Christmas in two days, but at that moment I was listening to my date blabbing for the past twenty minutes about her last class. She was the only girl I had asked out since I moved here. It was our first date. I needed to go back home knowing I tried to move on. No matter the outcome.

My date helped me understand that endless talking wasn't something only high school girls did, as I used to think. It was a girl thing. Period.

When she finished her story, she looked at me with anticipation.

"What do you want to do now?"

"Head back to my room?" I shot out immediately. She blushed and I clarified. "I mean I will take you to yours first. I'm tired."

"Oh, okay."

I couldn't miss the disappointed look on her face. It made me feel like a douche, but I just didn't feel any attraction between us.

"Sorry, I talk too much," she added.

I thought about Clementine and our secrets and soundless interactions.

"Don't apologize. It's not a bad thing. At least I know what you're thinking."

She stopped in front of her building's entrance and looked at me with a smile. She seemed kind and warm. A regular girl. Not a cheerleader with a nasty attitude or someone broken to the point of self-destructiveness.

"You're not going to ask me out again, are you?" she asked with a friendly expression on her face. "It just isn't there, is it?"

"What isn't?"

"The attraction," she shrugged. "The chemistry. Whatever you want to call it. It's not there." She pointed to the space between us. I nodded.

"I'm sorry," I sighed and ran a hand through my hair. "You are sweet and totally hot. I'm just not available I guess." I paused, then squeezed her hand. She squeezed mine back, and that was it. The summary of my dating life post Clementine Hartley.

I waited until she got inside her dorm and took a walk around the campus. It was cold, but I needed the fresh air. I checked my phone. I had messages from Chase and Hannah, who were also coming home for the holidays. Nothing from Clementine. Not that I expected her to text me, but every time I looked at my phone, I noticed she hadn't.

Two days later Hannah literally dragged me out of my house barely an hour after I arrived. She insisted we had to go eat waffles at this new place I had never heard of. She was way too excited, talked louder than usual, and just couldn't stay still. I thought it was some kind of mixture between her being back home and the whole Christmas spirit thing. She looked like a girl who loved Christmas.

"You need to get laid, Spencer, it will calm you down a little."

"Fuck off," she said with the biggest smile I had ever seen on her face as we entered the coffee shop. That was a bit of a stretch because my back was pressed to the door. The line was huge. I huffed.

"Do you have to eat a waffle here? Look at the line."

On the bright side, all the tables were empty, and I quickly noticed people were taking pies and cakes to go.

"Do I?" she pushed herself up on the tip of her toes and looked ahead. "You tell me, Cole."

My gaze followed hers. Standing behind the counter, laughing and selling pies, was the most beautiful girl in the world. Hannah started jumping and waving like she was trying to get the attention of the astronauts in the International Space Station from down here. And, of course, Clementine noticed us seconds later. She smiled at us with the sincerest smile I had ever seen on her face. Her eyes were shining from across the room and her cheeks reddened, but she didn't try to hide it.

I was standing like a piece of wood. She was working? I thought she went to school. What was that about?

"Excuse me," Hannah slapped my hand playfully. "I'll go kiss my girl. Don't move."

Like I could. I was mesmerized. But Hannah's words stung a little. She could go kiss Clem and call her *my* girl, while I was standing in the back of the line with the strangers.

Hannah returned a minute later and dragged me to a table.

"I ordered you a waffle," she said.

"Of course you did."

We sat, and I watched Clementine joke around with the customers. She looked so open and free. She laughed out loud. She didn't try to hide her emotions. It was like looking at a different person.

An old lady took over for her at the counter, and my beautiful nemesis motioned towards us with our order in her hands.

"Hey," she stood in front of me. She beamed.

Her voice was filled with joy and happiness that kind of seeped into me. Her eyes were glued to my face. I dropped my gaze to her neck. The daffodil pendant was still there but on top of her shirt, not under it as usual.

"You look so happy," I said without even thinking that my perplexity was showing through my voice. It only made her laugh.

"That's because I am," she sat down next to Hannah and squeezed her in a hug. "I missed you so much."

I knew that was meant for Hannah and not for me, but when she finally released her friend from her firm grip and took a look at me, I could swear she wanted to tell me those same words.

"I have to go back," she said instead. "We're closed tomorrow, so call me, okay?" she asked Hannah.

"Hell no. I will wait until your shift is over." It was Hannah's turn to squeeze Clem. "Are you going to keep me company?" She turned to me.

"Do I have a choice?" I tapped with my fingers on the table and pretended that the next hour I would spend here eating a waffle and looking at Clementine wasn't going to be the best thing that happened to me for months.

She returned to the long line of clients, and I couldn't tear my gaze away from her.

"Are you going to eat that?" Hannah pointed at my untouched waffle. I slid the plate in her direction silently, not even glancing at her. She laughed. "You're transparent."

"So are you. You dragged me here on purpose."

"Just tell her that you don't actually have a girlfriend already."

"How do you know I don't have one?"

"Even if you do have one, the way you're staring at my best friend kind of screams game over for every other girl out there."

"I just can't stop looking at her."

"Yeah," Hannah tapped my hand with her fork. "That's creepy, by the way. Maybe turn the obsession part down a notch."

"You moved to Boston for a guy that barely knows you exist, and you talk to me about obsession."

Hannah gasped and leaned back on her chair.

"Jerk," she shouted and everyone, including Clementine, turned to us. I winked at her, and she blushed. "Oh my God," Hannah dragged with annoyance. "Did you just wink at her?"

"Have you seen him since you moved?" I ignored her attempt to ridicule me, and I pressed her about Tyler. I slid my gaze to her reluctantly.

"No," she looked down at my now almost empty plate. "But we text from time to time. The thing is I'm starting to feel like he's treating me like I'm his sister."

"Probably because he's not into you."

"Wow. And here I thought you would be happy to see me, and I would enjoy my waffle without your insults, smartass."

"Open your eyes, Spencer," I said, implying she was lying to herself about Tyler.

"You sound like Clem. Maybe you two have to follow your own advice. But by the way you're looking at each other I'm judging it is already happening. I'm guessing I'm not going to see a lot from my best friend now, am I?" she pouted.

"She's all yours, Spencer. All yours."

***

I wanted to give Hannah and Clem space and let them catch up. Mainly because I was the reason Clementine took off for Thanksgiving and it was obvious these two missed each other like crazy. The thing was our mothers made it impossible for Clementine and me to keep a distance. The following day, there was a lunch in my house that we all gathered up for. I wasn't complaining though. I was enjoying this new version of Clementine so much I couldn't get enough of her.

However, watching her interacting with her mother was a bit weird for me. It reactivated my protective instincts toward Clem. But since I was kind of a friend to Sylvia, I decided I wasn't going to take sides.

"Don't forget," Sylvia said and looked directly at me. "Dinner. Tomorrow night. At our place." I lifted a brow in a silent question.

I had no idea about this arrangement. She ignored me. "Richard, Ty, and Maddie are coming too. And Adina..." Sylvia made a dramatic pause but in a funny way, and it showed she had no issues with her ex-husband's girlfriend. "So no excuses." Sylvia's tone was firm and suggested she wasn't taking no for an answer.

I had no intention of saying no to spending more time around the fun and easy-going Clementine. She still had that tendency of closing up in silence from time to time, but the darkness was gone. She looked at peace with herself.

After the news I was going to share another meal with Clem, I decided it was about time I approached her before things started feeling weird between us.

She was in the kitchen with my mom. I could hear them giggling, and I just couldn't resist the urge to peek. It was obvious she felt at home. She was digging in the cabinets looking for something, her back turned to me. She talked to my mother, who was the only one aware I was leaning a shoulder on the wall eyeing them.

"I don't see a box at all. I checked everywhere. Can we just eat on different dessert plates? I swear the cake is so good, they would eat it from the table." Clementine started opening the cabinets for a second time and added, "Or I could go home to pick up ours?"

"Or," I pushed off the wall and approached her. "You could ask someone who lives here to tell you where they are."

Clementine didn't freeze with the sound of my voice. She didn't take a step back when she turned around to face me, and I was pretty close. I could smell her pink grapefruit shampoo from where I was standing.

I loved that smell.

"Move. I know where the plates are."

She just smiled and made a hand gesture inviting me to help her. I rounded her and opened a cabinet she had already looked in. Twice. I wanted to tease her about it, but Mom killed the moment with her not-so-subtle exit.

"I'll go check if the others need anything," she said and winked at me on her way out.

"You don't actually live here anymore," Clem taunted me with a grin.

"I suppose that's true." I smiled back at her and placed the box on the kitchen island, then opened it. "These need a wash." I showed her the dusty plates she was looking for.

"Will you keep me company?" She asked and my eyes fell on her lips. I smiled.

She started washing the plates and we fell into the familiar silence between us for a moment. I was glad I didn't offer to wash the plates for her. This way I could just stare at her. So, I leaned on the counter and admired her pretty face. The warmth I felt inside my chest was spreading all over my body. Then she looked at me with a wicked grin. She was up to something.

"I went on a second date with Matt Pearson," she said. "He told me he stood me up because of you, just like I thought."

"Oh yeah?" I smirked and took a step closer to her. If the fact that I was invading her personal space did anything to her, she didn't show it at all. "And how was it?"

"You were totally right. We weren't a good fit."

"I bet I was right about the others too," I teased. She paused and then looked me straight in the eye.

"I bet you were." She bit her lower lip, suppressing a smile. I reached and released it like I always did. I felt her hot breath on my finger.

"You are flirting with me, nemesis."

I saw her blissfully closing her eyes for a moment when I used her nickname. Then she opened them, cocked her head sideways, and thought about it for a few seconds.

"I suppose that's true."

CHAPTER TWENTY-EIGHT

Clementine

I looked at my reflection in the French windows. We were at Chase and Amy's for the annual New Year's Eve party their parents were throwing. I envied my mother for her nonchalance. She waltzed in there like it was nothing. Like the man she made out with five years ago wasn't here with his wife. Like his wife wasn't our hostess for the evening. I managed to enter the house only because the twins weren't here.

I had no one else to spend New Year's with. Hannah got an invitation for some party and went back to Boston. So I was stuck with the married couples and the children who weren't old enough to attend a party on their own.

Dressed in my plaid dress in red and black, I looked like my mother always intended me to. I was pretty and presentable. I looked like a grown-up and not like a deranged teen with anger issues. And I liked it.

I had spent the last half-hour observing Troy trying to impress a girl, and I had to ask myself if Lucas and I looked so ridiculous when we were putting all our efforts into the task of hiding our feelings.

"That son of mine will be a man capable of great romantic gestures," Elizabeth's voice came from behind me.

"I think that can be said for both your sons." I took the daffodil pendant between my fingers.

"Probably." Her eyes followed the movement of my hand. "Sylvia just told me you decided to stay in California after graduation."

I had finally summoned the courage to share my plans with my mother. I told her about my dream of opening a bakery. I was skipping college after all. She didn't like it, I could see it on her face, but she kept her mouth shut, which was huge progress.

"I always thought I needed to go somewhere else to be happy," I tried to explain to Elizabeth. "To get away from my mother. Turns out I needed other things. I'm at a good place right now. I don't want to…"

"Screw it up?" she asked.

"Ah." I pretended to be shocked. "You've been under some bad influence I see."

Elizabeth laughed.

"I love it when Lucas comes back home from college, but it's so nice to live in a house where no one says the F word every ten minutes."

"He looked happy. He had a lot of fun on your account."

It was hilarious. He used every possible minute to tease his mother and it made everyone laugh their asses off.

"He's a smartass." She waved my comment off.

"Did you two talk about me?" I finally asked the question that was nagging me for days. Elizabeth's gaze moved around for a few seconds before she answered.

"I think I meddled enough in your relationship. I should stop."

"Now?" I cocked my head with a smile on my face. "I just want to know if he's still mad at me."

"Did it look like he's mad at you?" Elizabeth sounded amused.

"No. I even thought we were going somewhere, but he was probably just being friendly while I drooled all over him like a bulldog."

"You should ask him," Elizabeth suggested.

"I...I probably won't."

"Why not?" Elizabeth looked intrigued.

"It's too complicated now. Maybe if I hadn't left for England, things could be different. And he's probably over..."

Elizabeth looked at something behind my back and cut me off.

"Hm. Okay, honey. It's your call," she planted a kiss on my forehead and turned her back on me. "See you later."

Mm, okay. That was weird. I followed her with my eyes. I didn't see anything that would make her leave in the middle of a conversation about her son, but she must have had a reason. I focused back on Troy and the girl he was into, and they had melted the ice while I wasn't looking. They were watching something on his phone and laughing.

My mother was nowhere in sight, and I didn't want to look for her around the house. Too much trauma there. I didn't think she would pull the same shit from five years ago, but I wasn't risking it.

I went outside. The backyard had had some renovations. There were two sunbeds next to each other in one corner, and I decided that would be a perfect place for me. I could just lie around and think.

So, I positioned myself on one of them and I closed my eyes. The first image that popped inside my head was Lucas's face. His smile. The way he lifted his brow when he was provoking me.

"You are flirting with me, nemesis."

It felt so good hearing him say those words to me. We rarely had a chance to spend more than two minutes alone after that conversation, but I had the feeling he would actually want to talk before he left for Seattle. And then he just came yesterday morning to say goodbye. He waved at me like I was his grandma.

"What are you thinking about?" a male voice asked, and it melted my insides. I squeezed my eyes shut even harder.

"Are you really here or am I hallucinating?"

If it was a hallucination, I didn't want it to go away a moment sooner than it had to. A finger touched my collar bone and slowly slid down my chest to find my pendant.

"I love that you're still wearing it. It makes me feel like you're mine."

Lucas removed his hand from me and remained silent for a moment, then he chuckled.

"Are you going to open your eyes?"

"Still debating," I said, almost out of breath.

"What's there to debate about?" he tried to sound serious, but I heard the amusement in his tone.

"If it's worth the risk of waking up and finding out you're a dream."

I heard him sigh before he ordered me to move. He lay next to me on the sunbed, and his hand found my bare thigh and positioned my leg over his. His fingertips were slowly moving on my skin.

"I don't think our hosts would appreciate this behavior," I joked.

"At least one of them has done worse things at these parties," he said, and we both burst out laughing.

"About that...have you, by any chance, seen my mother? Because I haven't in a while, and I was too scared to try to find her."

"I had to occupy her attention for a while."

His voice was so low I finally opened my eyes, and I smiled at him.

"You're still here," I said like a total dork.

"Have I ever not been?"

I pressed my body even closer to him instead of answering his question with actual words.

"What did you want from Sylvia?"

"I told her you're spending the night in my bed." His eyes dropped to my mouth and he licked his lips.

"You're kidding," I giggled.

"Of course I am. I told her I'm taking you home to talk. I don't want to piss off the mother of my girlfriend. She is quite merciless."

I raised a brow mimicking his favorite gesture.

"The mother or the girlfriend?"

"The latter. She's my nemesis. I just can't get away from her no matter how much I try."

Lucas didn't give me a chance to say anything. His mouth covered mine. There was no anger this time. No desperation. No regrets about the time that we missed. There was just the feeling that lingered between us for what felt like a lifetime.

"I love you," I whispered into his mouth. He broke the kiss and looked at me, beaming. I loved when I made him beam. He closed his eyes and pulled me closer to him.

"Finally."

Two hours later we were lying in his bed naked. Arms, legs, and souls entwined like never before. We barely spoke after we left the party. Mostly because Lucas couldn't stop kissing me all over my body.

He rolled down and bit my waist. I giggled.

"You're tickling me," I wiggled in his arms. "Are you going to explain to me why you're here? You left for Seattle yesterday, and now you're back. What happened?"

Lucas was lying between my legs, kissing the lowest part of my belly, only inches away from the spot that couldn't get enough of his mouth.

"I was here the whole time," he said and looked at me with caution.

"What?" I sat up. "You didn't board the plane?"

"There was no plane. I mean there were obviously planes that flew to Seattle. I just never planned on boarding one of them."

"Why did you say you are leaving, then?" I asked, and he shrugged.

"I thought it would be romantic to kiss you at that party like it was originally planned, and I knew it would win me extra points if I did it out of the blue." He lifted a finger in the air, warning me he wasn't finished. "And before you jump all over me, it worked, so, you're welcome."

I rolled my eyes.

"And what am I thankful for now?"

"For the surprise. You were throwing yourself at me for a week. I had to pretend I was leaving to shake things up a bit. If you knew I was staying, that kiss wouldn't have been much of a surprise."

"Asshole!" I squealed and laughed at the same time. "I wasn't throwing myself at you."

"Oh yeah?" he asked, his voice husky and sexy, and he pulled me back down on the bed. "What were you doing then?"

"Seducing you?" I asked only half-jokingly.

Lucas hid his face between my legs, but I saw his grin, and I could feel his body shaking with laughter even before I heard it in his voice.

"If that makes you feel better," he said, and his tongue pressed my clit hard.

I moaned and continued the argument.

"You can laugh at me all you want, Cole, but you can't keep your hands off of me."

"I'm not even going to try."

EPILOGUE

Clementine

A year later

I arrived at Sea-Tac late in the evening. It was the beginning of December, and it was so cold I had to use a real winter jacket instead of what I usually put on back home in California.

Lucas was waiting for me at the airport with a huge grin as always. I ran to him, and he squeezed me in his arms, buried his nose in my hair, and inhaled deeply.

"Explain it to me one more time," I could hear the longing in his tone. "Why do we have to live so far away from each other?"

I smiled and kissed his chest. I was actually pressing my lips against his jacket, and I was pretty sure he didn't even notice I was kissing him.

"Because we love each other, and it doesn't really matter."

I wanted to say it like a statement, but it came out as a question. He narrowed his eyes at me.

"Liar. You hate it too."

He was right. I hated it. At the beginning, it made sense, him staying in Seattle and me in California. But I hated every minute we spent a thousand miles away from each other.

I smiled, threw my hands around his neck, and pressed myself to his body.

"I have a very important confession to make."

He closed his eyes with an annoyed look on his face, but I knew it was just an act. He knew I was messing with him.

"You and your secrets, nemesis. Shoot."

"I hate that." I tugged on his winter jacket. "I hate the cold. I don't want to live in a place where raining for ten days in a row is considered normal weather."

His laughter echoed around us. I loved it when he laughed because of me.

"Is that your problem? The freaking weather?" I nodded. "It's a good thing you don't have to live here then. If only your boyfriend was willing to come live with you in California, you wouldn't even have to spend a night in Seattle..."

He offered to transfer a hundred times, but I always stopped him. I loved the independence I had, but I missed Lucas. And I had enough of this back and forth we had been doing for the past year. Once a month, one of us was visiting the other. We had used the fact he was coming home for Christmas to make two visits this month. But it wasn't enough. I tried to imagine what it would be like if we actually lived together. And I started laughing.

"What's so funny?" he asked.

"I tried to imagine what it would be like for us to live together, and then I remembered we already had."

"That one doesn't count." He sucked my lower lip, and it made me squeeze my thighs. "This time around we would be alone." He wiggled his brows.

"That would be nice," I said with a tone that suggested I wanted to be alone with him that very second. He read my mind as always.

"It could be arranged," he said, and his hands tightened their grip around my waist, but otherwise he didn't move. He was just looking at me with a serious expression on his face.

"Are we doing this or not, Clementine? I want a straight answer and not that *we'll see* bullshit you've been feeding me for months now."

I took a deep breath. Everything felt so right. So I just placed my cheek on his chest.

"We're doing this."

In the summer, Lucas came back to California. My father got to use those connections he wanted to use for me before I left for England and helped Lucas transfer.

I was spending a lot of time in the bakery, *my* bakery, and Lucas balanced between his new job and his classes, so the only time we had for each other was on the weekends. So when one Saturday I had to wait for Maddie at the airport and drive her home to Mom, I felt guilty it took most of my day.

I finally got back home late in the afternoon, took the two steps that were the only space between the front door and our tiny living room, and I stopped. Lucas was lying on the couch with a satisfied look on his face.

At first, I blinked not really knowing how to react. But then I remembered this wasn't even really our apartment. It was a rental.

"Are you trying to get us kicked out?" I tried to sound calm and in control, which was hard because I was obviously living with a crazy person or a twelve-year-old.

"It's pre-approved," he deadpanned.

"Not by me," I snorted.

A huge daffodil flower sticker was decorating one of the walls. It looked bigger than our couch.

"You don't like it?" He was suppressing a grin.

"It's huge."

"The one on your ceiling was exactly the same."

I approached him and stood right in front of him.

"Is this about marking your territory? Because I'm pretty sure I could find another place to live with my next boyfriend, so he wouldn't have to look at that."

Lucas grabbed me by the waist and dragged me into his lap. I straddled him and he kissed my neck.

"And *I'm* pretty sure you won't have a next boyfriend, nemesis."

The words rolled off of his mouth more like a promise than a tease. I ignored the meaning behind them partly because I was way too excited about the thing he implied and partly because I was already thinking about the erection he was pressing against me.

"I want that thing off the wall now," I said and squeezed his hair in my fists to make him look at me. He was looking at my mouth with need. The same need that I felt inside my chest. I rolled my eyes. "Fine. First thing tomorrow morning."

He got up from the couch with me wrapped around him. A moment later I was pressed against the same wall the daffodil was on. Damn, that thing was huge. Lucas's gaze caught mine before he started talking.

"Get used to it. One day I'll put a ring on your finger, nemesis. And that thing stays on the wall until then."

***

Lucas

Two years later

I was standing on the street waiting. Someone bumped into me. Hard.

"Spencer," I said before I even turned back.

"Asshole," Hannah greeted me. "How's my girl doing today?" She kissed me on the cheek. "She doesn't expect it, right?" Hannah pointed at me with a finger and an expression that said I better not screw this up.

"First of all, I think you mean *my* girl. And second of all, I've been waiting for this long enough. No way in hell am I ruining it by hinting at her a second earlier than I have to."

We started walking towards the jewelry store. Hannah seemed excited. She was bouncing up and down, asking questions and making suggestions. I, on the other hand, was sweating everywhere I could possibly sweat, and we were just buying the fucking ring.

"Where are you going to do it? In a restaurant? Can I come watch? I swear I'll hide behind a menu the whole time. She won't know I'm there." She paused, then yelled. "No! I can shoot a video! You'll watch it with your children and grandchildren. Or even better! You could postpone a little and get the whole gang together, and we could all surprise her."

I had no doubt that by the whole gang she meant our families. No, thank you.

"Don't make me regret that I called you, Spencer. Just shut up and try the fucking ring. Are you sure you wear the same size?" I asked her for a millionth time.

"Yes, jackass. I'm sure. I tried four of her rings yesterday when I came to your place. We still wear the same size."

"Didn't she ask you why you're trying her rings?" I paused. "If she suspects something, it would be on you."

"I had a date later, and I asked her for a necklace to go with my dress. She just gave me the whole jewelry box and went to take a shower. She didn't even see me when I tried them on."

"Why the hell were you on a date? You live in Boston."

I honestly hoped Hannah wasn't moving back home right now. She would turn the wedding arrangements into a circus.

"Girls have needs," she shrugged.

"Don't you have a boyfriend?" I tried to remember a name that Clem mentioned some time ago. "Stew or something?"

"Steve," she corrected. "And no. I'm totally single. Again."

I sensed by her tone she wasn't loving that fact. But I wasn't about to pity her.

"Don't worry, Spencer. You'll find a nuthead who will want to be with you."

"Oh, you're so sweet." She pretended she was moved by my comment for a second and then her voice snapped back to her normal sassy one. "And brave. I could pick the ugliest ring there is in that store. Something to make Clem cringe every time she looks at it."

I threw my hand around her shoulders, and I laughed.

"You're a catch, Spencer, and you know it. And you're here only to try the ring, not pick it. Don't get ahead of yourself."

I knew exactly what I wanted to give my nemesis. I had already gone to that store to see the ring. It was perfect. White gold with a yellow diamond in the middle. I knew Clem would get it the moment she saw it.

Hannah tried the ring, confirmed it was the perfect size, and ten minutes later I shoved her into a diner for a thank-you-for-your-help chocolate waffle before I went back home.

"You never told me your idea. About the proposal," Hannah yelled back at me when we took off in different directions an hour later.

I turned to her and shouted.

"She'll tell you about it later tonight."

"Seriously?" she started jumping up and down again. "Tonight?"

I shrugged and smiled.

"I have everything I need. I'm not dragging this shit out a minute longer."

So I went back home, and I peeled the stupid daffodil from our living room wall. Some, and by some I mean a lot, of the paint came down with it.

She will be pissed.

I heard a key in the lock. She was coming home earlier than expected.

Fuck. Fuck. Fuck.

I wasn't ready. I had a whole thing planned. Peel the daffodil. Get a fancy dinner. Flowers. Candles. Shower and a new shirt.

All that gone with her putting the key in the fucking lock. I knew she would figure it out. Why the fuck did I peel the daffodil first?

I could have done everything else I planned, and she wouldn't have found out.

Seconds later she was inside, her eyes huge and pinned on the wall. Her mouth fell open as if to say something, but she closed it. I looked down at my hands. I had my sleeves rolled up to my elbows the way I knew she liked, so maybe the dirty shirt wasn't so bad after all. I had the ring in my pocket. I had the girl I always wanted a few steps away from me.

"You always fuck up my plans, Clementine Hartley," I half-smirked her way.

"Oh yeah?" she asked and her voice cracked. She knew. Just like I thought she would.

"Every time I come up with a plan to make you mine, you tear it to pieces," I shook my head and approached her slowly. "I planned to kiss you when we were fourteen, and you kissed another guy instead. I planned on making you my girlfriend when we were eighteen, and you moved an ocean away from me. And now..." I looked around the living room and laughed. "You managed to ruin my plans once again. Like a true nemesis. Always aiming for my downfall."

I took her face in my hands, and I placed a quick kiss on her lips. They were trembling, and I looked into her eyes. She was about to cry.

"You know I hate it when you cry," I said with a clenched heart just as her tears started falling down her face. I reached down to my pocket and fell to one knee. I had a totally different idea about what I was going to say to her. But my need to make her stop crying kicked in, and I improvised. "Nemesis, goddess of revenge and retribution," Clem laughed and wiped away the tears with her hands. First task completed. "Will you marry your Narcissus? I was always yours, and you were always mine. Just marry me."

She ran her hand through my hair, and I closed my eyes as the pleasure of her touch washed over me.

"Yes. I'll marry you."

I got up and took her in my arms and kissed the shit out of her. When we broke our kiss, she cocked her head, thinking about something. Then she narrowed her eyes at me and said, "Nemesis didn't marry Narcissus."

"Well," I grinned down at her. "You're smarter than that."

BONUS CHAPTER
LUCAS

Read how Lucas bought Clementine's necklace here:
⇒ VALERIAHEIGHTS.COM/BONUS-MERCILESS

BONUS: RECKLESS
CHAPTER ONE

Hannah

My plans for the evening: visit a bar I had never heard of in search of a man I hadn't seen in years.

The only problem was I couldn't recognize a single building around me and my phone was currently pressed to my ear, so I couldn't check the map I used to guide me to my final destination. Apparently, living in Boston for the past five years wasn't helping me in that particular part of the city. I remembered I had to turn left at some point, but I had no clue where exactly.

"It should take about four to five hours," my boyfriend Nick said over the phone. Killing the call so I could check the map again was an option, but it seemed rude to do it when details about a heart surgery spilled out of his mouth. He was about to save a life after all. I had decided to make that left turn and see if it got me where I needed to go, when Nick added, "I will be at your place around two."

"Great," I tried to fake enthusiasm. Not that I didn't want to spend time with him. I did. But he meant two in the morning. Lately, we had been seeing each other mostly in the middle of the night. I got that his residency pretty much dictated his entire life, but I had a nine to five job and these middle-of-the-night visits had started to become less and less charming and more and more exhausting.

"Do you have plans for tonight?" he asked. "It's Saturday. You should go out. Have some fun."

"I am out. I'm doing my friend Clementine a favor."

That was both a truth and a lie at the same time. I used the word favor because I honestly thought it would help her, but Clem hadn't asked me for it. In fact, if she knew where I was headed, she would probably call me all kinds of words for crazy and stupid. And rightfully so.

"The one with the dog?" Nick asked. It wasn't a surprise he couldn't tell the difference between my friends, my colleagues, and my family. He had never met any of them and we had been together for almost six months now.

"No," I said, doing my best to hide the disappointment. "That's my colleague."

I put him on speaker. I figured that if he couldn't make the effort to remember the name of my best friend, I was entitled to divide my attention between him and the task I had devoted myself to for the evening.

The app on my phone showed I was going in the right direction, but that couldn't be true. The buildings around me seemed too old and industrial, but it said I was only two minutes away from my destination.

"Oh, yeah. The colleague. You walked her dog while she was away for a long weekend. I remembered. Who was Clementine again?" I opened my mouth to explain yet again, but he cut me off. "Sorry, babe. I have to go. You will tell me later."

"Okay. Bye," I barely managed to say before he hung up.

Maybe I should have mentioned I was looking for someone. A man. But Nick focused on who Clementine was, rather than what I was doing tonight. He also knew nothing about Tyler Hartley. And I knew I couldn't explain Tyler Hartley in one sentence over a quick phone call.

My first crush. My childhood obsession that bled into my first years of adulthood. The love that brought me to Boston in the first place.

It was too much to unpack in a two-minute conversation.

I didn't plan on searching for him. That thought never even crossed my mind. Until earlier that day when I saw his photo on social media. A girl had posted it in the middle of the night in a private group I was a member of, with the following text: *The cutest bartender in Boston.*

I stared at that photo for longer than I should have. Cute didn't even begin to do him justice. He was gorgeous. His blond hair looked messy, yet somehow perfect. Probably because Tyler Hartley was a total mess himself and it just suited him. His green eyes looked straight into the camera. He was pouring a beer with a carefree smile that I wanted to erase from his flawless face.

Clementine called him for two weeks straight, trying to talk to him. He never returned any of her calls. Didn't even bother to send her a message. She worried her older brother might be in trouble, and that son of a bitch ignored her because he was busy charming the girls he was serving drinks to at some shady bar.

I finally stopped in front of the questionable establishment Tyler worked in, wondering if I should be feeling bad for acting like a stalker.

That was the first time I would be cornering him like that, and I had been in love with the guy for almost a decade, so I decided I shouldn't make a big deal about it.

Besides, ever since Clem got engaged two years ago, I started preparing myself for the inevitable rendezvous. He was a shitty brother, but he wouldn't miss her wedding. And yet the nuptials were kept on hold for so long, I forgot about our impending get-together.

I opened the door of that bar without any hesitation, and just waltzed in.

My first impression? The place looked old and neglected.

My second impression? The waitresses were naked.

What a douchebag must the manager be to make them dress like that? They were wearing a top that resembled a bra and shorts that showed half their asses.

The place was a typical man cave. I bet married men going through their midlife crisis loved it. It smelled of wood, leather, alcohol and sweat. Naked women serving them drinks in dimmed lights.

The misogynist's paradise.

I walked past people, stepping over peanuts and who knows what else on my way over to the bar counter. And there he was, pouring drinks to a group of women. One of them wore a wedding veil. A banner hung over their heads. *Last fling before the ring.* Why would any woman have a bachelorette party here of all places?

The women burst out laughing, heads flying back, at something Tyler said, and it hit me. They were here for the *cutest bartender in Boston*. Charming.

These girls were going to stay there for a while by the looks of it, so I took a deep breath and marched over there. I wouldn't choose to start the conversation in front of an audience, giving our history, but I had no choice apparently.

Somewhere in the back of my mind, I imagined Tyler lifting his gaze and meeting mine before I reached the counter, but that didn't happen. He didn't even glance in my direction. He was focused on his customers.

I sat right next to the bachelorette and her friends. They were having a good time and I couldn't help but smile. I would have to throw a bachelorette party for Clem at some point.

Minutes passed and Tyler seemed unaware of the fact a new customer was sitting there, waiting for a drink. So I cleared my throat and tried to raise my voice enough for him to hear me without sounding like I was desperate to get his attention.

"Excuse me?" I waited for him to turn and notice me. He didn't. "Excuse me? Hello?" I waved my hand in his direction, determined to catch his gaze.

The girls were too loud. He was flirting with the one wearing a Maid of Honor crown on her head, leaning closer to her, whispering something in her ear, while she batted her eyelashes.

I didn't want to make a fool out of myself by calling him a third time, so I just lifted my butt from the wooden stool I was sitting on, leaned over the counter putting my entire upper body in front of the girls.

The laughing and shouting stopped. So did my heart the moment his eyes met mine. The good thing was my brain was still working properly so I managed to say something instead of just staring at him.

"Can I have a drink and a word, please?"

My voice sounded soft and smooth, like I wasn't affected by the fact we just saw each other for the first time in so many years.

He squinted for a moment, then a half-smirk formed on his lips. He tore his gaze away from mine and looked back at the girls.

"Ladies, can I offer you a table?" He was already waving his hand at a waitress. She practically ran over to him. "Chloe, could you please help the girls move to a table? I need to take care of an issue."

The word *issue* was accompanied by his thumb pointing at me. I pursed my lips together, suppressing a smile, not at all offended. On the contrary. I loved the fact I was causing him inconvenience.

The maid of honor took her drink with one sharp movement and sent me a death glare. I cocked my head and flashed her a grin.

"Oh, come on. He's not that cute. Nor is he that funny."

I was the last person on the planet to have the right to say something like that to any woman regarding Tyler. My infatuation with him had been of the worst kind. The kind you couldn't shake off until it completely destroyed you. And perhaps in some cases not even then.

Fortunately for me, I managed to shake it off *after* he destroyed me.

The girl just scrunched her nose at me and followed her friends to a free table. Chloe gathered the drinks and left me and Tyler alone.

He took a glass and started wiping it dry absent-mindedly. His eyes were slightly narrowed at me. Someone who hadn't spent years of their life obsessing over his beautiful face wouldn't even notice. But I did.

"I am not that funny, huh?"

I lifted my chin up. "And I am an issue?"

He put the glass on top of a pyramid of shining glasses, ready to be used. "What do you want, little Spencer?"

That nickname. I used to be so annoyed when he called me that. It made me feel like I was nothing but a little girl to him. When I finally got rid of my ridiculous feelings for him, I found out he never thought about me to begin with, let alone analyze how he perceived me. He didn't attach a meaning to that nickname. It was all inside my head. Just like the connection I believed we always had.

"I would like a drink." I wiped a drop of something sticky from the countertop with my middle finger, buying time.

Tyler stepped to the side and waved his hand in the air pointing to the bottles behind his back.

"Scotch, please."

He barked out a laugh but took two glasses and poured us both a drink.

"Won't you get in trouble for drinking?"

"I'm the manager," he gulped his scotch in one go and slammed his glass on the counter, his eyes clinging to my face. "You got your drink. Why are you here?"

"You are the manager?" I asked, thinking about those uniforms the waitresses wore. It didn't make any sense. Tyler wasn't the type of man, or should I say pig, to make women expose themselves like that.

"Yes," he crossed his arms over his chest. "I doubt you came here to ask me about my professional life. So? Care to share?"

He wants to get rid of you. Just tell him and leave.

"Clem wants to talk to you and you're ignoring her."

"I've been busy."

"She thinks you might be dead." That one was a huge stretch and the look on his face told me he was well aware of that. I opted for another tactic. "You're hiding." My audacity made him arch a brow and I added. "Busy or not, you can take a phone call."

"That's not for you to decide, little Spencer."

"Yeah, but now I know where you work. And so will your sister. You're not unreachable anymore."

Tyler's face went from patronizing to annoyed in a blink of an eye.

"How did you find me?"

"I have my ways," I reached for my glass, hoping he wouldn't pressure me for a real answer. His eyes followed my movement. I took a sip from my scotch, a drink I actually hated, and forced myself not to wince from the awful taste that deprived me of all my other senses for a few seconds there. Lowering my glass to the counter, I secretly took a few deep breaths.

Inhale.

So what if he found out you are here on pure luck? He doesn't matter.

Exhale.

You are here to help your best friend. That's all.

Inhale.

You are not betraying Nick in any way.

Exhale.

You just haven't had the chance to tell him about Tyler.

"So you walked in here thinking you would tell me what to do and I would obey." I couldn't miss the mockery in his voice. "What exactly made you think that?"

My face started burning, it had reddened for sure. What was I really thinking? That I would waltz in here after five years and make him call his family? Something that they hadn't managed to do themselves.

"Well, no. I thought you might do it for Clem. She really is worried. I wouldn't be here if she wasn't."

We both knew that much was true. I would never seek him out for anything or anyone else. We stared at each other for a few seconds. Then Chloe, the waitress he asked to move the bachelorette party to a table, appeared next to me and recited orders. Tyler prepared the drinks, and she spent her time eyeing me.

And what the hell was her problem?

"Are you going to call her?" I asked the moment Chloe turned her back on us. I wanted to get this over with and leave.

"Good to see you, little Spencer," Tyler knocked on the counter with his knuckles. "The drink is on the house." He turned around and went to talk to a man sitting five stools away from me.

Well, that was a disaster.

I poured the drink in my mouth, immediately regretting my impulsive decision to appear tough, and left cash next to my empty glass. I almost bumped into Chloe on my way out while I mumbled profanity about her boss. Consumed by my anger, I didn't even bother to apologize.

"Tyler is not a bastard," she shouted at my back referring to what she heard from my rambling. I turned to face her. "He does everything for the people he loves."

"His family would disagree."

"Are you a part of it?"

My throat bobbed. Her tone, her hostile posture made it clear she knew very well I wasn't.

I wouldn't usually run away from confrontation, but I felt like a complete failure at that moment. I ignored her question and got out, bolting down the street back to where I came from. When I decided I was already a safe distance away, I stopped, fished my phone out of my purse and called Clem.

"Hey! What's up?"

"I accidently found your brother and I went to see him," I didn't bother with any greeting.

"I...I'm sorry. What?"

I told her about his photo on social media, the bar, and my visit. I didn't tell her he basically kicked me out, but expressed my doubts he would return her calls.

"I think I pissed him off by showing up."

"Most likely," Clem sounded amused. "Tyler doesn't like to be pressured."

Clem knew all about my feelings for Tyler, but I never got the courage to tell her about our last encounter five years ago. She always advised me not to waste my time and feelings on her brother. I didn't listen and I got smashed.

We talked on the phone while I walked back home. She didn't seem worried about Tyler's reaction. I however was deeply unsettled, but it wasn't him who caused my uneasiness.

He does everything for the people he loves.

I repeated Chloe's words inside my head over and over again.

Years ago, I used to defend Tyler with that same passion. With that same belief that he was better than the man he chose to show to the world. I wanted to go back there, shake her, and scream at her that Tyler Hartley doesn't love anyone. But I knew it would be my ego speaking. I knew he loved people. He loved Clem.

He just didn't love me.

Acknowledgements

I started writing this book almost two years ago. It changed a lot over that time and it took many people's support to make it the best version it could be.

The first person I would like to thank is my editor, Cate Hogan. Cate, I feel so lucky I got to work with you. Your guidance and feedback gave this story the polish it needed to become an actual book. Clementine wouldn't be the same without you.

My friends and beta readers Steph, Martina and Mariya, thank you for reading the not so perfect draft and share your thoughts on Clem and Lucas. I needed the boost of confidence you gave me. It means the world to me.

I am incredibly grateful to my alpha reader and husband, who graciously tolerated my endless chatter for those countless months. You always believed I could do it. Thank you for the cheering and encouragement. Thank you for kicking my ass every time the anxiety got the best of me. You're my rock.

And to everyone who picked up my book and gave me a chance as a storyteller, I'm so grateful. And I would love to hear your thoughts. Please take a moment and send me an honest review to valeriaheights@gmail.com.

Printed in Great Britain
by Amazon

59515038R00189